SHADOW THIEF

FLIRTING WITH MONSTERS
EVA CHASE

BOOK
1

Shadow Thief

Book 1 in the Flirting with Monsters series

First Digital Edition, 2020

Copyright © 2020 Eva Chase

Cover design: Yocla Book Cover Design

Ebook ISBN: 978-1-989096-74-1

Paperback ISBN: 978-1-989096-75-8

1

Sorsha

The story of how I was going to end the world began not with a bang or a whimper but a kerplink.

The kerplink came from the latch of an arcanely ancient window lock hitting the sill as it disengaged. Adjusting my position on the ledge outside, I withdrew my equally ancient wedge and probe—gotta have tools that fit the job—from beneath the sash. At my tug, the window slid upward with a faint rasp.

Shadows draped the hallway on the other side even more densely than in the backyard below me, where the glow of the mansion's security lamps cut through the night. Less work for me. Dressed in black from head to toe, with my hands gloved to avoid fingerprints and my vibrant red hair tucked away under a knit hat, I blended in perfectly.

I slipped from the flutter of the warm summer breeze into the stillness of the hall and eased the window shut. The ceiling loomed high above. The tangy scent of wood polish tickled my nose. No doubt the floorboards that showed at the edges of the Persian rug gleamed like glass in daylight.

The thick rug handily absorbed my footsteps as I slunk along it, eyeing the doors. If I'd been able to get a good view from outside, I'd have snuck straight into the room I was aiming for, but with the coverings on the other windows, it'd been impossible to know whether I'd hit the jackpot or stumble onto inhabitants I wasn't looking to meet.

Looking around now, there were a couple of signs that this wasn't the home of your typical collector. Most of them kept the rest of their living space free of anything that would hint at their secret interests, a portrait of normality. Here, paintings of eerie, twisted forms with glowing eyes hung on the walls. Farther down, a patch of thicker darkness streaked across the pale paint of the ceiling as if it'd been scorched. What the heck had this dude gotten up to?

But then I spotted the door that had to lead to his collection room, and that question fell away behind a tingle of exhilaration.

I couldn't tell exactly what kind of security I was dealing with until I got right up close and flicked on the thinnest beam on my flashlight. The sight made me grimace. Son of a donkey's uncle.

In my experience, there were two kinds of collectors. Some went all in on traditionalism, preferring esoteric fixtures and devices of times past—the older the better—to match the nature of the creatures they'd stashed away. Others valued modern tech over keeping a consistent ambiance and secured their collection areas with the most up-to-date electronics.

I preferred the former. Forget fancy do-dads hacking digital codes—it was much more satisfying getting to tackle concrete objects hands-on, like a puzzle I was putting together... or, more often, pulling apart.

This guy clearly leaned that way too. Except he leaned it way too far. One look at the mass of interlocking metal around the door's handle told me my standard picks weren't getting anywhere with that lock. I didn't encounter many that required more forceful methods. Tonight's collector was awfully paranoid about protecting his treasures.

Or he had something in there that was so special it justified the lengths he'd gone to.

A prickle of apprehension quivered down my spine. You know the feeling when you realize that the thing you're in the middle of doing might actually be a horrible idea—but you're so committed already that stopping would feel even worse? Yeah. I lived there so often I might as well have made it my permanent address.

Which meant I shrugged off the uneasiness and

reached into the cloth bag hanging from my belt. I had ways of defeating even a ridiculous lock like this, and I wasn't going to let some wannabe master of the macabre get the better of me. Once I set out on a mission, I saw it through. And so far I always *had* seen them through, no matter how tricky the situation got.

I broke a pea-sized bead off my lump of explosive putty and poked it into the deepest cranny in the center of the mechanism. "Beating you with some goo, eat your fill," I sang at a whisper to the tune of Duran Duran's "A View to a Kill." Mangling '80s song lyrics always put me in a better mood.

Hey, everyone needs a hobby.

Bracing myself, I aimed my lighter at the cranny and flicked on the flame. The putty burst with a crackle and a puff of smoke—and the tinkle of several antique fittings shattering apart. I held myself totally still for several seconds, my ears pricked for any indication that someone in the house had noticed the sound, but the hall stayed silent.

When I pressed on the handle, the lock creaked, balked, and then crunched with a harder jerk. At my push, the door swung open.

Holy mother of mackerels, this was a collection room all right. I'd seen a lot of them, but even so, I couldn't help gaping.

The "room" looked as if it had actually been three or four rooms with the walls taken down between them, stretching like some grand ballroom into the distance.

Built-in wooden shelves stuffed with books, trinkets, and other objects lined the walls on either side of me from floor to vaulted ceiling. In front of those shelves at regular intervals, globe-like lights beamed down into glinting cages not so different from those you'd expect to house birds. Their vertical bars rose into domed tops, and their bases ranged from the size of my palm to the length of my arm.

I counted at least a dozen of them spread out down the vast space. It was rare to come across a collector who'd managed to get his hands on more than a few shadow creatures. This dude had been busy.

I tore my gaze away from the cages to skim the wall and note the thick velvet curtains that covered the room's narrow windows in the few gaps between the shelves. There were my possible escape routes.

Another, more massive velvet curtain hung across the entire width of the room at the far end. What in Pete's name lay past that?

A reddish blotch caught my eye in the middle of the blue-and-gold patterned rug. That maroon shade verging on brown—it was a bloodstain. One so big I could have lain down on it and not covered the whole thing.

A fresh twinge of nerves shot through my gut. It wasn't at all unusual for collectors to experiment with all kinds of supposed supernatural rituals, including blood-based spells, but this guy appeared to have gone all out and not made any attempt to clean up afterward. He'd left the evidence on display as if it were a valuable part of the exhibit.

There was creepy, and then there was "here's a fellow who might very well enjoy wearing other people's skin as a three-piece suit."

Before I returned my attention to the cages, I took a few moments to browse the shelves and pocket artifacts from the dude's non-living collection—whatever looked both valuable and not so distinctive it'd be easily recognized when I sold it on the black market. I settled on a gold bangle, a large ruby set in ebony, and a handful of antique coins.

That should cover at least a few month's room and board while I figured out my next heist. A gal's got to pay the rent somehow. It seemed fitting that the collectors indirectly funded my efforts to shut them down. Call me the Robin Hood of monster emancipation.

Because that was what lurked in those cages under their spotlights. At least, the collectors called them monsters. And to be fair, for the most part the creatures that slunk through rifts from the shadow realm into our mortal one did fit the standard criteria.

Those of us who both knew of the creatures' existence—and had bothered to speak at any length with the ones capable of talking—chose our terminology with a little more respect. "Shadowkind" came in all shapes, sizes, and inclinations, and most of them were a heck of a lot *less* monstrous than the worst human beings I'd tangled with.

It was difficult to tell what exactly this guy had caged in his extensive menagerie. Shadowkind could literally meld into our world's shadows and travel through them, hence the name, but they had to be able to reach those shadows first. The spotlights were positioned to fill each entire cage and the space beyond the bars with light, preventing that sort of escape.

Distressed by their incarceration and that constant glaring light, the creatures shrank in on themselves. I could only make out a blurred, flickering smudge of darkness in each: a glimpse of spines here, a flash of fangs there. When the collectors wanted to gloat over their prizes, they dimmed the lights just enough to coax their captives into showing themselves more clearly without allowing any full shadows to fall into range.

Silver and iron twined together to form the cages' bars and base—true to mythology, most otherworldly beings recoiled from one or both metals to some degree. Most creatures of this size weren't strong enough to leap into the shadows through the narrow spaces between those bars even if they'd had shadows to travel through. That meant freeing them was a multi-stage process.

I started with the nearest cage, drawing a dense black cloth from the larger bag on my belt and wrapping it around the light to blot out the illumination completely. Breaking the thing obviously would have done the trick faster, but even the lovers of antiquities often resorted to higher levels of tech when it came to ensuring their most valuable possessions didn't escape. Chances were high an alarm would go off if the flow of electricity were interrupted.

The same possibility existed for the cage doors. Instead of messing with the lock, I unhooked the juiced-up knife I kept at my hip, hit the button to flood the blade with heat, and applied it to the bars on the side.

The titanium tool had been enhanced not just by black-market skills but a sorcerer's supernatural efforts as well. Its blazing edge sliced through five of the bars in less than a minute. They bowed upward at a push with the flat of the blade.

The second I'd lowered the scorch-knife, the creature inside sprang through the gap. I got a clear look at it in that instant—a ball of raggedy gray fur from which six spindly legs and two bat-like wings protruded, a glitter of yellow eyes—and then it flitted off into the thicker shadows to enjoy its freedom far from here.

With a roll of my shoulders to loosen them up, I let out my breath. One down, a hell of a lot more to go.

Using the same technique, I made my way down the room one cage at a time. It was only when I'd hacked through what turned out to be the thirteenth—what a fitting number—that I glanced up and realized I'd come to the end of the line. Well, almost. I'd reached that vast curtain.

Bracing myself, I nudged one edge of it aside—and froze. More spotlights gleamed off more silver-and-iron bars ahead of me, but the three cages that awaited me there... I'd never seen anything quite like them. Set back at the far end of the room, a good fifteen feet from where I was now standing, they loomed almost as high as the ceiling and wide enough that I couldn't have reached from one side to the other with my arms straight out.

My breath stayed locked in my lungs as I slipped past the curtain and walked toward them. What was this dude keeping in *there*? It'd have been hard enough keeping his collection of thirteen minor "monsters" properly fed and exercised so they didn't totally dwindle away. Any creatures big enough to require cages like these—they could have gobbled him up the second he made a wrong move, if they were so inclined. And it wouldn't take very long shut up in a cage to so incline them.

I'd already thought he was over-ambitious and possibly insane. Now I'd have to go with completely cuckoo, and not just for Cocoa Puffs.

As with the smaller shadowkind, the beings in the huge cages had contracted into blurry dark forms. I couldn't tell whether the cages' height was overkill or if all three were simply hunched down in that space, but they all looked like big balls of, well, shadow condensed in the lower third of the space. The ball on the left was about twice the width of the one in the middle, the one on the right somewhere in between. I caught a flicker of pale hair, a glimmer of neon-green eyes—

My foot landed on the smaller rug between me and the cages, and an electronic shriek pierced both my eardrums.

Shit! I scrambled back so quickly I could have given a

professional tap dancer a run for their money, but the alarm continued blaring through the room and no doubt the whole of the mansion. A pressure sensor under the rug must have triggered it. I hadn't even thought—I probably *should* have considering the maniac I was obviously dealing with here—

No time to curse him out. No time to do anything except the bare minimum I'd come for. Whatever the hell was in those cages, they deserved their freedom just as much as the smaller beings I'd released did.

With the alarm already shrieking around me, I could throw caution to the wind. I sprinted to the first cage, chopped at the lock itself with my scorch-knife, and managed to sever it with several sawing motions. At my yank, that door flew open. To ease the captive's escape, I hurled my blackout cloth at the lamp overhead. It covered the light for only a moment before it slipped back down for me to catch it, but in that moment a presence hurtled past me so large and so close the hairs on the back of my neck stood on end.

No time to make any formal introductions. I dashed to the second cage, sliced through that lock a little faster than the first, flung my cloth, and raced to the third without stopping for a "How do you do?" No sounds of approaching doom reached my ears through the wail of the alarm, but it was practically deafening me, so that wasn't much comfort. It wasn't a question of *whether* the master of the house was charging toward the room, only how quickly he could get here—and how lethal the reinforcements he'd bring would be.

As I snatched back my blackout cloth for the third time, I was already digging my final gambit out of my bag. With a pop of the bottle's lid, I tossed a splash of kerosene across the traitorous rug. Then I whipped the flame of my lighter at it.

The damp patch caught fire with a whoosh of heat. I glanced around one last time to make sure no living things were left in the place—I hoped my signature farewell would destroy as much of his *inanimate* collection as possible, considering the uses he'd put it to—and realized that in my rush I'd nearly cut off my route to the nearest window.

Heat licked my face. I dodged to the side as the fire shot up higher. Smoke seared down my throat, and my pulse thrummed through my body with its own inner burn of adrenaline. If the flames would be kind enough to travel more to the right than to the left, attack those rows of books before it snatched at the window curtains...

Luck was on my side. The thought had barely crossed my mind when the flames flared with sharper intensity toward the bookshelves at the opposite side of the room, giving me a smidge of an opening. A shiver passed through my nerves at just how convenient that was, but who was I to argue? I dove around the growing wave of fire and whipped the curtain aside.

Without needing to think, my grappling hook was in my

hand. I slammed it into the pane, and the glass burst with a rain of shards onto the patio below. As I leapt onto the ledge, I was already sighting the utility pole just beyond the nearest wall of the backyard. One swing of my arm sent the hook soaring to latch onto the fixture at the top of the pole.

A shout of rage reverberated through the room behind me. Adios, asshole. With my hands tight around the rope, I launched myself out into the much more temperate night air.

I aimed myself at the perfect angle to catch hold of one of the metal bars protruding farther down the utility pole. Piece of cake. A flick of my wrist detached the grappling hook overhead. I clicked it onto the back of my belt, dropped down onto the sidewalk, and vanished into the shadows as completely as the creatures I'd come to save had, all ties to the place behind me severed.

At least, that was how it'd always worked before.

Despite the weirdness I'd encountered on the mission, everything about my escape appeared to go perfectly smoothly. I arrived back at my apartment in the wee hours of the morning, showered the smoke stink out of my hair, and curled up in bed. When I woke up, the sun was beaming outside, the birds were chirping, and I had new treasures to sell sitting on my desk.

I poked at them, grinning at the thought of the cash they'd bring in and the collector who'd now hopefully be agonizing at least as much over his loss as his captives had in their cages, and headed down the hall to grab some breakfast singing, "How wrong, how wrong was that dinged-up dong. How wrong, how—"

My voice jarred in my throat. I jerked to a halt a few steps from my kitchen, which was currently inhabited by three inexcusably stunning—and unfamiliar—men.

2

Sorsha

To be clear, I was all for shockingly handsome men as a general principle. I enjoyed resting my eyes—and sometimes other parts—on them as the occasion presented itself. Just not when the occasion was them randomly appearing in my apartment without prior invitation or me having any idea who in the wide blue yonder they were.

These three had certainly made themselves at home. The brawniest of the bunch, a hulking dude with several scars marking his chiseled face and white-blond hair that grazed his considerable shoulders, had pulled out one of the chairs at the kitchen table. He sat there with his legs sprawled out and one of my dinner knives held to the light from the window.

Next to that window was a young man who could

have been a sun god, all golden curls and radiant beauty. He'd perched his tall, slim form right on the counter, one knee drawn up and the other—bare—foot dangling. His long fingers curled around my last banana, now half-eaten.

Beside him, the last of the trio was poised by the sink, the sleeves of his collared shirt rolled up past his elbows and his well-toned arms submersed in the mountain of bubbles he'd stirred up under the running water. His eyebrows arched nearly all the way to the fringe of his messy chocolate-brown waves as he met my eyes.

"Have a good sleep?" he asked in a voice that was equally chocolatey: smooth, dark, and sweet.

They were all watching me now, the bubble enthusiast smirking, the sun god beaming like, well, the sun, and Mr. Brawn forming an expression as if he were trying very hard not to frown but his face wasn't quite sure how to do anything else.

My body had tensed with that good old fight-or-flight instinct, faced with uncertain and potentially dangerous circumstances. "What the hell are you—" I started. Then my gaze caught on a couple of details that threw my understanding of the situation for a loop.

Paler shapes, more caramel than chocolate, poked from amid the bubble guy's wavy hair. They were the curves of two small, pointed... horns, just above his ears. And the sunlight was glinting not just off my dinner knife in the hulk's hand but also off his knuckles, which had crystalline edges even harder than his face and a blueish white tint like ice.

You could still have called them men, yeah, but a substantial portion of the population would have also called them monsters. I had three of the higher shadowkind camped out in my kitchen.

Which still begged a whole lot of questions, but also meant a different level of caution. I backed up a step. "Just a second. Stay right there."

I hightailed it back to my bedroom and snatched up the undershirt I'd been wearing beneath my cat burglar outfit last night. The badge of silver and iron I wore over my heart was still pinned to it. I plucked it off and fixed it to my current T-shirt in the same spot.

The metals' effects wouldn't make me impervious to shadowkind powers, but the badge did deflect most attempts to manipulate human minds and emotions. While I believed in letting the shadowkind live freely, that didn't mean I trusted them to keep their voodoo to themselves. Some of them had *earned* the label "monster." And even the sweetest of shadow creatures often didn't understand kindness and consideration the way we mortals did.

My hasty preparations woke up Pickle where he'd been baking in the sun on my bedroom windowsill. The kitten-sized, dragon-shaped creature, whose scales were as green and bumpy as his namesake, blinked at me, stretched his wings, and scrambled up into a jumping position.

I hesitated and then leaned toward him. "All right. But you might not like what's out there." He wouldn't be much help if it came to a fight, but his response to their presence might tell me things my mortal senses didn't register.

Pickle leapt into the air with a clumsy flap of his wings and landed on my shoulder. He hooked his claws—gently, after a couple of years of trial and error—into the fabric of my shirt and nudged my jaw with his flared nose. Sometimes it was hard to tell whether he saw me more as a helpful companion or a steed.

He settled in happily with his cool cheek tucked against the crook of my neck until I'd reached the threshold of the kitchen. The three gorgeous men had stayed exactly where they'd been when I first saw them. At least they were capable of following direct instructions.

Pickle flinched and sprang away from me—and away from his much larger shadowkind brethren—with a squeak that released a puff of sparks. He landed on the shoulder of the mannequin that stood just inside the living room.

I'd emancipated that object from the long-abandoned store my apartment sat on top of, a place that used to offer fabric and clothing alterations. The headless, armless figure looked almost as unsettling in my apartment as it had amid the dust and darkness downstairs, but I'd decked it out in one of my shirts, unwashed to keep my scent, so that Pickle had somewhere to perch other than on me, which was where he'd have wanted to be every waking moment otherwise.

Apparently he preferred substitute-me to the real deal if it meant getting farther away from the beings in the kitchen. Once on the mannequin, he hunched his back, his beady black eyes fixed on them and another, fiercer squeak escaping him.

Okay, so he thought they were pretty scary dudes. Of course, that might have been more to do with the fact that they were about a hundred times bigger than he was than any horrifying powers he'd picked up on.

The men still hadn't moved, but Mr. Brawn's expression had shifted into total frown territory as he considered my pet dragon. The bubble enthusiast with the chocolate hair and voice appeared to focus on my protective badge for a moment before he caught my gaze again with another teasing arch of his brows.

I'd worn it on the outside of my clothes on purpose, so they'd know I knew what I was dealing with—and how to defend myself if I needed to.

I crossed my arms over my chest. "All right. What are you doing here?" They seemed tame enough so far, Mr. Brawn's scars aside, but with the higher shadowkind, you really couldn't go by appearances. They were capable of hiding their more monstrous forms beneath a nearly fully human veneer, only one tell-tale characteristic like those horns or those knuckles showing through. I could be dealing with any manner of demon, shapeshifter, fae, vamp, or the many rarer but equally caution-worthy types.

"You let us out," the slim sun god said in a bright, awed voice. "It was fantastic." He took another bite of the banana, and I realized he hadn't bothered to peel it. He was downing it skin and all.

His tongue flicked across his lips—was it *forked?*—and his smile turned swoony. "This is fantastic too. What did you say it's called?"

He glanced at the guy at the sink, who answered with obvious amusement. "A banana. While we're working on B-words, what do you think of these?" He lifted his hand and blew a stream of the dish-soap bubbles into the air. As they floated along with more airlift than I could have managed, the godly guy's eyes followed them. He reached out to touch one bubble's glossy surface and guffawed when it popped.

Mr. Brawn had set aside the dinner knife and gotten to his feet without any sign he'd noticed the others' chatter. He looked even bigger standing up—at least a foot taller than me, and I was no shrimp at five-foot-six. He bobbed his head, his expression as somber as before. His voice came out deep and gravelly.

"My name is Thorn, and my companions are Snap"— he indicated the sun god—"and Ruse"—the bubble enthusiast. "After the efforts you took and the repercussions you risked to ensure our freedom, we owe you a great debt. We'll repay it to the best of our ability, m'lady."

Had he really just referred to me as "m'lady" like some courtly knight? I might have questioned the title, but I was too distracted by the larger implications of what he'd said. Ensure their freedom—let them out—*oh*.

The pieces clicked together. The three huge cages in the collection room. The glimpse of pale hair I'd gotten—that could have been this Thorn guy's. The brilliant green eyes... Snap's were a more subdued mossy green, but in his more monstrous form they might very well take on that neon shine. Shadowkind tended toward extremes in their natural state.

I *had* freed these three. And then apparently they'd followed me home like a pack of lost puppies. Extremely hot lost puppies, but still. Pickle was enough trouble.

My arms relaxed a little, but I didn't move from my spot on the threshold. "You shouldn't have come after me. I wasn't looking for repayment. I let you and the lesser beings there out because you didn't deserve to be caged in the first place. You can go on back to the shadow realm now."

Ruse blew another waft of bubbles into the air. "No can do. You see, we lost our boss."

Snap's cheerful expression dimmed at that comment. He downed the last of the banana like it was a shot of tequila.

"Your boss?" I repeated, knitting my brow.

As far as I'd gathered, the shadow realm didn't operate with much social organization, let alone jobs and employers. There were higher shadowkind who'd come over to the mortal realm permanently and lived alongside humans with most of the trappings of mortal life, but this trio didn't fit that mold. From Snap's awe at the basic contents of my kitchen, I'd guess he'd spent very little time outside his own realm at all. Thorn's formal way of speaking and outfit of tunic and trousers suggested any significant time he'd spent here had been a few eras ago. Ruse might have fit in all right, though his fitted shirt and slacks were more clubwear than work uniform, but he'd said *our*.

"We were brought together for a specific cause by another of our kind who suspected treachery was being carried out by certain mortals," Thorn said. "The fate that befell him suggests he was right. On our third cross-over, he was ambushed by attackers well-prepared to combat our abilities. We were able to avoid the fray, but before we could track down him and them afterward, we were trapped by another party." His face darkened, his head dipping.

"I did tell you I had a bad feeling about that building," Ruse put in.

Thorn glowered over his shoulder at the other guy before turning back to me. "Techniques have changed since I last engaged much with mortals. They've become more... potent." He sat back down as if over-burdened by that admission.

Snap gave a little shudder as if trying to shake off the tension of the moment and hopped off the counter. He reached into my fruit bowl on the table, the glow of curiosity coming back as he examined his finding. "What's this one called?"

"That's a peach," Ruse said dryly. "They're nice too."

Snap took a bite and hummed delightedly. I did my best not to ogle the pale curve of his neck and that heavenly face as he held the fruit up to let the juice drip into his mouth. I might not have invited these guests, but I could be polite enough not to openly leer.

"Omen brought us together," Thorn went on from his chair. He aimed his mournful glower at the dinner knife as if its dull blade offended him. "We can't return without him. And if he's right about the sort of people who captured him, many more of our kind are under grave threat."

An uneasy prickle ran down my spine. Collectors and the hunters who supplied them didn't normally deal in higher shadowkind. Too risky and too much effort required. If there was some kind of organized campaign underway to seize beings like these—if it was happening enough that some shadowkind were starting to realize... It didn't bode well that none of the people I worked with had noticed.

I shifted my weight from one foot to the other. "I can see why you'd feel that way. The last thing I'd want to do is get in the way of that mission. By all means, go off and search for him." And I'd check with my contacts to see if they had any idea about the bigger picture here.

"We will of course continue our search," Thorn said.

"But we can see to it that you remain protected and aided in any way you require in the meantime."

Three unexpected, monstrous house guests—not what I'd signed up for. "That's really not necessary," I said, holding up my hands. "I'm sure I'll be fine. Don't worry about me."

"Oh, but we owe you," Ruse said in that smooth voice of his. I thought there might be a teasing note in it. "If it's simpler for you, we could sink into the shadows to stay out of your hair."

"Her hair," Snap murmured. He looked from the partly-devoured peach to me and sidled close enough to lift a ruddy lock that had fallen across my shoulder. His head cocked as he rubbed it between his lithe fingers.

My pulse stuttered despite myself. Thorn might be ruggedly handsome and Ruse devilishly stunning, but up close, Snap's divine face was literally breathtaking.

"It's almost the same color," he said, sounding pleased with his observation. He held the strands up to the peach's red skin. "And just as soft."

I managed to catch my breath, but the only sound that came out of me was, "Er." I should probably step away, but I couldn't quite convey that message to my legs.

Ruse chuckled. "I'll bet she tastes just as sweet too."

There was no mistaking the suggestiveness of that comment, but Snap's head jerked toward him with a flicker of horror. "You can't eat her!"

Thorn stirred at the table as if tuning in to his companions' asides for the first time. "No one should even be *thinking* about eating anyone around here," he commanded.

Ruse rolled his hooded eyes. "I'll have you know that in my entire existence, I've never eaten a person—not like that, anyway." He winked at me. "I apologize for my associates' inability to follow a metaphor."

I held up my hands, finally convincing my feet to back away from Snap. "Enough. Let me think."

No way in hell did I want these guys lurking around in the shadows, keeping an eye on me for my "protection" without me having any idea where exactly they were. I valued my privacy, thank you very much. At least while they were visible, I'd know when I was actually on my own.

As the entire conversation had demonstrated, shadowkind didn't have the same concepts humans did of social niceties... or basic legalities, for that matter. The fact that they had no right to occupy my apartment and that I might not *want* them hanging around "repaying" me meant zip. If they'd decided to temporarily adopt me, I wasn't sure there was anything I could do to convince them otherwise—not without provoking hostilities I wasn't prepared to contend with, anyway.

Because I'm nothing if not stubborn, I had to make one last attempt. "Can you really not believe that I'd rather you put all your energy into finding your 'boss' instead of looking out for me?"

Thorn blinked at me as if I'd said something

completely preposterous. "It's not about *believing*. It's about what's right."

He said it with such solemn commitment that I barely held back a laugh. What was right, according to him: crashing the home of a woman they barely knew and insisting on watching over her despite her protests. Welcome to shadow logic.

Ruse and Snap looked equally disinclined to budge. I inhaled sharply and squared my shoulders. In that case, I'd just have to do what I could to get them moving on with their other responsibilities.

"Fine," I said. "There are some people I can meet up with tonight who might have information that'll help you track down this Omen guy. In the meantime, I'd prefer if you did your protecting from the kitchen."

I slipped into the room just long enough to grab a muffin out of the breadbox for my breakfast, waved Pickle onto my shoulder, and stalked back to my bedroom to figure out how to get myself unadopted ASAP.

3

Ruse

"Well, that went just spectacularly," I said, leaning back against our savior's kitchen counter.

"Really?" Snap looked toward me with that dopily hopeful expression of his.

Thorn shifted forward in his chair as if debating whether to spring into action right now. "I thought so."

Unfortunately, my current associates understood sarcasm about as well as they comprehended metaphors. I wiped the lingering bubbles off my hands. The lemony scent made my nose itch, but at least the stuff had entertained Snap for a little while. Not that he was all that difficult to impress.

"I was joking," I said. "She all but told us to take a hike. Repeatedly." Her noxious silver-and-iron brooch might have deflected most of my ability to read her emotions the way I generally could with mortals, but from the moment she'd retreated to put the thing on, her wariness about our presence should have been perfectly obvious to anyone with functioning eyes.

Anyone other than these two. Why had I let Omen rope me into this posse again? I hadn't taken into consideration the possibility of being snared and shut away in a cage for darkness only knew how long.

Longer than was good for my health, the more insistent itch in my chest suggested. The ravenous sensation I'd been fighting off for days was producing claws.

"She told us to stay," Thorn said, which was the most generous possible interpretation of the young woman's instruction for us to keep to the kitchen. "She even offered to help look for Omen, not that she should feel obliged."

I sighed. "I'd imagine she's counting on us leaving as soon as we've found him, and she'd like to hurry up the process."

Snap's eyes grew even rounder than usual. "We can't leave. What if the mortals that attacked us come after her because she freed us?"

"I get the feeling she'd prefer to take her chances with them more than us," I replied, but I couldn't help smiling as I said it. Our rescuer had plenty of spirit in her. I'd pass up a seduction or two for the chance to watch her face off against those asshole hunters.

At Snap's crestfallen look, I added, "It isn't your fault. She hasn't had the chance to see all we have to offer."

Our mortal-realm neophyte was easily reassured. He nodded with earnest determination and popped the rest of the peach into his mouth. The pit crunched between his teeth.

I didn't have the heart to tell him he was eating it wrong. His jaws could handle it. He was a devourer, after all.

Thorn's determination was much grimmer. "Whether she appreciates our company or not, we must ensure she doesn't suffer because of the immense favor she did for us." He paused. "But we must also come to Omen's aid as quickly as we can. The trail will have grown cold. It's been too long already."

The twist of his mouth showed how his opposing duties tore at him. Having a sense of loyalty was awfully troublesome, as far as I could tell. I was glad I'd never cultivated one.

I pushed myself off the counter to amble over, and a tremor ran down the back of my legs. I tensed them before I could visibly wobble. My jaw set.

Oh yes, *that* was a perfect reminder of why I'd agreed to join in on this operation—and why I wasn't going to shirk the duty I'd pledged to carry out even if the job had gotten much more complicated than expected. It wasn't loyalty; it was self-preservation.

Thorn could stick to our mandate out of higher principles, and Snap out of his desire to please or whatever exactly drove him, but for me, being able to slip between the realms was a matter of survival. Shadowkind like me relied on mortals to sustain us. I might not be capable of *dying* while I was in my native realm, but I wasn't sure that wasting away into a sliver of a shadow would be any better. It might be worse.

And any of us could die on this side of the divide.

I made sure my body had steadied and then stepped toward the table as I'd planned. The scrabbling of my hunger burrowed deeper between my ribs. No piece of fruit would satisfy it.

"The answer is perfectly clear," I said to Thorn. "The last time we went searching, our poking around got us caught. Neither of you is really prepared to navigate this realm without guidance, and I know you don't want to listen to my advice. Our host, reluctant or not, knows this world far better than any of us, Omen included."

"What are you suggesting, then?"

I shrugged. "She's offered to make inquiries. She's motivated to see us on our way. We should let her take the lead in the investigation, and we can see that no harm comes to her by following along behind. Two birds with one stone, as the mortals like to say."

"What do the birds want with a stone?" Snap asked.

"It's more what the stone wants with the birds." I reached over and spun the knife Thorn had left on the table. It rattled around to point its blade at him. "So? Can you agree that my approach makes sense even though it came from me?"

Thorn gave me one of his long-suffering glowers. I'd gotten plenty of practice at ignoring those. But it seemed he couldn't come up with any actual argument.

"Your proposal sounds reasonable," he said after a moment. "We'll see where her connections can take us."

"Excellent." I straightened up and sauntered past Snap toward the hall, alert for any new tremors in my muscles. The last thing I needed was Thorn picking up on my current weakness.

His gaze swiveled to track me. "Where are you going? She said to stay in the kitchen."

I smiled sweetly at him. "And as you well know, I'm not very good at following orders I never agreed to in the first place. I'll go see if I can't spin our dropping in on her home into a more welcome visit."

And if I could sate my vital appetites at the same time, we'd all win.

4

Sorsha

Expecting my new shadowkind entourage to follow *all* my instructions to the letter was obviously too much to hope for. I'd only just wolfed down my breakfast and opened my laptop to get down to business when a knock sounded on the door. Biting back a sigh, I got up to answer it. Was there the slightest chance they were stopping by just to tell me they'd reconsidered and would be taking off now?

Nope. I eased open the door to find just Ruse standing on the other side in a casual stance, his heavy-lidded eyes languid. Up close, I couldn't help noticing that the chocolate theme extended to his scent. A bittersweet smell like pure cacao mixed with caramel filled my nose—and made my mouth water despite myself.

He wasn't as tall as hulking Thorn, but he still had a good half a foot on me. As he gazed down at me, his lips quirked into a smile that cracked a dimple beneath one of those high cheekbones. I wouldn't be surprised to find out that grin had melted the panties off thousands of women around the world.

"I'm sorry our initial conversation went so poorly," he said in that smooth but slightly teasing tone. "If Thorn had been named 'Prick,' it would have been a lot more fitting. I thought I should make an attempt at a proper introduction. I can't believe we didn't even get *your* name. So—"

He made an elaborate flourish with one hand and dipped in a playful half bow. "Ruse of the shadow realm," he said when he'd straightened up again. "A pleasure to meet you. And you are?"

"Sorsha of the mortal realm," I said, bemused. I couldn't return the sentiment about it being a pleasure.

"Sorsha," he repeated, trying out the syllables as if they were a rare delicacy. The richness he gave to them sent a tingle down my spine. "I think you're the first with that name I've encountered."

I felt abruptly awkward and annoyed by that awkwardness. "It's from an old movie." My parents had apparently been as obsessed with '80s media as Luna had been. "Is that all you wanted—to get my name?"

"Well, no, I have to admit I have an ulterior motive." He shot me that smile again, even slyer this time, and damn it if *my* panties didn't melt just a tad.

Resting his hand on the doorframe, he leaned into the room as if to indicate that this part of the conversation wasn't meant for the ears of those down the hall. "I have a small predicament. Unfortunately, it means asking for your help when you've already gone above and beyond, but I can promise it'd be very enjoyable for you too."

I crossed my arms and raised my eyebrows at him the way he had at me when I'd first encountered the trio. "Oh, yeah? And what exactly is this favor?"

"The trouble is, our former jailor didn't offer the kind of food that can actually sustain me. I need a different sort of nourishment."

His warm hazel eyes took on a meaningful gleam, and I connected the dots.

"You're an incubus," I said, mentally kicking myself for not figuring it out sooner. The guy did ooze sensuality, after all. "You need to have sex to survive." Like a vampire needed blood. Fair enough. But why would he— Oh. "And you're propositioning *me*?"

His grin stretched even wider. "You are a sharp one, aren't you, Miss Blaze?" He reached out to gently tug a strand of my hair, which might have inspired the nickname as much as my farewell to the collection room had. "The feeding won't hurt you. We leave our intimate companions better off than when we found them, not worse."

His fingers nearly grazed my cheek. The closeness set off a much headier pulse of attraction than Snap's heavenly beauty had provoked.

I'd rather a love bite than one with fangs, and to be totally honest, I *had* wondered from time to time just how much a supernaturally sexual being could bring to the table. But all the same... "I'm flattered, but no thanks. We did only just meet. And that might complicate things even more than you just staying in my apartment out of the blue. I'm not going to stop you from heading out on the prowl, though. By all means." I motioned toward the apartment's front door beyond him.

Ruse's mouth pulled into something more like a grimace. "Given what my companions and I have already been through, I'd rather not risk taking my needs to the streets. Any potential lover I encounter out there is also a potential jailor. I know *you* have my best interests at heart."

I wasn't sure I'd put it exactly that way, but he did have a point. That didn't mean I had to go along with it, though. "You've toughed it out this long. You can't hang in there a little longer while we get this whole Omen situation sorted out?"

He shrugged, the twinkle coming back into his eyes. "I could, but I'd rather be at my full capacity, so I can properly contribute and all. Is the thought really so distasteful?"

He was definitely teasing now. I doubted he could sense much from me using his powers while I was wearing my badge, but certain parts of me *were* responding to his appeal. From the heat creeping up my neck, I suspected I had a flush coming on. Lord only knew how dilated my pupils might be right now, taking in that striking face.

I was only human, after all. And it'd been months since I'd last gotten it on with anything not battery-powered, let alone a master of the sensual arts.

That was exactly why I shouldn't give in to temptation, wasn't it? I couldn't be completely sure Ruse had *my* best interests at heart, and I wasn't sure how clear a head I'd keep in the heat of the moment.

At the very least, I should take a little time to think about it. He and his friends clearly weren't planning on going anywhere anytime soon. Maybe someone at the Fund would have an idea of extra precautions to take with the cubi type of shadowkind.

Vivi would love to know what had provoked that line of questioning, wouldn't she? I was definitely going to have to keep this unexpected roommate situation on the down low when it came to my best friend. If the trio had gotten themselves caught up in something dangerous, which it sounded like they had, the last thing I wanted was to drag her into the mess too. She had no idea about any of my totally illegal nighttime crusades.

I opened my mouth to tell my attempted paramour that I needed a rain check until at least tomorrow, and my gaze snagged on the hand he'd set on the door frame. The hand that wasn't simply resting there now. A faint twitch of his fingers had caught my attention—a trembling he must have mastered by grasping the frame harder, because his hand had stilled, but his knuckles had whitened.

The second my gaze landed there, he jerked his hand away and tucked it behind his back in another flirty pose. But now that I was alert to the possibility, that stance looked a tad more rigid than fit his laissez-faire expression.

He'd talked as if he wasn't doing that badly, but how much was he downplaying his weakness? He was aiming to win me over with charm, not pity.

A sudden flicker of concern gnawed at my hesitations. I didn't enjoy seeing any being in pain. And it would make a hell of a lot more trouble for me if one of my new volunteer bodyguards collapsed on my watch. That was the main reason I was reconsidering: a totally practical consideration.

Oh, come on—would your resolve really be unshakeable in my position?

That didn't mean I was going to leap straight into bed with the dude, of course. I prodded his chest—ooh, he was packing some muscle under that silky shirt. "Maybe I'd be open to, let's say, making out a bit. Nothing too intense. I wouldn't want you using any voodoo on me. Can you feed while I've got this badge on?"

He cocked his head, considering the circle of twined silver and iron. "A little energy would seep through—more a light snack than a meal, but it'd help. And I can provide plenty of satisfaction without any extra-worldly influence necessary. All I ask is that you reconsider the whole protective amulet thing once I've proven that. If you don't want me affecting your emotions, I have no problem staying out."

He could say that all he wanted, but that didn't mean he'd stick to it. The thought of him meddling with my mind sent a cold jab of panic through me. I stifled it and the shiver that came with it. "Badge stays on. That's the limit of my trust right now. Keep in mind that you did barge into my apartment without an invitation or even asking."

He lowered his head in mock shame. "Point. The limits are yours to set. So..." He grinned at me again, making his face somehow twice as handsome than it'd already been. My pulse hiccupped. Maybe this wasn't such a great idea after all...

What the hell. I'd pretty much committed already. It'd make a great party story someday. *Did I ever tell you about the time I made out with an incubus?*

I stepped back from the door. "Come on in, then."

Ruse sauntered inside and kicked the door shut behind him. His eyes shimmered with a golden cast now —a little of his mortal façade fading away to reveal the shadowkind form underneath.

He brought his hand back to my face, letting his knuckles tease across the line of my jaw in a way that left my nerves shimmering too. He set his other hand on my waist. With our bodies just a few inches apart, the heat of his washed over mine, setting off a fresh flare of desire. I swallowed hard, resisting the urge to meld right into him, and he tilted my chin up to meet his first kiss.

Holy fucking cannoli. I'd thought I'd been kissed pretty skillfully in the past, but just the brush of Ruse's lips set all those past encounters into pale relief. My mouth tingled, more heat swelling in my chest, and he drew me closer. The perfect pressure turned the shimmer of my nerves into outright sparks.

Before I'd realized I was moving, my fingers had curled into the front of his shirt, holding him in place as if I had any reason to worry he might be going somewhere. I kissed him back, instinctively seeking even more, and he hummed encouragingly. With a small shift in angle and a stroke of his tongue, he coaxed my lips apart.

If he was feeding off the intimacy of this interlude already, I couldn't sense it. All I could feel was the blissful heat and the delicious curl of his tongue around mine. The hand on my side trailed higher until his thumb traced the curve of my breast.

More sparks shot through me at that touch. I swayed into it automatically.

He caressed my cheek once more and then tangled his fingers in my hair in a gesture that was somehow both confidently controlled and wild. The passion stirring inside me spread further, pooling between my legs with a growing need.

How could I give up everything he could offer now that we'd started? How could I possibly ask him to stop?

A fresh flash of cold broke through the haze of

pleasure that'd been consuming me. Those questions were exactly why I needed to stop it—now.

I pulled myself back with agonizing effort. My face was definitely flushed now. As I pursed my lips, my mouth tingled with the after-effects of the kissing. I gathered myself enough to say, "That's enough. We'll leave it there."

The incubus didn't make any move to persuade me otherwise. He simply studied me with an expression halfway between amusement and approval. A little more color had come into his previously pale skin—a sign that my contribution had given him enough of a "snack" to make a difference?

"For now?" he suggested, with an implied, *until later?*

I wet my lips without meaning to, sending a renewed quiver of bliss through my body. "We'll see," I said, ignoring all the parts of my body screaming, *Yes, pretty please, with multiple cherries on top! And also, let's see what you can do with those cherries...*

I'd enjoyed that little make-out session—hoo boy, understatement of the year—but I'd rather be sure I didn't come to regret the gamble before I rolled the dice again.

5

Sorsha

Monster advocacy wasn't exactly the type of work you could openly advertise. Technically, the group where I did almost all of my socializing—along with picking up tips for new collectors to target—called themselves the Shadowkind Defense Fund. Outside of the four walls in which they held their twice-weekly meetings, we usually shortened that first word to "SK" or simply referred to the group as "the Fund."

Those four walls were contained in a discount movie theater that showed second-run films. Tonight, the warble of a recent Marvel soundtrack filtered in from the showing beside us, all epic orchestration punctuated by the occasional explosion. The small popcorn machine brought in for our private party filled the air with a salty buttery smell—and something spicy that tickled my nose.

Ellen, co-owner of the theater and unofficial co-president of the Fund alongside her wife, had a thing for experimenting with new popcorn flavors. We Fund members served as her guinea pigs. As I strolled around the rows of red-velvet-padded seats to check out her current attempt, a petite figure bounded to join me with a swish of her buoyant curls.

"Sorsha!" my best friend cried, catching me in a hug I returned with a laugh. From Vivi's enthusiasm every time I showed up, you'd have thought my attendance was a rare occurrence. The truth was, I rarely missed a meeting, since the people in the Fund were pretty much the only people I could talk to without having to lie about the vast majority of my life. And even with them, there was plenty I edited out.

When I'd first showed up at a Fund meeting as a much more hesitant and recently traumatized sixteen-year-old, Vivi had immediately swooped in and taken me under her wing. I'd even ended up living with her and her parents for a while. Two years older, she'd been the next youngest in the bunch, but she'd seemed awfully mature and worldly to me. Over the more-than-a-decade since, we'd come out on more equal footing, bonding over our unusual senses of humor and our mutual love for cheesy old movies and Thai food.

"It's chili pepper and brown sugar tonight," she said, nodding to the bags of popcorn already filled to the side of the machine. "It'll roast your tongue like a rack of honey ribs and then set the barbeque on fire."

I'd never met a lyric I couldn't mangle; Vivi had never met a simile she couldn't stretch to the breaking point.

I grinned back at her and swiped a Coke from the mini-fridge as well as my bag. "Thanks for the warning. I see you survived."

"Only barely," she said in a dramatic undertone, but her eyes still twinkled merrily. She struck a pose, one hand on her hip, the other in the air. "What do you think of the new get-up?"

Today's outfit consisted of a sleek white tank top with a pearly sheen and trim white capris. Vivi only wore white—"It's my calling card," she'd told me way back when—which to be fair did set off her smooth brown skin and dark features amazingly. She emphasized her eyes with thick liner and mascara, and her black hair ran tight along her scalp in braids before bursting into a gush of curls at the back. Perhaps most amazing was the fact that she somehow managed never to get a smudge or a stain on all that pale fabric.

"You look incredible," I said, "like you always do. Got something special happening later?"

"I'm supposed to meet this guy for drinks. We've talked a little online. I don't know. Hard to tell how you're going to feel about a person until you can see and, like, smell them, right?"

My mind tripped back to Ruse's bittersweet cacao scent, and a warmth I hadn't wanted to provoke flickered up from my chest. I tamped down on it in the same instant, but Vivi knew me pretty well.

"Huh," she said with a teasing tilt of her head. "What have *you* been up to, missy?"

I waved her off. "Nothing, nothing. Just thinking about times past and all." I didn't have to mention how recently past they were. Time for a subject change! "Hey, have you heard anything through the grapevine about hunters getting more organized or people trying to trap higher shadowkind as well as the little beasties?"

Vivi frowned. "I don't think so. Maybe someone else will have. Why, do you think something like that is happening?"

"Just seems like it could. Something to keep an eye out for." I scrambled for an excuse that wouldn't perk Vivi's curiosity too much. "It's coming up on the anniversary of Luna's death, and I guess that got me thinking."

My best friend's expression immediately softened with sympathy. She gave me a gentle tap of her elbow. "That's got to be tough. But it's been a long time and we haven't seen more incidents that were anything like that, so I don't think there's a pattern. Just a bunch of assholes who must have thought better of making that kind of move after things went wrong."

"True," I said. It could also be true that what had happened to the trio who'd crashed my apartment and their "boss" was an isolated incident, not part of a larger conspiracy, no matter what the guy in charge had believed.

"Can't hurt to ask, though, if it makes you feel better.

Come on." She motioned for us to head back to the front
of the room where several other Fund members were
scattered across the folding seats, munching popcorn and
chatting. The projection screen flashed briefly as Ellen
and Huyen must have fiddled with their weekly visual
report, which they would share once the meeting really
got underway.

We'd only made it halfway down the aisle when one
of the lounging figures yanked himself to his feet and
ambled our way. My steps slowed. "Here comes the rain
again," I murmured to Vivi, but my heart wasn't in the
joke.

"Hey," Leland said as he reached us, his voice light
but cool, his expression outright cold. The muscles in his
stout frame, which a bodybuilder would have envied,
flexed beneath his polo shirt. I forced myself to smile, but
his gaze only rested on me for a second before flitting to
Vivi and staying there.

Ever since we'd broken off our friends-with-benefits
arrangement, emphasis on the benefits, months ago—or
rather, since *I'd* broken it off after he'd started snapping
at me for not doting on him like an actual girlfriend—he'd
turned to ice around me. Somehow he couldn't stop
making a point of shoving that ice in my face at least once
a meeting. Did he think I was going to throw myself into
his arms with sobs of regret because of his pointed
demonstrations?

I wasn't, because honestly, I didn't miss even the
casual relationship I'd lost all that much. I'd always found

Leland easy on the eyes, that soft face and schoolboy haircut paired with his tough-guy physique, but in personality? We'd gotten along well enough when all we'd had to discuss was where we'd be hooking up on a given night. We hadn't had much to talk about otherwise. The fact that he'd apparently wanted more had thrown me for a loop.

But it still stung that I hadn't picked up on the signs soon enough to avoid his obvious hurt and that I'd managed to disappoint him so thoroughly even when we'd seemed to be on the same page... It wasn't the first time. No matter what kind of relationship I ended up in, it always turned out I wasn't giving enough.

I'd been doing my best to show *I* had no hard feelings and wanted to co-exist peacefully, so I ignored the intended snub with my smile still in place. "Hey. Looks like it's going to be a busy meeting tonight."

He responded with a noncommittal grunt, nodded to Vivi, and veered closer to the seats to pass us on her side. As he stepped by, his foot must have caught on the base of the nearest chair. I didn't see it happen, but one second he was striding along, and the next he was sprawling forward onto his hands and knees with an audible "Ooof!", ass in the air.

As Leland picked himself up, one of the old members who'd come over to the popcorn machine chuckled. "Watch yourself there, kid!" Leland brushed himself off with a briskness that showed his embarrassment and hustled on giving the chairs a wide berth.

Vivi wrinkled her nose and leaned in to talk under her breath. "Maybe if he paid more attention to where he was walking than to giving you the cold shoulder..."

"At some point he's got to forgive and forget," I replied. I sure hoped so. For now, I could stick to giving him whatever space he felt he needed. It was a big room —plenty of chairs for everyone.

Shaking off the gloom of that exchange, I continued on to the other familiar—and much more welcoming— faces gathered near the screen. With Vivi looking on, I phrased my questions about new hunter behavior carefully, but all I got were shaken heads and doubtful expressions. If a larger than usual effort to confine the shadowkind was underway, word of it hadn't reached our group yet.

Which meant it either wasn't happening... or the people involved were covering their tracks incredibly well.

"All right, folks," Ellen called out as she and Huyen emerged from the projection booth. "Let's see what we can put in motion today. We had an incident earlier this week that should remind us all why none of the beings that cross over into our world deserve to be left in the hands of people who see them only as supernatural collectibles. A member of the Defense Fund in L.A. joined a group of mortal-side higher shadowkind who shut down a hunter ring, and this is what they encountered."

At the press of a button, a video started to play on the

screen. It'd clearly been taken with a handheld camera, probably a phone, and the hand that held it was shaking.

The recording swiveled to take in a small, dim room. A couple dozen cages stood stacked against one wall. At the other, several furred or scaled forms sprawled on the steel table, bones protruding from their flesh like ghostly knobs.

"Oh my God," the video-taker mumbled with obvious horror.

My own stomach churned queasily at the sight. Some collectors were too nervous or fastidious to want to deal with living shadowkind. For them, the hunters carved up their haul to provide polished skeletons or taxidermy shells. Two sales for one catch. Some hunters even preferred those dealings.

There wasn't much we mortals could do to take down these hunter rings—or independent hunters and their clients—directly, especially a larger scale operation like in the video. They'd have at least one sorcerer on staff: one of the rare human beings who'd mastered the art of summoning shadowkind from their own realm and bending their powers to the sorcerer's will. Their magic would deflect any typical law enforcement we tried to sic on them.

Those of us in the Fund had all come to know about shadowkind in various, personal ways we couldn't have convinced the general public to believe. Maybe if the higher shadowkind had wanted to show off their powers and prove they existed, we could have made more headway... but understandably, they had much more of an advantage in keeping their true nature secret.

The best we could offer was to interfere with the hunting and collecting as well as we could in roundabout ways, gather money to buy and release caught creatures when we had the chance, and inform the higher shadowkind who'd taken up residence in our world of activities we'd uncovered so they could step in if they felt it worth the risk. At least this bunch had taken action before the people who ran the facility could torment any more unwitting beings.

A solemn mood had descended over the room when the video finished. Then a chart popped up on the screen showing our latest fundraising efforts—not a bad week, considering *we* had to keep secret what we were actually raising those funds for.

"One of the big old homes in Walnut Hill halfway burned down last night," someone piped up as the screen went dark. "We've seen signs that the owner was a collector. That's the third fire this year—do we still have no idea who to thank?"

I bit my tongue. I definitely had nothing at all to say about that.

If I wanted to continue my more vigilante-style interventions, it was best if no one else had any idea I was responsible. The other Fund members might joke about approving, but if they knew one of their own was committing the crimes, I'd be kicked out for "crossing too many lines" in two seconds flat. I'd seen it happen to a guy who'd leaned too far into vigilante territory not long after I'd first joined.

"If it's a higher shadowkind taking matters into their own hands, as we've discussed before, it's understandable that they're not advertising the fact," Huyen said.

A guy farther back clapped his hands. "I say we leave them to it. They can police what happens to their own in their own way."

Being raised by a higher shadowkind for thirteen or so years made me pretty much an honorary one, right? That was my story, and I was sticking to it. Auntie Luna hadn't deserved what the bastards had done to her, and I'd be damned if I let any other shadowkind suffer while I could prevent it by any means necessary.

Vivi glanced at me and must have caught something in my expression. "Still fretting?"

I shrugged. "It's okay. If no one's heard anything, then there's nothing to hear."

"We could always spread the net a little farther. I was thinking of stopping by Jade's on Friday night. Wanna come with? It's been a while since we let loose anyway."

Yes, Jade's would be the perfect spot to dig a little further—and hopefully solve my uninvited monster roommate difficulties. I smiled. "You're right—let's do it."

6

Sorsha

Popcorn was hardly enough to fill a gal up, scorch-your-tongue-off spicy or not. As I tramped up the stairs past the fabric shop to my apartment, my stomach grumbled about how long I'd delayed dinner time. It was definitely time to eat.

I fit my key into the lock, singing to myself: "When the meal's in sight, I'm gonna run all night, I'm gonna run to chew..."

I pushed open the door half expecting my new shadowkind roomies to be waiting on the threshold all but wagging their tails to see me home. Instead, the hall was vacant, the apartment totally silent, no movement even in what I could see of the kitchen.

For just a split second, my spirits lifted with the hope that the trio had changed their minds about the whole glomming-onto-Sorsha plan and gone off to pursue their rescue efforts on their own. Just a split second, because an instant later, three distinctive forms wavered out of the shadow cast by the front door like watercolor paints condensing into a sharpened image.

Pickle scampered out of my bedroom, saw the much larger shadowkind, and cringed before flinging himself the rest of the way toward me. I'd have been surprised he didn't flee right into the shadows, except he'd gotten so attached to me that he stuck to his physical form all the time these days. I wasn't sure he even remembered how to vanish into the darkness.

I scooped him up to set him on his preferred shoulder perch and eyed my obstinate guests. "You decided you'd rather lurk?"

Thorn was wearing the dour expression that seemed to come so naturally to his rugged face. He squared his broad shoulders as if his form wasn't intimidating enough up close. "It's much easier—and more discreet—for us to travel through the shadows."

Snap's moss-green eyes were lit with a neon sparkle. "Such a fascinating place," he said with an errant flick of his tongue that, yes, I was sure now was slightly forked at the tip. "So many chairs—and what is the purpose of them swinging up?"

Chairs that swung up...? My stance tensed, Pickle's claws jabbing my collarbone as he echoed my reaction. "You followed me to the theater?"

Thorn gave me a baleful look. "We could hardly

ensure your protection if we stayed in the apartment when you've left it, m'lady."

I'd definitely heard him right that time. "*M'lady?*"

"Excuse the archaics," Ruse said with his typical amused smirk. "Our friend here hasn't spent much time mortal-side since the Middle Ages."

Thorn had said it so stiffly I got the impression he resented the honorific anyway, not that I'd required it. "Well, I'm not your *lady*," I said to him. "And I told you I don't need your protection. You can't go sneaking around after people without them even knowing—"

Except they could, because they were shadowkind, and that was how they worked. Even now, in the face of my irritation, Thorn and Snap only appeared to be various degrees of puzzled. I had the feeling Ruse understood my protest, but that didn't mean he sympathized. His smirk suggested the opposite.

"We didn't interfere with your activities," Thorn said. "I would like to know, though, what business that congregation of mortals has with the shadowkind."

"And how were those images put on that wall?" Snap put in. "So large and—moving!"

He drew in a breath as if to exclaim more, but Thorn cut his gaze toward the slimmer man with a firm glower. Snap shut his mouth with an apologetic dip of his divine head.

Suddenly I was twice as annoyed as before. Who'd put Mr. Brawn in charge of any of us? If their "boss" had brought all three of them on, then no doubt the apparent sun god here was just as capable as the others no matter how much the mortal realm amazed him. I'd rather answer Snap's awed questions than listen to Thorn's demands for information.

"You should have been able to figure that out if you'd been paying any attention," I said to the hulking guy, brushing past him on my way to the kitchen. They weren't going to stop me from grabbing the dinner I'd been looking forward to, even if my enthusiasm had dwindled. "The Fund is an organization of mortals who are aware of the shadowkind's existence and do what they can to help the creatures who've run into major trouble here. Whoever nabbed your boss, they'd be among the most likely to have heard something."

I snatched a frozen dinner from the freezer and shoved it into the microwave. I definitely wasn't in the mood for an extended cooking session right now.

The trio had followed me into the kitchen, Thorn in the lead. He folded his bulging arms over his chest. "It didn't sound as if they relayed any information that would direct us."

"They didn't," I agreed. "Because either your friend Omen got grabbed by some regular if particularly ambitious hunters and it's all a coincidence that he was talking conspiracy theories beforehand, or the conspirators are keeping their plotting incredibly quiet. I've got other people I can check with, though."

"You told the woman in white that you'd accompany her to a place called 'Jade'?"

Sweet jackrabbits and hares, how closely had he been eavesdropping? I gritted my teeth as I got my fork. The microwave dinged, not a moment too soon.

"Jade's," I said. "As in Jade's Fountain. It's a bar run by one of your kind, with other shadowkind as frequent clientele along with various mortals, most of whom have no idea. She doesn't like to get involved in inter-realm conflicts, but she'll pass on observations if she doesn't think it'll come back to bite her—or she might point me to someone else in the know."

Thorn didn't look convinced. "Are you sure this is the most fruitful avenue you could take? Talking hasn't resulted in any progress so far."

I resisted the urge to mash my newly heated container of pad thai into his face. Satisfying as it might briefly be, it'd be a waste of the food.

"It's the best strategy I can think of. If you want to keep busy in the meantime, how about tomorrow you show me the spot where Omen got ambushed and maybe we'll find something there?" Maybe I could move these three along before I even got to Jade's, and I could spend my time there chatting with Vivi instead of digging for clues.

"I highly doubt our attackers would have left obvious identifying ephemera behind," Thorn, his glower deepening.

Of course he'd take offense to the slightest hint that he might have missed something. I shrugged. "Well, maybe I'll pick up on something you all wouldn't have. If you have other avenues you want to pursue, get to it. Now I'm going to go have dinner. Alone."

Since I wasn't likely to get privacy in the kitchen, I marched back down the hall. But my "protectors" couldn't take a hint. They trailed after me as if connected by a magnetic force.

I spun around when I reached my bedroom doorway, about to tell them off. Before I had the chance, Thorn barreled ahead with his interrogation.

"That young man you spoke to momentarily before the images on the wall started—he gave me the impression of hostility. Is there any chance he might have something against the shadowkind after all?"

Could I stab him with my fork? I did have plenty of those. Of course, who could say whether the guy's commitment to keeping me safe would hold firm in the wake of a direct assault. I settled for clenching the handle tighter and aiming my best death glare at him.

"Leland's hostility has nothing to do with his feelings about *you*, only about me. Believe me, if I'd thought he was relevant, I'd have mentioned him. There isn't *anything* else worth mentioning, so why don't you all go raid my kitchen again and give me a break?"

Thorn's face tightened, but he inclined his head. "If that is what you require. We will ensure your living space remains secure while you dine."

I couldn't help rolling my eyes, but he'd already turned his back. Snap slipped away too, still with a confused air that I couldn't help feeling a twinge of guilt over.

Ruse had eased back a step, but he lingered in the hall, his head cocked.

"You deserve much better than that dingus anyway, you know," he said. "He didn't have the slightest concern for *your* well-being or pleasure, only what he felt he was missing out on."

My hackles came up. "I told you to stay out of my—"

He held up his hands with a softer smile than usual. "I didn't need any mystic awareness to pick up on your discomfort," he said. "My regular senses work just fine. And you never said I shouldn't see what I could make of *other* people's emotions. His weren't subtle at all. I guarantee I could take you to heights he'd never even have bothered to attempt."

The seductive timbre of his voice sent a giddy shiver through me, stirring up the memory of our short interlude this morning. But he didn't stick around in any attempt to persuade me, just popped his dimple at me and turned to follow the others.

As the disdain he'd shown for Leland sank in, something clicked in my head. "You tripped him, didn't you? In the theater?" I said, remembering how Leland had gone sprawling out of nowhere. He'd never been particularly clumsy—and he'd been walking where the shadows of the chairs fell. It wouldn't have been hard for a shadowkind to extend just enough physicality to knock a mortal off his feet.

Ruse glanced back at me with a cheekier smile. "I figured he had it coming to him."

He'd acted on my behalf—because the way Leland had treated me and thought about me had actually bothered him? If it'd only been a ploy to win my affection, he'd have brought it up himself. I could easily have never realized.

The incubus was continuing on his way. "Wait," I said before he could reach the kitchen.

He stopped and turned all the way around, lifting an eyebrow in question. I didn't normally find myself speechless around the shadowkind or, well, anyone, but just this once, my mouth had gone dry. I scrambled to sort out the mess of emotions and impulses racing through me.

Ruse needed this. Maybe I did too. Why should I care what Leland or any guy before him had thought? If heights were being offered, I wouldn't mind going flying. I didn't know much about the incubus, but I was pretty sure at this point that, at the very least, he wasn't out to hurt me in any way.

And when would I get a chance like this again? Tomorrow they might find the lead they needed and give up the whole protection scheme.

"You think you can do so much better?" I said. "Let's see you try."

A pleased glint lit in Ruse's hazel eyes. He strolled back to me. At my gesture, Pickle leapt onto the bookcase just inside the bedroom and tucked himself away in the felt cave of a cat bed that sat on the top shelf, filled with rags he'd shredded. I raised my chin to meet the incubus's gaze in challenge.

"I'm so glad you've reconsidered," Ruse said, all smoothness and charm, but I thought I caught a hint of relief in his expression too. The earlier "snack" had only delayed his starvation a smidgeon. Of course, if I was going to give him anything more than that, we had a negotiation ahead of us.

I eased farther into the room so Ruse could come in after me and set my dinner down on the vanity. It could wait a little longer with this other hunger stirring inside me. I fingered the fabric of my blouse over the badge I'd returned to my undershirt. The incubus might not be able to see it, but the presence of those metals would prickle at his senses.

"It'll be even more enjoyable with the special effects," he said. "But if you're uncomfortable with me using any of my influence, I can hold back without your protective patch. My skills would hardly be worth bragging about if I didn't know how to ply my trade with the same parts any mortal can put to good use."

My hands dropped to the hem of the blouse. "You can feed, however exactly that works, but I don't want you peeking at anything inside my head—or heart—or creating feelings with your powers." A flicker of that icy panic passed through my chest. "Not even a tiny bit. Are we clear?"

"Crystal," Ruse said, with a grin that practically

sparkled. "We can make this all about you, Miss Blaze. My most important need will be fulfilled perfectly by *your* fulfillment."

My body quivered in anticipation. The heat already rising through me overcame the chill of my worries. Why should I let events from decades ago dictate what I got to enjoy right now?

I grasped my blouse and tugged it up over my head. When I'd tossed it over the bed post, I reached for my undershirt, but Ruse touched my hand to still it.

"Allow me," he said, so low the words washed over me like a caress. I hesitated and then let my arms fall to my sides.

He leaned in, catching my mouth with his in the most delicate of kisses, like the brush of a butterfly wing. It shouldn't have affected me much, and yet it set off a sizzle through my lips and a pang of longing sharper than I could ever remember feeling before. At the same time, he drew the thin cotton of my undershirt up, skimming over my skin and grazing my nipples through my unpadded bra just firmly enough to provoke a jolt of pleasure through my chest.

He drew back for a second to flick the item aside, and despite my best efforts, a whimper of protest at the loss of contact spilled from my throat. Ruse smiled brilliantly as he gazed down at me.

"You're lovely," he said.

A giggle tumbled out of me. "I think we're past the point of you needing to seduce me."

"I'm simply making an honest observation."

He tucked his arm around me as he claimed another kiss. My head reeled with it, but I didn't intend to be the only one naked around here. As I drowned in the dark sweetness of his lips, I found the wherewithal to get to work on the buttons of his shirt. When I reached the collar, he shrugged it the rest of the way off for me without releasing my mouth.

Holy mother of miracles, his chest was as stunning as his face, all lean, sculpted muscle beneath creamy skin I couldn't resist running my fingers over. It felt as good as it looked, firm and smooth. The flames of desire kindling between us set off another flood of heat through my body.

Ruse kissed me again, this time so hard it left my head spinning. Then he tucked his face close to mine, nipping my earlobe and murmuring, "There is one other power you might appreciate me employing. If you'd like, I can make sure no sound travels out of this room while we're... occupied."

Um, yeah, that sounded like a good idea. "Be my guest," I managed to say over the eager thump of my heart.

He made a small motion with his hand and then brought that hand to the back of my bra. As the cups slipped from my breasts, he lowered his head to kiss my jaw and then my neck with careful attention.

His lips found every perfect point to spark bliss through my nerves. His hands stroked my breasts, his thumbs swiveling over both nipples at once, and a shuddering gasp tumbled out of me that made me abruptly glad he'd offered his soundproofing skill just now.

My hands settled on the incubus's head of their own accord. As he trailed his mouth down the slope of my chest, my fingers curled into the thick waves of his hair—and brushed against those small horns that protruded on either side. Their curved surface was as hard as bone and faintly textured to the touch, but warm as skin. I grasped them instinctively.

Ruse let out an encouraging growl and swept me off my feet. For a second, I really was soaring—in his arms, from the middle of the room to the middle of my bed.

The incubus bent over me, his gaze intent. His eyes flashed golden. The bright hue only stayed for a second before he blinked as if purposefully willing them back to their mortal-appropriate hazel.

I teased my fingers along his horns and back into his hair. "You don't have to hide it. I know what you are. Let out your regular form if you want."

Ruse smiled wryly at me. "Better not to when you aren't quite as swept up in sensation as I'd usually ensure. It's pretty... intense."

I studied him. "Do you normally need to magically sweep women away before they'll fall into bed with you?"

He dipped his head, teasing his mouth along the crook of my jaw, my earlobe, my cheek. "No," he murmured between the tantalizing kisses. "I happen to only pursue women who are whole-heartedly interested in the general experience. Shame and regret spoil the meal. But certain aspects are better accepted by the mortal mind when I can bring all my powers to bear."

I was about to argue that I could handle intense just fine without any voodoo, thank you, when he claimed my mouth again. The press of his lips was plenty intense on its own. Why argue when I could simply enjoy this?

He fondled my breasts as his tongue tangled with mine, alternately gentle and forceful at just the right moments. My skin was all but singing by the time he slid down to suck one nipple into his hot mouth, and then my nerves might as well have been performing a symphony. The only sound I managed to produce was a wordless moan.

His deft fingers made short work of the fastening on my jeans. As his lips and tongue drew every particle of bliss from my chest, the sensations flaring hotter and deeper with the graze of his teeth, he tugged my pants off me. One hand came back so he could work over both breasts at the same time to even greater effect, and the other drifted across my panties with a caress so light I couldn't stop my hips from arching up in a plea for more.

"Patience," Ruse drawled, the vibration of his voice bringing my nipple to an even stiffer peak. I clung to his hair. As he stretched out his torturously pleasurable attentions to my chest, I emitted all kinds of sounds I'd never have thought any man could drive me to produce. But this wasn't a man, not really.

Right then, I'd have said give me a shadowkind lover over a mortal one any day.

Just as I reached the verge of begging, the incubus eased even farther down my body, and I realized what he'd meant about this encounter being all about me. He hooked his fingers around my panties to drag them down, and then his breath was tingling deliciously over my core. Every inch of me quivered in anticipation. I barely held myself back from yanking his face to me.

He didn't extend the blissful torment too long. The tip of his tongue flicked over my clit at just the right angle. My hips jerked, and he held them while he brought his whole mouth down on me.

Lips and tongue and just the right hint of teeth, from that sensitive bud to my slit and back up again. The wave of pleasure that rolled through me shook a deeper moan from my lungs. Just like that, I was a goner. My head arched back, my eyes rolled up. I'd swear I saw shooting stars as I came.

Ruse wasn't done with me, though. He chuckled against my sex and lapped his tongue over me. I shuddered and whimpered, clutching his horns again, and he penetrated me with a skillful swipe. The ripples of the orgasmic aftershock swelled into a renewed surge, rushing through me higher and faster as he brought his hand to bear too. The pleasure built with each thrust of his fingers and press of his lips until I was bucking to meet him with abandon.

The second wave of release raced through me from

toes to head and then crashed with a shower of ecstasy. I cried out with it, just shy of sobbing. I didn't know whether I deserved this bliss or whether I'd ruined myself for any regular man after this, but in that moment, I wouldn't have traded the experience for a million dollars.

Ruse lifted himself up over me. The flush in his cheeks and the satisfied gleam in his eyes told me he'd achieved everything he'd been looking for out of the encounter even if he hadn't gotten off. He leaned in to give me one last kiss on the cheek.

"That was perfect. I won't keep you from your dinner. Adieu, until tomorrow's adventures."

He stroked his fingers down my side in a final caress, pulled his shirt back on, and left with a soft click of the door closing behind him. My gaze lingered there for a moment longer.

Who would have thought? When all this was over, I might actually miss one of these intruders, just a little.

7

Sorsha

Even at midday with the summer sun beaming, we only passed a couple of dog walkers on the narrow path the trio led me down through the city's largest park. By the time Thorn came to a stop, we were completely alone in a denser stretch of trees. No sound reached us except the chirping of birds.

He motioned to where the path veered down a sharp slope ahead of us and passed beneath a broad concrete bridge. A vine clung to the rough cement surface. The drape of its leaves darkened the passage's opening even more.

"Welcome to the jungle," I muttered to myself. Despite the brightness of the day, this spot felt almost gloomy. "Is there a troll we should be paying a toll to?"

Ruse chuckled, but Thorn only frowned at me. "No trolls. Only enemy mortals, at least on certain occasions."

The guy had no sense of monster humor. I glanced around. "This is where the hunters—or whoever they were—grabbed your guy?"

He nodded, pressing one hand against the other palm. To cover his unusual knuckles while we were out where mortals not in the know could see him, he'd pulled on a pair of fingerless leather gloves, the same fawn-brown as his skin and thin enough not to draw too much attention on their own. Having his hands even slightly confined appeared to irritate him.

"Omen had noticed something unusual in this area. There's a rift between the realms not far from here, so shadowkind often pass through this area. We were... patrolling, searching for evidence. He told us to always remain in the shadows unless we needed to physically interact with an item. He slipped out for a moment just under the bridge—and they came at him from all sides in an instant."

"You hadn't noticed they were there?"

Ruse gestured to the trees on either side of the path. He was sporting a baseball cap to hide his horns, but somehow the sporty headwear didn't diminish his roguish good looks in the slightest. "We were farther back, spread out away from the path," he said. "I didn't even see what was happening until they were already on him. I'd guess they were waiting on top of the bridge, ducked down behind the wall."

Snap paused, his stance tensing as he eyed the structure. He'd seemed to take joy in just about everything he'd encountered in the mortal realm, but the attack here must have really shaken him.

"I could test the bridge," he said, his voice more subdued than usual too. "Over and under. Even with the time passed, if I'm thorough I might be able to taste something about them."

He walked on down the slope without waiting for our agreement. I glanced at Ruse. "Taste something?"

The incubus shot me a grin that set off a flicker of heat in my loins despite the situation. He'd disguised any weakness he'd been suffering from before well, but I'd definitely noticed more spring in his step since our encounter last night.

"You'll see," he said. "Come on. We did rush in after we heard the attack—let's see how much of the scene we can reconstruct."

"If we'd intervened in that first moment instead of holding back..." Thorn rumbled as the three of us followed Snap.

"We've been over this," Ruse said. "Even *you* held back because Omen specifically ordered us not to fight any battles we weren't sure we could win, and you could see that our chances were slim. Those jackasses were clearly prepared to fight—and capture—shadowkind, and there were at least twice as many of them as of us. They'd have taken us all, maybe to a worse fate than those ridiculous cages."

Thorn grimaced. "More than twice. There were ten. But in days past, I could have taken that many on my own. Perhaps I could have still. That's why Omen brought me on."

"You saw how quickly their methods subdued Omen —and he can put up a good fight when he needs to. I remind you again, you were following his orders." Ruse flashed another grin, this one at his beefier companion. "So really, if it's anyone's fault Omen got captured, it's his own."

Thorn made an inarticulate sound of derision, but he stopped arguing. Before he could grouse about anything else, I waved my hand toward the arch of the bridge. "What exactly did you see when you made it over here?"

Thorn tilted his head to the side as he considered the scene. His eyes, so dark I could barely make out the pupils within the irises, went distant as he drew up the memories. The breeze stirred his moonlight-pale hair.

When he wasn't talking or outright scowling, he really was something to look at. The scars that mottled his tan skin—one slicing across the bridge of his nose, another bisecting one of those hard cheekbones, various nicks dappling his brow and the edges of his jaw—only added to the valiant warrior vibe.

"There were the ten of them," he said. "All wearing a sort of plating of silver and iron over their entire torsos and like helmets on their heads. When Omen lashed out at them, it burned him. He still managed to take one down—slashed through his throat just under his chin—

there." He pointed to a spot just beside the base of the bridge. No trace remained of the skirmish that I could see, but it'd been weeks, maybe months, and these people were obviously skilled at removing evidence.

"They didn't have just armor," Ruse put in. "Weapons too. Nets—not the dinky ones they use on the lesser creatures but like they were meant to haul in a boatload of fish, with silver and iron barbs all over. And these sort of whips that swung streams of light. I hadn't seen those before. They caught Omen up in the bindings before he had a chance to escape into the shadows."

Even powerful shadowkind had trouble using their powers if they were bound with iron and silver. As for the rest... As Thorn grunted in agreement with Ruse's account, a chill washed over my skin. *I'd* seen glowing whips in the past. A memory from much longer ago swam up: muttered commands, Auntie Luna's cry, and the arc of searing streams of light swinging at her to bind her in place.

That didn't necessarily mean anything. If there were new weapons that could disable higher shadowkind, anyone who set out to capture or kill them would be using them, with no connection to any other group implied. But I was about to press the men for more detail anyway when Snap leaned over the railing on the bridge above us.

"I think I've got something from that evening here," he said, and then, I swear on a unicorn's ass, he dipped his head lower and flicked his *tongue* across the concrete.

It darted from between his lips farther than any human tongue could have, and he sucked in a breath with a snake-like hiss.

"Um," I said, momentarily lost for words.

Ruse was smirking now. "I told you that you'd see. Omen brought him on board for a reason too. One of his kind's primary talents is picking up impressions of the past from any object they encounter."

By "tasting"—right. I'd never heard of that talent among the shadowkind before. There mustn't be many like him.

The thought of licking that grubby cement made me wince, but it didn't appear to bother Snap any. "Yes," he said dreamily. "At least one of them was crouched here— she bumped her foot against this spot as they all vaulted over. A leather shoe, a little too tightly laced. Pushing fast."

"And probably no one else has touched that exact spot since then," Ruse said. "That's why Snap can still pick up something from that long ago. The most recent impressions end up overwhelming things from farther back."

Snap's gaze refocused on us. An apologetic note came into his voice. "That's all I've been able to find up here from the ambush. It doesn't seem as if it'd help us find Omen."

"The actual battle happened on the ground," Thorn said. "See if you can discover more beneath."

Snap leapt down to join us, landing on his feet more

lightly than you'd expect from a guy that tall. He peered into the thicker gloom beneath the bridge. I found myself staring as his tongue flitted from between his lips to test one patch of wall and then another.

"He can't get sick from doing that, can he?" I asked Ruse. Lord only knew what microbes had taken up residence under there.

Ruse chuckled. "As offensive as it might look, he's not actually making contact, just tasting the energies clinging against the surface. As far as I know, *they* can't do anyone any harm."

That didn't sound so bad, but I couldn't have said I was entirely offended anyway. A certain amount of fascination was involved too. Especially when the dreamy tone came into Snap's voice again.

"One knocked his shoulder here in the struggle—a spot where the armor didn't cover his clothes. His shirt was torn. A piece falling. It might still be..."

He dragged his foot through the scattered leaves, twigs, and other natural debris that had collected along the edge of the passage. With a victorious exclamation, he fished out a small scrap of fabric. As he held it level with his face, his tongue flicked out again, not quite close enough to make the scrap stir with the motion. He inhaled deeply.

"Cotton. Blood from a cut underneath—Omen's claws. The one wearing it bought it—I can see the store— All Military Surplus."

I'd been in that place once or twice—a big warehouse

type store on the industrial side of town. "That doesn't narrow things down much. There've got to be thousands of people in the city who've shopped there."

Snap's face fell. He looked so disheartened that I had to add, "It's amazing that you can tell all that in the first place, though."

"I can taste more when there's a stronger emotional association," he said. "He didn't care about this shirt very much."

"You're giving it your best shot," Ruse reassured him. "Anyway, that tidbit could end up being useful in some way we can't anticipate yet."

"I'll see if I can find more." Snap turned and ventured farther along the passage.

I turned to the others. "Can you remember anything else about the people who staged the ambush—any identifying details at all?"

The incubus spread his hands. "Unfortunately, my skills are fairly short range. I didn't get a detailed read on any of them—nothing beyond the expected aggression and fear."

Thorn studied our surroundings again as if searching for something to jog his memory. "Their faces were mostly covered. From their movements, they were thoroughly trained in combat. A few of them carried silver daggers as well, and one had—I'm not sure what to call it. Like a metal stick that shot electric sparks from one end."

"Some kind of taser."

"I don't know that word." His forehead furrowed. "It had some sort of symbol on it, didn't it? I only saw it for a second—it was mostly covered by the fighter's hand. But the swords in the design caught my attention."

Another, sharper chill prickled through me. "A symbol with swords?"

"Yes. Like a five-pointed star, but the two most horizontal points were drawn as the blades of a sword with a simple joint hilt in the center."

He picked up a stick from beside the path and dug its end into a clear patch of dirt. With several strokes, he sketched out an image so familiar it made my stomach flip over.

The star with the sword points. The hunters who'd come for Luna—I'd caught a glimpse of that symbol on one of the metallic bands they'd worn around their heads. And never found any reference to it since, even with all the searching I'd done in the first few years after her death.

I'd given up on getting justice for her, other than in the roundabout way of striking back against hunters and collectors in general. But the people who'd come for her hadn't just been a particularly vicious group of hunters after all. The symbol connected them to the trained fighters who'd come for the trio's boss as well, eleven years later.

They'd only captured Omen, not slaughtered him, as far as his companions knew. Maybe they hadn't been attempting to kill Luna either. What *were* they doing with the higher shadowkind—and what else had they been up to in the decade in between?

My three lost puppy dogs might be the key to getting answers, and to more questions than I'd even known to ask until now.

My heart had started thumping faster. "After they captured him, didn't you follow to see where they were taking him?"

Thorn let out a huff. "As far as we could. We can move quickly through the shadows, but not swiftly enough to keep pace with your mechanized vehicles."

"They drove off in a big truck," Ruse clarified. "No logos or anything useful there."

Snap emerged on the other side of the passage under the bridge. His tongue darted toward a spot at the corner, and he hummed to himself.

"One leaned back here briefly. Breathing hard. But he was pleased. Very pleased and a little relieved. They must have bound Omen by then." He paused with another flit of his tongue, and a faint smile crossed his face. "He said something—quietly, to a man next to him. 'Let's get it back to Merry Den.'"

Both of his companions stepped closer. "You could hear that?" Ruse said.

"Yes. The sound's blurry, but—he was so eager, the words stuck. Is that good?"

Thorn clapped Snap on the shoulder, so forceful in his enthusiasm that the slimmer guy both beamed and winced. "A name is excellent! The name of where they were taking him." He looked at me. "Do you know a 'Merry Den'?"

The bastards who'd come hunting didn't stand a chance now. I rubbed my hands together as a waft of elation filled my chest. "I don't, but you'd better believe I can find it."

8

Sorsha

Given that we had pretty much no idea who we were dealing with other than that they were formidable as fuck, discretion seemed wise. I held in all other questions until we returned to my apartment with the door shut and locked behind me.

"That symbol you saw on the one man's weapon," I said to Thorn. "The star with the sword points. Have you seen that anywhere else before? Any of you?" I cast my gaze to include the other two shadowkind.

Snap shook his head, a slight crease forming on his brow. Of course, from the way he responded to most things in the mortal realm, I didn't figure he'd seen much of anything on this side of the divide before this recent visit. Ruse contemplated the question for a few seconds longer before indicating no as well.

"I can't remember a time," Thorn said. "Why? Do you think it's especially significant, m'lady? Have *you* come across it before?" As he studied my expression, his near-black eyes darkened even more.

My chest tightened. I wasn't sure how much I wanted to tell them about that part of my life. I'd never gone into much detail with Vivi and the rest of the Fund members, even though they were the ones I'd run to—the ones Auntie Luna had told me to run to—after I'd lost her. My shadowkind guardian and I had kept so many secrets for so long, it was hard to break the habit.

But while I could hardly call these three friends, and they were by at least some definitions of the word monsters, they'd shared everything they could about their own catastrophe with me. I'd seen them at their most vulnerable, pinned by spotlights in giant cages. It wasn't as if sharing the story could hurt me other than the pain that came with remembering those times.

What I did know wasn't going to help us all that much on its own, though. Before I started making inquiries farther abroad, I should see if I could dredge up anything else from the past that might guide that search.

"I think so," I said. "Just once, a long time ago. But all I can tell you for sure about the people who had it is that they came after a higher shadowkind just like your bunch did. I don't know why or even what they meant to do with her. But maybe..."

I glanced at Snap. Ever since I'd seen his talent in action, the thought of other ways he might put it to use had been niggling at me. "Would you be okay with testing a few things I have here with your power and seeing what you can pick up from them?"

He brightened at the suggestion. "Of course," he said. I could see now how carefully he spoke so that his forked tongue barely showed. One of the first things all higher shadowkind seemed to learn was how to disguise their true nature among mortals. "What would you like me to examine?"

"I'll get the things. Why don't you sit down in the living room?" It'd be less cramped than my bedroom, especially since the other two would want to observe.

He tipped his head in agreement, his golden curls jostling against each other, and all but bounded through the doorway. You'd have thought I'd offered him a year's supply of ripe bananas, not asked to put him to work.

I ducked into my bedroom to dig into the back of my closet shelf. From what the trio had indicated, Snap's ability mainly picked up the most recent impressions. For there to be any real chance of him gleaning something about Luna's life, I'd need to give him objects I hadn't handled much in the past eleven years. I grabbed an Amazon delivery box I hadn't gotten around to tossing yet and plucked up a pair of sparkly sneakers and a purple scrunchie to set inside so that I didn't have to touch them too much now as I carried them over.

My attention stalled on a small, pearly box tucked in the corner of the shelf. There wasn't any practical reason to have Snap test that...

I wavered, a lump rising in my throat. Then, not letting myself second-guess the impulse, I wedged it into one of the hip pockets on my cargo pants. If I changed my mind in the moment, I didn't have to take it out at all.

In the living room, Snap had sat down on the plaid sofa, giving off definite eager puppy vibes. Ruse dropped into the not-at-all-matching polka-dot armchair that stood kitty-corner to the sofa; Thorn leaned against the wall by the doorway with his arms crossed. I set my box down on the wobbly coffee table in front of Snap and turned to the CD rack next to my little TV. I was pretty sure that at least one of these...

Ah ha, that one would be perfect. I slid the case out, touching as little of its surface as possible, and added it to the box.

"It doesn't matter what order you go in," I said. "Just see if you can pick up anything about someone who used them other than me. There might not be anything, but... it seems worth a try."

Snap set his godly face with such determination that his gorgeousness made my pulse flutter despite my nerves. "I'll do my best." He picked up the scrunchie first, giving it a curious look before raising it closer to his mouth.

Luna's devotion to '80s culture had included not just music but all forms of art and fashion. I'd rarely seen her without her light auburn waves pulled high in one of those contraptions. The purple one had been mixed up in my emergency-bag clothes—I'd only found it days after

I'd fled. I didn't know how often she'd worn that one, but I'd never used it.

Snap's tongue flicked from his lips, and his moss-green eyes hazed. I stood beside the coffee table, trying to keep a relaxed stance, but my shoulders kept stiffening despite my best efforts.

I'd told him to look for impressions that didn't involve me, but that didn't mean he wouldn't still pick those up. When I'd pulled the thing out of my bag eleven years ago and realized what it was, I'd bawled for a good half hour.

The chance of him seeing that was worth the embarrassment if he also sensed anything that might tell us who'd been after my guardian—and what they'd meant to do to her.

Snap drew in a breath and paused. The corners of his mouth tightened. He shifted the scrunchie in his grasp and tasted its energies again. A restless itch crept under my skin.

Then his eyes widened. His voice came out as dreamy as it had at the bridge. "A shadowkind wore this. Yellowish-orange hair. A light sort of energy—she was fae. She fixed a flower into her hair with this once: an iris. *Purple goes with purple—I can coordinate at least that well.*"

His voice wasn't at all like Luna's high soprano, but he hit the melodic cadence just right. A shiver ran down my back, equal parts thrilled and pained. I hadn't expected to be offered an echo of the past quite that potent. What I wouldn't have given to really hear her voice—to have her still with me. What would she think of the woman I'd finished growing into?

Thorn stirred, his jaw flexing as if he wanted to say something, but he held himself in check while the other shadowkind continued his inspection. Finally, Snap set the scrunchie back down. When he looked at me, I saw more than just an apology in his gaze.

The lump in my throat came back. Everything else he'd gleaned must have had to do with me. Not surprising after all that time.

He might have been clueless about a lot of mortal things, but he was shrewd enough—and kind enough—to keep whatever private moments he'd uncovered to himself, no acknowledgment other than that hint of sympathetic sorrow. "I couldn't find anything else from her," he said. "She's the one you were hoping I'd reach?"

I nodded, not totally trusting my voice to stay steady. Thorn cleared his throat imperiously before Snap could reach for the next item. "Who *was* this fae? Do you believe she was captured by the same group that took Omen?"

I inhaled slowly, making sure I had a grip on myself, before I met his demanding gaze. Stick to the facts, keep it short, and there was no need to get emotional about it. All of this was more than a decade past anyway.

"My parents died when I was three," I said. "They were involved in the same kinds of activities the Fund is —helping the shadowkind. One of those was a fae woman named Luna. I don't remember much from back then, but

I know they stayed close friends with her. She came by the house a lot, played with me... She was with me when my parents were attacked, and she got me away from there."

That day had become reduced to a few fragments in my memories: chasing fireflies in the backyard, their glow and the beat of their wings against my hands, a scream carrying through the back door, my mother's ragged voice crying, "Luna, go!" Luna's skinny arms around me as she'd leapt up with supernatural speed to carry me over the fence and away.

"Luna didn't like to talk about what happened, but from what I gathered, some hunters found out that my parents had interfered with their business and came after them in revenge. After that, she raised me. We moved around a lot because she was always nervous, but no one bothered us for a long time... When I was sixteen, she somehow knew people were coming—we grabbed the things we had packed to run for it—but they'd already reached the house."

"They captured her as they did Omen," Thorn filled in.

I shook my head. "I don't know what they were planning. At the time, I thought they were trying to kill her for being a shadowkind passing as human. They came at her with those whips of light like you said, and one of them had the star symbol on his clothing... They'd almost managed to bind her up when she must have decided she'd rather die on her own terms than theirs—and distract them so I'd have more chance to escape."

That knowledge came with a pang of guilt. I swallowed hard and managed to go on. "With her magic... She burst apart, like a firework."

It had been stunningly beautiful and horrifying at the same moment. I'd been so stunned myself that I'd frozen in place. Thankfully Luna's last act had also literally stunned her attackers, who'd stumbled around dazed for long enough that I'd remembered I needed to get the hell out of there if I'd wanted her sacrifice to mean anything at all.

"Maybe they were only going to capture her, though," I added. "If they were the same people who ambushed your boss. Hell, if they've been up to some kind of larger scale illicit dealings for even longer, it could have been their operations my parents disrupted—they could be the ones who murdered them too."

"Are you sure your parents *are* dead?" Ruse asked, his voice carefully gentle.

"Yeah. Luna wouldn't have kept me away from them. And, my dad at least... They cut off his head."

I had no visual memory of that moment anymore, only the fact of what I'd seen and the *thunk* of it hitting the ground after it'd been flung out the window. After I'd woken up nearly every night for weeks sobbing hysterically from nightmares of that moment, Luna had used some of her magic to wipe the image itself from my mind. *I don't want to take all of it*, she'd said. *You need to remember why it's important that we stay cautious. But the whole thing is too much.*

All three of my guests were silent in the wake of that comment. The weight of their hesitation filled the room. I motioned my hand vaguely as if I could wave their reaction away. "If it's the same people, then all the more reason I'll be happy to help you track them down. I just wanted to see if any impressions from Luna's things might be useful."

Snap took my cue to move along. "Let me try the others, then." He picked up the CD case and swiveled it in his hands.

Luna had indoctrinated me with a lot of her tastes, but I'd just never been able to get behind Def Leppard. Whenever she'd put that album on when I was a kid, I'd groan until she gave in and turned it off. I suspected *she* only liked them because of their name—she'd had a thing for big cats too.

Yet of course she'd kept it in the assortment of "essential music" that stayed in my emergency duffel bag. One of her top twenty, apparently.

Snap gave the case the same thorough examination as he had the scrunchie and frowned. "I hear a little laughter and the sense of her opening it on a couple of spots, but nothing more than that."

"That's okay. I knew not to get my hopes up."

He'd left the sneakers for last. I wasn't sure whether to have the most or the least hope for those.

Luna had adored them, called them her "fairy dust

shoes"... but I'd also worn them for the most traumatic moment of my near-adult life. Sixteen-year-old me, with typical teenage rebelliousness, hadn't left my shoes where I could easily snatch them up the night we had to flee. It'd started to seem so ridiculous that Luna insisted on so many precautions. Instead of waiting for me to search the piles of clothing around my bedroom, Luna had tossed that pair of hers at me on the way to the door.

They were too small for me by at least one size, maybe two. My recollection of the run away from the house she'd been renting was punctuated by the pinch of my constricted toes, sharper with each step.

No doubt Snap tasted that fraught impression first. He glanced at me again, his divine face haunted by a brief sadness, and then went on with his investigations. I resisted the urge to fidget.

"It's only fragments," he said after a while. "I think because it's been so long—I'm sorry. A lot of happiness when she wore them. And... I get a hint of missing someone they reminded her of, someone who was fae like her maybe? Did she have shadowkind friends? Someone else who might have been taken?"

"I don't know." I was a little ashamed that it'd never really occurred to me to wonder about Luna's social life or lack thereof. "Except when I was at school, she was always with me, and we never visited anyone. We never stayed in any city for more than a couple of years to make close friends."

But maybe there'd been someone she'd left behind in

one of those cities—or way back in the shadow realm—
that she'd never mentioned to me. Another sacrifice she'd
made, one without my ever knowing.

"This line of investigation does not appear to be very
fruitful," Thorn declared gruffly. He stalked over to the
window to survey the street outside as if he felt he'd find
more sense of direction there.

"It wasn't a bad idea," Ruse said more encouragingly.
"When we've got this little to go on, can't leave any stone
unturned." He flashed me a smile before getting up.

As the incubus slipped out of the room, Snap put
away the shoes. He sighed, all this enthusiasm over
contributing having faded away, and stood up. My
stomach twisted, but if nothing else, he'd shown he could
be respectful of my past traumas. Thorn didn't appear to
be paying attention anyway—and what did I care what *he*
thought, the big grouch?

I touched Snap's arm. "Wait. There's something else
—not to do with Luna. Just, for me... It's even more of a
longshot, but anything you pick up from it that doesn't
involve me would be more than I've got now."

I pulled out the trinket box with its pearly shell
casing. Snap took it from me with tentative fingers. He
considered it and then my face.

"This wasn't the fae's," he ventured. "It belonged to
your parents?"

"Yeah," I said. "It's—it's the only thing I have of
theirs. They'd given it to Luna to keep for me, just in
case."

There was a letter inside, one I'd pored over so many times I couldn't imagine it held any impressions that weren't of me. Telling me that if I was reading it, they were sorry they weren't there with me, but they hoped I was staying safe with Luna. That what was most important to them was me getting to live my life as fully as I could.

They'd known the hunters might retaliate. They'd been prepared. But I hadn't been. I remembered my mother's scream and the sound of my father meeting his death more clearly than anything else about them.

Snap dipped his head so low it was almost a bow. "I appreciate your trusting me with this. I'll handle it carefully."

He began his testing even more slowly than before, his tongue flitting here and there, his breath sucked in and expelled. I stuffed my hands in my pockets as I waited. Finally, he lowered the box.

"You're right," he said. "There isn't much. But they had a lot of feeling around this object, so a bit of it clung on even across that many years. They were very sad about the thought that you might need to receive this. Afraid of losing their time with you—but not of the course they'd taken. They were proud of that, of taking risks..." He took another taste as if to clarify that thought. "I get the sense they felt they wouldn't have had you in their lives at all if they hadn't taken those risks."

"Maybe they met through the Fund, through the shadowkind work they were doing," I said.

"That makes sense." He offered the box back to me. Our hands brushed as I took it, and he offered me a smile so soft but bright that I lost my breath like I had that first morning when he'd compared my hair to the peach. "The one thing I can tell for sure is they loved you more than anything else in all the realms."

I choked up abruptly. "Thank you. For all of this. I'll do whatever I can to find the people who took your boss."

"I know you will." He touched my hair again, just for a moment, still smiling. "I thought so when you broke into my cage, but I think it even more now. You're meant to do good things, Peach."

Then he ambled away, leaving me wondering why I felt as if I'd needed so very badly to hear someone tell me that.

9

Thorn

If I were not beholden to our liberator's efforts on our behalf, there were many things I could have complained about in regards to this mortal woman. The way she rattled the ends of the twig-like things she'd called "chopsticks" against the sides of one of the boxes our dinner had arrived in. The squeak of the kitchen chair's feet as she periodically tipped back her weight in it. The little laughs she made to herself while she prodded her "laptop" into producing information that apparently was more amusing than useful to our quest.

She made a lot of jokes, this one. Here in her home, out at the bridge, in that large room full of padded chairs where she'd met with the rest of her "Fund" friends. And always singing her silly songs too. As if Omen's life might not depend on how quickly we could decipher what had happened to him. As if so many other lives might not hang in the balance based on what we discovered.

But none of those things were worth putting into words, not when I knew that without her I'd have still been locked in a cage. I might not appreciate her attitude, but I'd ensure no harm came to her on my watch. If it itched at me that I wasn't out scouring the streets for our leader right now, I had only to remind myself that the mortal had uncovered far more connections in the past day than we'd managed in the many weeks before. The fact that most of those weeks had been spent in captivity only compounded that failure.

Omen had counted on us. He'd counted on *me*, specifically, to defend our group and subdue any enemies we encountered. It didn't matter what the incubus said— he was made to cajole and placate. I *had* failed, again, and if I didn't correct that failing quickly, it could turn into an even greater disaster than the time before.

"Ah ha!" the lady crowed, and waved her hand rather wildly at the glowing screen of her device. "There's a flea market in a town near here called Merry Den Market."

I couldn't imagine there being much of a demand among mortals to buy fleas, but she seemed satisfied with the discovery. I stirred in the chair I'd taken across from her. "You believe the people we're looking for could be keeping Omen there?"

"I don't know." A thin line formed on her pale brow as she tapped one of those chopsticks against her lips. "It doesn't look like the kind of place hunters or anyone else dealing in shadowkind would operate out of... but you can't always tell by appearances. That could make it a perfect cover. It's closed now, but we can go check it out tomorrow. I won't be able to stop by Jade's until the evening anyway."

Ruse straightened up from where he'd been lounging against the doorframe. "A little road trip. I'm looking forward to it."

Since we'd finished our meal, Snap had been puttering around the mortal's living room asking the incubus about every object he encountered. Now, the devourer poked his head out, his eyes eagerly wide. "Road trip? Does that mean we'll take one of those... cars?"

The lady grimaced. "I don't have one. Not much need for it when you're living downtown—and you can make stealthier getaways on foot. I actually never even got my license." She looked vaguely embarrassed about this admission, as if there were any honor in burning gas through a metal shell to make wheels spin.

"I suppose it's too much to hope that there might be horses we can make use of?" I said.

Her mouth twitched, because apparently she found that remark amusing as well. "Sorry, but no. It looks like there's a bus that should drop us off right outside, though."

"Should we ever find ourselves with a car of some sort, I can manage to drive," Ruse offered. "I may even be able to help with the finding one part."

She shot him a skeptical glance, still smiling. "You mean you'd seduce someone into giving us theirs?"

He spread his hands with a smirk in return. "I'd rather think of it as reminding them of the potential generosity in their nature."

I shifted in my seat again, tamping down on my irritation. The incubus never took anything all that seriously either. His skill at reading and manipulating emotions *would* have come in handy if we'd gotten farther into our investigations with Omen, but he was no use at all in a battle.

"Let's see if I can turn up any other promising results, in case the flea market isn't what we're looking for," the lady said, returning her attention to the computer.

Snap was still peering into the kitchen. "What's a bus?" he asked.

Ruse motioned him back into the living room, following at his heels. "Let Sorsha do her computer magic. I'll explain."

"The computer runs on *magic?*"

The incubus chuckled before their voices faded out with the closing of the door. The lady's smile turned wry. "Sometimes it does seem that way. Including the unpredictable element. Oh, hey, Pickle."

She clucked her tongue, and the little green creature that appeared to follow her all around the apartment scrambled up to her lap and then her shoulder. She plucked one last morsel of sauced chicken out of the carton and offered it to him. He gulped it down with a bob of his long throat and a pleased thrum of his chest plates.

Watching, I found I couldn't quite hold my tongue about *that* gnawing complaint.

"You freed us and the lesser beings in that prison from our cages," I said. "Why do you keep this creature at your beck and call?"

She reached up to scratch the underside of the minor shadowkind's chin. "Beck and call? You haven't been paying attention if you think Pickle listens to me any more often than he wants to."

"He is confined here, is he not? You don't let him leave." I'd never seen him so much as dip into the shadows, though I couldn't see any evidence of how she might have forced his physical presence.

The mortal fixed her gaze on me more steadily then, with a puzzled blink. "He stays because he wants to. It's a pretty good gig—food and cuddles for doing a very half-assed job as a guard dragon."

Did she suppose that made her possession of him acceptable? "The 'collector' who imprisoned us fed us as well."

Her free hand balled where it was resting on the table. "You're comparing me to *those* pricks? Are you kidding me?"

Any trace of humor had left her voice. I'd clearly offended her. That seemed only fair, when the sight of her carting around her pet shadowkind offended me at least as much.

"You're welcome to educate me on exactly how it's different," I said.

Her jaw tensed. For a second, I thought I might see a flare of anger as scorching as that hair of hers. Then she appeared to master herself. She stroked the creature's flank.

"I don't need to justify myself to you," she said, her tone more cold than fiery. "*I'm* doing *you* all kinds of favors. But since you brought it up—Pickle can't survive on his own. The hunter who sold him or the collector who bought him had his wings clipped so he can barely fly, and he wasn't made to get around by walking—if you can even call that waddle 'walking.' Would anyone back in the shadow realm make sure he had all the food he needs and that he didn't go stumbling through a rift into a hunter's snare again?"

I had noticed the creature barely used those wings, but I had to admit I'd assumed it was laziness due to his captivity, not a disability. As to her question... I gritted my teeth before I answered, "No, I don't suppose there would be."

"Exactly. I wasn't looking to take on a pet, let alone one I'd have to hide from any regular person who comes around the apartment, but he was there in one of the houses I set fire to a couple years back, and he obviously couldn't look after himself, so I wasn't going to just abandon him."

She brandished her chopsticks at me. "You should be glad I'm not in the habit of kicking shadowkind to the curb, or imagine where you could be. If you want to be mad at someone, make it the assholes who thought mangling Pickle's body was a reasonable way to treat another living being."

She was obviously mad at them. Her voice had stayed flat, but a tartness had crept into her tone, and the bright flash of her copper-brown eyes— I wasn't sure I'd envy any mortal being who went up against her. Imagine what she might do with a sword.

Perhaps, under the jokes and frivolity, she did care quite a bit.

"My apologies," I said, with a stiffness I couldn't smooth out. "I shouldn't have leapt to such a conclusion. You've been very generous with us—and it seems you are with your little green companion as well."

Sorsha eyed me for a moment longer as if confirming that I was being genuine. Then she relaxed in her chair. Now that I recognized the bond as one of protection rather than incarceration, it was impossible not to see the affection with which she tipped her cheek toward the creature to meet his nuzzle.

No, I hadn't been fair at all. I grappled with the twist of discomfort that acknowledgment brought and then leaned forward. If she could surprise me that much, I'd like to discover what else I might have missed.

"Tell me more about this 'flea market,' would you, m'lady?"

10

Sorsha

As we stepped off the bus by the flea market's gate, Thorn tugged at his fingerless gloves as if he'd like them better if he adjusted the fit for the one hundredth time. I checked Ruse's cap to make sure it was hiding all sign of his horns. Catching my examination, he tipped the brim to me in a jaunty salute.

"All monstrous features well hidden away," he said with a grin.

The four of us had gotten into a bit of an argument about them accompanying me at all. The trio had promised to keep their nature under wraps, but given Ruse's casual attitude and the others' inexperience with modern life, I wasn't convinced they'd keep it. I'd done my best to stress how ill-prepared most of my fellow twenty-first century mortals were to cope with the idea of supernatural beings in their midst.

I pointed a finger at him, just shy of waggling it. "I'll be watching you."

In some ways, Snap had both the easiest and the hardest time of it. Concealing his tongue didn't require any awkward fashion statements, but on the other hand, it also meant he had to rein in his enthusiasm at least a little—and refrain from using his power. From the way he gazed around us as we stepped under the awning that shaded the outer half of the market, he'd have liked to test a whole lot of the objects around us.

"Remember," I said quietly to the trio. "We're looking for any sign of shadowkind or that sword-star symbol. Try to stay focused."

Ruse gave me a thumbs-up. Thorn frowned as if he resented the reminder and strode on slightly ahead of the rest of us.

I had to give Snap a little nudge to get him moving again. He tilted his head at a curious angle, taking in a used electronics booth and a table stacked with scented candles. Farther along, pendulums swung on intricately carved wooden clocks. He couldn't seem to help stopping to follow the rhythm of one for a few seconds.

As I tugged him along the crowded aisle, he leaned close to me. His warm breath tickled my ear. "There are so many things here—and each array is so different from the others! Are they really all being sold? What were those objects with the numbers and the ticking?"

"Clocks," I said, scanning the shoppers and stalls around us. "They're for telling time. And yep, pretty much everything here is on offer—they'd probably even sell the tables if someone put up the cash."

"Telling time," Snap repeated in a puzzled tone.

"Like, how long it's been during the day. It took us an hour to get here on the bus."

"Ah! That *would* be good to keep track of." He peered back over his shoulder at the booth, so avidly I half expected him to bound back over there and grab one for himself. I guessed shadowkind didn't worry much about the passage of hours—or days or sometimes even years—while they went about their business in their own realm. From the way Auntie Luna had described it when I'd badgered her for information, things there didn't work in ways mortal senses understood.

The best I can describe it is that it's like a vast dark cave, one you'd never reach the walls or back of, she'd said. *You're aware of who and what's around you, but everything feels somewhat... flat. You could almost say it's like a dream, one interaction and another bleeding into each other without much logic to it.*

Do you miss it? I'd asked her, and she'd laughed and said, *Not while I can be here with you.* But after what Snap had gleaned from her glittery shoes, I wasn't sure how true that was. No matter how flat and random the shadow realm was, how could you not miss the place where you came to be?

She would have loved this market. When I was a kid,

she'd drag me off to garage sales and church bazaars and the like: anyplace where you never knew what you might stumble on that could be bought for not much money at all—not that she ever used real money when her illusionary magic could transform a few pieces of blank paper into a payment. She might even have gotten her fairy dust shoes at one of those places.

By the time I'd hit my teens, all I'd seen was a bunch of junk. I hadn't been to a market like this in years. So far, I hadn't spotted anything to make me think shadowkind other than the three who'd come with me had ever passed through.

Snap's slim fingers encircled my forearm with a gentle squeeze. "What are those for?" he murmured, his eyes almost round.

He was staring at a rack of bikes and—if you can believe it—unicycles in the corner of the market we'd just reached. The man behind the rack motioned to a kid I figured was his, who hopped up on a small unicycle and showed off her skills pedaling back and forth, her body swaying over the seat. Somehow Snap's eyes managed to grow even larger.

"Most people don't use those anymore," I said. "Not the things with one wheel, anyway. The two-wheeled ones are for getting around, like buses and cars, only they don't go as fast."

"Why use them, then?" Snap said as I ushered him onward.

"Well, speed isn't everything. You don't need any

fuel to make them go, which saves money, and they're good exercise to keep your body in shape. And you don't need a license, so there's a lot less hassle and paperwork."

"Paperwork." His puzzled tone had come back.

I elbowed him playfully. "Believe me, you don't want to get into *that*. Come on, Thorn and Ruse are leaving us behind."

The other two had only made it about three booths ahead of us, but Snap took the warning with all seriousness. He darted between the other shoppers to reach them, faster than I could match. Then he stopped in his tracks, faced with a stall offering stacks of gleaming honey jars.

The woman behind the table held out a little plastic spoon. "Want a sample?"

Snap accepted the offering as if he wasn't quite sure how he'd gotten so lucky. He carefully dipped the spoon into his mouth so his forked tongue could stay hidden. Oh, boy.

If I'd thought I'd seen his face lit up with joy before, it was nothing compared to the expression I saw now. His eyes outright sparkled. He glanced over at me, not just reveling in the sweetness but wanting to share it, and my heart skipped a beat.

Oh, boy, indeed. That sensation wasn't just the awe I'd felt seeing his full beauty. Nope, the giddy tingle that had shot through me had at least as much carnal desire in it too. What would it be like to taste that honey off those godly lips? To experience his divine eagerness in all sorts of other ways?

I shook the giddiness and the questions off as quickly as they'd come. This wasn't the time for it. But when I dragged my gaze away from Snap, it caught Ruse's. He was watching me with a knowing smirk.

I gave him a light punch as I caught up with him. "Shut up."

"I didn't say anything," the incubus said, all innocence other than that damned smirk.

"You were thinking it very loudly."

Ruse tucked his arm around my waist as if we were some kind of couple. The slide of his hand across my back left me tingling all over again.

"It's nothing to be ashamed of," he said under his breath. "The boy's got something special. If I swung in that direction, I'd be angling to get him into my bed too."

I resisted the urge to kick him as a follow-up to the punch. "Did you miss the part about shutting up?" What if Snap overheard? Would he know what the hell we were talking about? I could only imagine trying to deal with *those* sorts of questions.

As far as I'd been able to determine, sex wasn't really a thing in the shadow realm. Shadowkind emerged from the ether, or whatever it was, rather than being born. The cubi kind had to venture into the mortal realm to sate their hunger. I'd never seen anything like a carnal longing in Snap's demeanor. He probably had no idea that kind of pleasure was even possible.

How ecstatic would he look when he discovered it?

Nope, nope, not chugging along with that train of thought right now. But I did let myself smile as Snap rejoined us, exclaiming over the spoonful of honey. His joyful sense of wonder might be catching.

Maybe places like this weren't all junk. I shouldn't let my former teenage cynicism color how I looked at it now. There was a sort of magic to the possible treasures you could stumble on—even more so when it was all brand new to you.

I spent most of my life dealing with paranormal creatures from an otherworldly realm. I had a pet miniature *dragon*, by all that was holy. I really ought to revel in that magic a little more myself, in between the difficult bits.

Thorn had marched deeper into the crowd. He doubled back just outside the doorway to the inner market.

"Did you spot something?" I asked.

His expression was slightly more grave than usual. I was learning to read the Thorn range of emotions, from vaguely discomforted (his happiest) through to "the apocalypse is nigh" (his most severe, I was assuming in the hopes of never seeing it).

"Not any sign that we were seeking," he said. "But I have a sense that a man several paces behind you has started following us."

I restrained myself from glancing back. Giving away that we'd noticed a potential tail was an amateur's mistake. "How sure are you? Everyone's kind of moving in the same direction along the stalls."

Thorn's frown deepened a tad more. "My instincts are well honed. I will observe more closely."

He headed off before I could say anything else. I glanced at Ruse. "Do you think we should get out of here?"

The incubus shrugged. "It's not as though anyone stalking us could have realized what we're looking for, since *we* haven't found any trace of it yet. I haven't picked up any ill intent toward us from anyone we've come near. And our disguises are firmly in place." He tweaked his cap. "I think we're fine. Let's keep going and see what they do next."

That sounded like a reasonable enough plan. Especially since while we'd been distracted, Snap had already wandered ahead into the sprawling building that contained the other half of the market. I hustled to reach him before he became so overwhelmed by amazement he forgot to tone it down to reasonably acceptable levels.

Somehow he managed to be equally fascinated by old leather jackets and the artwork on retro video game cases. But we kept him moving, studying the stalls as well as the walls and ceiling of the building around them. We'd made it up and down two of the four aisles when Thorn returned.

"Have you sufficiently defended our honor?" Ruse asked him.

Thorn glowered at him, but there wasn't much

conviction to it. "The one I thought was following us went in a different direction and left."

"Ah. So either he's very bad at this whole following thing, or he wasn't interested in us in the first place."

"I might have misread the situation," Thorn admitted. "But I think it's equally likely someone else was monitoring us, and I simply attributed that awareness to the wrong target."

I scanned the crowd. "Do you feel like we're being tracked *now*?"

He paused, his gaze making a similar trajectory across the market. "I'm not sure. Not strongly enough to narrow down the source, in any case."

Ruse patted him on the arm. "That, my friend, is called 'paranoia.'"

The remark earned him a whole-hearted glower. Before they could get into a real squabble, I nudged them both. "Come on. We're going to lose Snap at this rate. Let's just get through the rest of the market."

My expectations had already been low. By the time we emerged from the market building's back door, they'd bottomed out. Even Snap's high spirits flagged as he took in our expressions.

"This wasn't the right place?" he said.

He was the one who'd given us the name. I couldn't bring myself to completely nix any usefulness he'd felt. "It could be that the sword-star bunch only used it the one time to pass Omen on to someone else or to get a different vehicle to transport him. It just doesn't look as if anyone with shadowkind connections has a regular presence here."

"I will—" Thorn started, and seemed to catch himself. He frowned, his gaze settling on me and jerking away again. "I'll endeavor to bring on a shadowkind or two willing to survey this location across the next few days to confirm that conclusion."

I suspected he'd been going to say that *he* would keep an eye on the market but then remembered his commitment to watch over me. It was hard to argue with him about that when he hadn't outright said it, though.

"You'd better let me do the smooth-talking," Ruse said. "That's *my* job here, after all. I'm sure I can find a willing candidate." As we meandered back toward the bus stop, he slipped his hand into his pocket. "And our expedition wasn't totally fruitless. For the lady."

He held out his hand to me with a little bow, his tone an obvious mockery of Thorn's formal courtesy. A gold chain with a pendant dangled from his fingers: a pendant in the shape of a curled dragon, its one visible eye a glinting ruby.

"Given your choice of pet, I thought you might appreciate it," he said, grinning.

It was a charming enough gesture that my chest fluttered—but also completely unacceptable. I admired the necklace for a moment longer and then tucked the pendant back into his palm. "You stole that, didn't you?"

"I liberated it from its display rack."

I rolled my eyes at him. "Stolen goods don't make a great gift, FYI. You can't go around just taking whatever you want." A decency you couldn't count on any shadowkind recognizing.

"You lifted some pretty trinkets from our collector," he pointed out.

I hadn't realized he'd noticed that. That didn't change my answer, though. "It's not the same thing. The collector had money coming out of his ass, and he was using it in horrible ways. The people who set up shop in that market—most of them are barely making ends meet. And even if they're doing all right, they don't deserve to be robbed. Take it back."

Ruse let out a little huff, but his eyes still gleamed with good humor. "As the lady requires." He stepped toward the trees beside the sidewalk and wisped away into the shadows to do so.

Snap had cocked his head. "Can mortals really produce money out of their—"

"Just an expression," I said quickly. "Don't worry about it." Especially when we had so many other things to worry about. I couldn't help studying the street around us in case Thorn's possibly imagined follower had trailed us out here.

No one I saw appeared to be paying any attention to us at all, other than a teenage girl who openly ogled both Thorn and Snap as she sauntered past. I could hardly blame her for that.

Well, our next course of action had already been decided. I exhaled, making a silent plea to the fates that today wouldn't be a total loss. "We've still got the bar tonight. Jade is a better bet than the market was anyway."

11

Sorsha

I wouldn't have called Jade's Fountain exactly *posh*, but it did have a vibe you needed to dress to match if you didn't want to stick out like a total rube. Inventive but sophisticated was probably the best description. I didn't get dolled up very often, but over the years I'd picked up a few suitable dresses for my nights on the town with Vivi.

For this evening, I pulled on the forest-green one that set off my hair—and my collarbone with its square neckline. The geometric element was repeated in the black buckle of the dress's wide belt and the cut-out pattern in the bottom few inches of the knee-length skirt. Flashes of my thighs in their silky black tights showed through those peepholes as I turned in front of my bedroom mirror.

Between the outfit and the makeup I'd carefully applied, toeing the line between striking and overboard, I looked a lot more sophisticated than I generally felt. Luna would have liked it, though, even if the colors weren't the bright ones she adored. I adjusted the cap sleeves, pepping myself up with a murmured lyric: "Neat seams are laid to please. Who am I to disagree?"

It wasn't just Jade's clientele this get-up would please, apparently. The moment I stepped out of the bedroom, Ruse let out an approving whistle from where he'd been hanging out by the living room doorway. "Not that I had any complaints before, but you *do* clean up nicely, Miss Blaze."

I pressed my hand to my chest in a mock swoon, although the appreciation in his voice had given me a quiver of pleasure too. "Be still my beating heart."

The incubus ambled closer. I could almost feel his eyes roving over me like a whisper of a caress. "I think it's much more fun to speed that pulse up. I hope you'll be down for some fun alongside all your hard work. You'll deserve it."

"Not at the bar," I reminded him with a jab of my finger. "You're staying put." I'd insisted that my entourage let me navigate this part of the investigation alone. They might be able to pass for mortal among people who weren't in the know, but there were bound to be at least a few shadowkind—including Jade herself, of course—enjoying a night out at the bar.

And Vivi. If she found out about my new roommates,

I'd never keep her out of the perilous situation I'd stumbled into.

Ruse winked. "I'll just have to wait up for you then."

Thorn came out of the kitchen, where he seemed to have declared the one chair his official domain, to see what the fuss was about. His gaze skimmed over me and shifted to the incubus.

"She isn't going out to make merry or invite intimate relations," he chided. "This is about finding—and rescuing—Omen."

Ruse rolled his eyes. "Forgive me, my lord, for daring to distract the fine maiden from her quest. I'll just have to find another young lady to bestow my affections on." He sauntered back to the living room and swept Pickle's mannequin into his arms.

"You look absolutely exquisite tonight, my darling," he said. "No one could possibly compare. May I have this dance?"

I raised my hand to my mouth to cover a giggle. The incubus dipped the headless, armless figure low, filling his voice with exaggerated passion. "How can I resist you? And yet—how can I possibly kiss you when you have no mouth? My heart breaks!"

My giggle turned into a full-out laugh. Thorn's scowl deepened. "You're ridiculous," he informed Ruse, and turned back to me. "And you do look as if you've fashioned yourself to draw attention."

My amusement dampened. I folded my arms over my chest. "I don't see how what I'm wearing could be a problem, but maybe you should remember that I know a lot more about what I'm walking into than you do. This is how people dress at Jade's. People will trust me more if I look like I belong there instead of like I'm some clueless newbie."

Thorn let out a grunt that was barely conciliatory. He cut his gaze toward Ruse before returning it to me. "I suppose it's for the best that this one won't be along to divert you, then."

Something in his tone pricked at me. He hadn't said it in so many words, hadn't given any indication before now that he knew what Ruse and I had gotten up to in the privacy of my bedroom, but he knew what the incubus was. It wouldn't have been hard for him to guess. I was abruptly certain that I'd heard disapproval of our prior diversions under that statement.

As if there was something wrong with me getting a little enjoyment out of the company I'd been forced to accept. While I was running around the city and beyond it trying to solve their mystery for them, on top of that.

I let my lips curve into a smirk I intended to rival Ruse's. "Maybe I *should* bring you along. You could obviously use some practice in loosening up. Constantly going around like you've just put your best friend in the ground doesn't help us find your boss any faster, you know."

Now I was getting the full Thorn glower. "Do you have a problem with my comportment, m'lady?" he asked stiffly.

"Yeah, actually, I do. Considering all the favors you're asking of me, the least *you* could do is act like you're at least a little happy for the help."

"And what would 'happy' look like to you?"

I waved my arm in his general direction. "Allow a few words to come out of your mouth that aren't criticizing or ordering people around. Convince your face to appear somewhat less solemn than a gravestone. Just as a couple of options."

Thorn drew himself up even straighter, which with his considerable height meant that his head nearly brushed the top of the doorframe. Even Ruse, who'd set the mannequin back in place, tensed at the sight. Snap peeked out of the living room and promptly ducked away to return to the TV he'd become enamored with.

"I haven't meant to disturb you," Thorn said, his voice even deeper and more gravelly than usual. He motioned to the living room. "I'm not one for chatter like these two. I say what I need to in order to see important matters through. And right now the matters we're facing give me no cause for happiness. The one who set me on this quest is lost, I was wrenched from my attempts to locate him for so long the trail has gone cold, and at any moment I might lose any of you as well—"

He stopped abruptly, his expression shuttering, as if he'd said more than he'd meant to. I'd definitely heard more than he'd actually said this time, but it hadn't been derision. The undercurrent of pain and fear had been palpable.

He blamed himself for what had happened to Omen. He felt responsible for his companions—and for me—and no doubt he would beat himself up all over again if we got hurt.

I could have told you those things already, as facts, but I hadn't grasped how deeply he felt that shame and commitment until just now. It wasn't simply an abstract idea of loyalty he was following to the letter. He was truly worried—about whether we'd find Omen, and also about what might happen to me at the bar tonight, to Ruse and Snap if we didn't unravel this mystery in time.

My own frustration simmered down. I still had the urge to give the guy a cheeky prodding and tease him into cracking a smile, but I could accept that it wasn't going to happen. And why should it? I hadn't felt like joking around or chatting or anything much besides lashing out when I'd first lost Luna.

"If you let yourself show a little more of *that* emotion from time to time, it'd be easier to take the grimness," I said, without any bite. "I admire your dedication. It's pretty impressive that you're working so hard to keep us all safe. Maybe we've all been a little on edge for good reasons."

His stance relaxed a smidgeon. "Perhaps."

"Well, then all I can say is that I've been figuring out how to keep myself safe for twenty-seven more years than you have, so I hope you can trust that I'm the authority on the subject. And I can handle asking a few questions around Jade's bar just fine like this." I gestured to my clothes and then couldn't resist arching an eyebrow. "I promise I won't stay out past curfew."

Ruse muffled what sounded like a snicker. Thorn sighed but inclined his head. And I reached for the front door with a sudden burst of nerves.

I'd been to Jade's dozens of times. I'd never run into any real trouble there. But somehow as I walked out to the stairwell, I couldn't shake the twist of anxiety that Thorn might be right to worry, and everything else might be about to go horribly wrong.

12

Sorsha

Y ou've never seen a bar like Jade's, guaranteed. And not just because of the shadowkind clientele—or the human clientele, who were pretty unique beings in their own right.

Jade had taken the name "fountain" very seriously—and literally. Filtered water streamed in a waterfall across the entire back wall in front of granite bricks sparkling with mica. It was totally drinkable, and Jade encouraged customers to refill their cups there to hydrate between cocktails and shots. She'd also set up a little knee-deep pool in the center of the space, framed by matching granite tiles and curved limestone benches. People used it as both a wishing well and, when they'd had enough to drink, a wading spot.

Features like that attracted a pretty unusual bunch,

but that worked in Jade's favor. It helped her and the inhuman customers, who had their own quirks no matter how well they'd adapted to mortal-side life, blend in with the rest.

Only about half of the limestone tables that stood at random intervals across the rest of the floor were taken when I stepped through the front door. The burble of the waterfall filtered through the upbeat chatter, and the sour tang of beer and spirits mixed perfectly with the mineral scent in the air. I dragged in a deep breath of it, letting it wash away the worst of my nerves. It was hard to feel all that stressed out at Jade's.

My gaze didn't catch on any explosion of tight curls or startlingly white outfit, so Vivi hadn't turned up yet. For all her fastidiousness about her clothes, she wasn't great at arriving on time.

That was okay. In fact, I'd been counting on it. I wanted a chance to chat with Jade one-on-one.

Jade might have owned the place, but she took a hands-on approach. Every night except Saturday, the busiest, she also served as the only bartender. Right now, she was ringing up the bill for a couple who must have stopped in for early drinks before heading on to other nightly exploits. Her dark green hair, almost the same hue as my dress, hung in neat coils halfway down her slim back.

Most people probably thought she'd picked the color to go with her name, but I suspected it was the other way around. If anyone ever asked, she gave credit to a special dye her stylist mixed for her, but I happened to know her hair grew in like that. It was the one shadowkind feature she couldn't hide away in her mortal form. In this company, no one batted an eye at it. The color complemented her smooth skin, the same rich brown shade as the tequila she was now pouring.

I sat down on the stool at the far end of the gleaming counter, which appeared to have been carved out of a single immense slab of quartz. That seat was a little removed from the others, and it had a splash of supernatural influence on it that would discourage any mortal not wearing a badge like mine from taking it. The understanding was that if you wanted to talk to Jade about shadowkind matters, you sat yourself down there and waited until she was ready.

It only took a few minutes before she moseyed over, giving me a crooked smile. "Sorsha. It's been a while. You're looking well. What's new in your part of the world?"

"Not a whole lot, but I was hoping to run something by you." I motioned to the rack of drinks on the wall behind her. "Jack and Coke, please." Only a cheapskate asked for info without offering their patronage first.

Jade mixed the drink with graceful efficiency and slid it across the counter to me. I took a sip and enjoyed the sweet-and-sour burn all the way down to my stomach. She never skimped on the quality of her ingredients, which was also part of what made this place popular.

She leaned her elbow onto the counter. "What's on

your mind?"

Talking with her about Fund business or anything similar required a careful hand. Jade might have been shadowkind, and I was sure she cared at least a little about her people's well-being, but like most of the higher shadowkind I'd met who'd transitioned to living in the mortal realm, her own survival and that of her immediate friends was way higher on her list of priorities than any thought of the greater good. If she could lend me a hand without any consequences, she'd happily do so, but if the subject sounded at all risky, she was likely to clam up.

"I got a tip there might be something worth checking out at a place called 'Merry Den'," I said, pitching my voice low enough that the growing bar-room din would cover it. "That might be just a nickname, not something official. Any idea what that is or where I could find it?"

Jade's thin eyebrows drew together. She tapped the glass stir-stick she was holding against her lips. "That doesn't ring any bells," she said in a tone that sounded genuinely apologetic. "If it comes up, I can give the Fund a ring?"

"This is more of a private matter," I said. "Call me directly."

"Not a problem."

I sucked my lower lip under my teeth, trying to figure out how to phrase the next question in nonthreatening terms. "Has there been anything new in talk among the kind in general—about unusual behavior from hunters or anything like that?"

Her pale blue eyes went even more distant, and then she blinked, a flash of inspiration crossing her face. "You know, I have heard—and if anyone asks, it wasn't me who mentioned it—that there've been advertisements going out on the down low that offer collectors big bucks if they happen to have a particularly potent shadowkind in their stash. It sounded like some mega-collector trying to create the ultimate zoo." She gave a little shudder.

Huh. It was communications about a possible transaction to purchase shadowkind that had brought my attention to the guy who'd had my trio caged up. The way the pieces I'd seen had been worded, I'd assumed that collector was the buyer, but maybe he'd been considering selling one or more of his prizes. A higher shadowkind was about as "potent" as you could get. I might be able to get my black-market contacts to trace the other side of that conversation.

"Thanks," I said. "That could be just what I need."

"Just what you need for what?" The bright voice came with a skinny arm slung across my shoulders. Vivi leaned in beside me, shooting a grin at Jade. "Hey, Jade. Looks like you two are having a good chat. Anything interesting come up, Sorsh?"

I caught Jade's gaze for just a second with a twitch of my mouth I hoped she'd recognize as a plea to keep quiet about my inquiries. "Nothing major," I said. "But I'm glad I checked." I took a swig from my Jack and Coke. "What are you having? First one's on me."

"Well, now, that's an offer I can't refuse." My bestie

laughed and drummed her hands on the counter. "One Cosmo, please, with extra lime."

As Jade went off to assemble the drink, Vivi tipped her head close to mine. "Come on now. It sounded like she said something you thought was worth pursuing. Is there a big bad hunter for us to sic the gangs on—if any of them will go for it? An illicit auction we could crash?"

I shook my head, shrugging her off as lightly as I could. I had to tell her something, but in a way that wouldn't invite her to join in. Going with a sliver of the truth seemed like the best tactic.

"It wasn't anything for the Fund," I said. "Just a bit of info that might help me find out a little more about Luna's life in general."

"Oh, hey! I've been dying to know more about her. Shadowkind woman takes in a mortal toddler and raises her for years—that's not your typical story."

My throat tightened. It was partly because of that attitude that I didn't feel totally comfortable getting into the details I did have about Luna with my best friend. To Vivi, it was a fantastic story. To me, it was the only life I'd known.

Vivi's childhood hadn't exactly been normal either, growing up with both parents already in the Fund and bringing her into that world, but she *had* two human parents still living—just enjoying a surprisingly ordinary retirement in Florida as of two years back—and never interacted with the higher shadowkind except for briefly.

In some ways, she probably hoped my weird history

would bring some spice into her life the same way I'd been drawn to her relative normalcy.

"I'd like to look into this stuff on my own, at least to begin with," I said, as gently as I could manage. "It's pretty personal, and when I don't know exactly what I'll stumble on..."

"Oh, sure, of course." Vivi patted me on the shoulder as she grabbed her drink from Jade, but she didn't quite suppress her wince at my brush-off. Guilt twisted my stomach, knowing I was doing more than brushing her off —I was outright lying. Even if she couldn't totally understand where I came from, she was a good friend. And when I'd first come to the Fund, I'd needed that more than anything.

"How'd your date go?" I asked, switching to a safer topic.

Vivi pulled a face before sipping her drink. "Like watching paint dry while his grass grows. Why do they all turn out to be so *boring* when I actually get to know them?"

"Maybe because you've got a more unusual life than most people even know is possible?"

"I'm not asking that much." She sighed. "And it's not like the stuff we get up to is all that exciting most of the time. Fundraising and passing on anonymous tips—so thrilling! You know, my parents went busting up hunter clubhouses and all that when they were young."

The corner of my lips quirked up. "I'm pretty sure they only did that once—they just like telling the story an awful lot. I must have heard it about a hundred times while I was crashing at your place."

"Maybe so. But seriously. I'm going to be thirty in a few months, and I've never pulled off anything like that." She rested her elbow next to mine companionably. "You remember all the plans we dreamed up back then—epic rescue missions to free the shadowkind, sabotaging the hunters left and right?"

It'd be hard to forget those long-ago nights staying up in Vivi's room, chatting away until one of her parents had knocked on the door and told us to get to sleep already. She'd been the first real friend I'd had, the first person I'd talked openly about my life with other than Luna.

"What was it we were going to call ourselves?" I asked. "The Shadow Avengers?" We'd been too old to see the name as more than a joke, but the kernel of the idea, going out and literally fighting for justice—that eager rebelliousness from our teens resonated through me from the past.

I'd been seeing it through as well as I could, without her.

Vivi laughed. "Yeah. Like some kind of superheroes." Then her mood dampened. "We were going to track down the people who came for Luna too. You know, I'm really sorry the Fund never caught them. You'd think we'd be able to pull off at least that much."

The regret in her eyes made my throat tighten. Vivi might not totally understand what Luna had meant to me, but she knew how badly her loss had shaken me, and she'd truly wanted to make it right however she could. I hesitated against the urge to spill the beans after all—to at least tell her that I was probably on the track of those villains right now. It would be *nice* to share my hopes and worries with her.

While I grappled with the idea, a guy wearing a purple top hat bumped into Vivi as he passed her. She flinched toward the counter. "Hey, watch it with that drink!" she said, peering over her shoulder to make sure his beer hadn't stained her ivory jumpsuit, and my mouth stayed firmly shut.

If I told Vivi much of anything, she'd want to know everything—and could she handle getting into a *real* mess? These might be the same people who'd not only ambushed Omen and Luna but slaughtered my parents as well. If anything, it'd be selfish of me to involve her. This once, I could protect the person who meant the most to me.

I raised my glass, opting for distraction instead of a confession. "Enough about the past—drink up! It's time to hit the dance floor."

A few of the patrons were already swaying to the music in the open area next to the pool. When Vivi and I had downed our cocktails, I slid a twenty across the counter to Jade, told her to keep the change, and headed over to join them.

Vivi grasped my hand and swung me around with her, laughing. The broad legs of her jumpsuit swished around her calves. I focused half my attention on keeping up with her and the other half on scanning the bar-goers around us.

Jade wasn't the only being here who might have information they could share—and another shadowkind who wasn't as tied to this spot could be willing to say more. The tricky part was identifying the actual monsters amid the mortals who made themselves up like one.

I considered and then dismissed a guy with yellow cat's eyes—contacts, I was pretty sure—and a woman with a wolf's tail pinned to the back of her skirt that was obviously fake when I got a closer look. My gaze settled on an older woman with a dappling of shimmering scales across the back of her neck, only visible when her hair shifted with the motion of her head. She could have passed those off as a tattoo, but if they'd actually been one, I'd have expected her to show it off more.

Before I could think up an excuse to leave Vivi and sidle over to her table, four new figures marched through the bar's front door together. And by "marched," I mean they had the air of a military squadron.

An apprehensive prickle ran down my back as I watched the quartet in their business casual button-ups and slacks spread out through the bar. Each of them stopped by one of the nearby patrons, but from the other people's expressions, they didn't know these dudes. I got the impression the four were asking as many questions as I'd have liked to.

There was no reason to assume their arrival had anything to do with me. The clientele here could have been mixed up in all sorts of unusual dealings. But Thorn's warning that we'd been followed at the market came back to me with a nervous jitter. Any second now, one of those guys would come over this way and spot me. What would they do then?

It seemed wisest not to stick around and find out. At the very least, I could slip around to the front of the bar and watch them on my own terms—see if they focused in on someone else, and if they didn't, where they went after they'd finished their rounds.

I checked my phone, pretending I'd gotten a text, and wrinkled my nose at Vivi. "I've got to get going. Sorry to take off so early."

"Hey, we still had fun," Vivi said, but curiosity still shone in her eyes. "Need any help?"

"No, I'm good. Just going to duck out the back to avoid the crowd."

"Talk soon, then. And you know if you ever do need me, I'm all in." She made an air kiss at my cheek. "Ditto."

The corner of my lips quirked upward. "Ditto." We'd taken that as our way of saying, "Love ya!" ever since watching the movie *Ghost* together way back when.

I gave her a little wave and took off for the back door as fast as I could jet it without catching the preppy squadron's eyes.

13

Snap

T he place Sorsha had called a "bar" didn't look anything like the long, straight pieces of metal I'd used that word for in the past. Even viewed from the shadows, the images slightly warbled and the sounds and scents faded, it was much more interesting. Interesting enough that I couldn't quite bring myself to ask Thorn whether it really was a good idea for us to be slinking through these shadows.

Sorsha had insisted it wasn't safe for us to come along. I'd have thought she should know, since she'd been here before and we hadn't. But Ruse knew a lot about the mortal realm and Thorn knew a lot about danger, and neither of them seemed concerned that we'd run into any trouble here. I could follow their lead.

Especially when it meant getting to take in so many new aspects of mortal-side life.

I slipped through a patch of darkness under an empty table to tip my head close to a glass that one of the mortals had left there, a trace of amber liquid ringing its base. I couldn't taste anything while remaining in the shadows, directly or with my deeper senses, but the sour smell tickled my nose.

"Why are they drinking these liquids?" I asked Ruse, a languid presence nearby. "They smell almost like plants gone to rot."

The incubus's chuckle came with a distant tone. "In some ways, that's what they are. It's called fermenting. It brings out some... interesting qualities that help mortals relax and find courage."

I peered at the people socializing in the room around us. "Are they bolstering themselves to head into some kind of battle?" Sorsha's world hadn't appeared to be the sort of place where masses of warriors took up swords against each other on a regular basis, regardless of the hints Thorn liked to drop about his past adventures in this realm.

Ruse laughed again. "Only battles with their own self-esteem and other people's opinions of them. Mortals come to establishments like this to enjoy themselves with friends and to pick up potential mates. Usually short-term ones, but for some reason many of them get much more anxious about that than looking for marriage material."

Mates. Like that couple over there, two men with their arms twined as they rocked with the music a few paces from where Sorsha and her friend were dancing. You could tell they were mates and Sorsha and her friend weren't because of the amount of closeness... and also a sort of energy around them that I could taste without even using my tongue.

Sometimes Ruse and Sorsha generated that kind of energy between them. But not always. I didn't fully understand what it accomplished other than that they seemed to enjoy something about it, which maybe was reason enough to want it. Like eating food I didn't need but that tasted so delicious.

Did they decide to create the energy or did it just happen? What did it feel like when you had it? I didn't think I'd ever encountered it in myself.

I might have asked, but as I turned in Ruse's direction, I spotted another shadowkind—not in the shadows like us but sitting at one of the stone tables with a drink of her own. A dappling of scales showed across her skin. From that along with her pose, I expected she was some sort of reptilian shifter.

"There are other kind here," I said, nodding toward her. "Should we avoid her?" We'd already known the being distributing drinks from behind the shiny counter was one of us, but she stayed on the other side of that large, carved crystal slab.

Thorn shifted closer to me, his presence looming as large in the shadows as it did on the physical plane.

"Sorsha said our kind often come here. Why would any of them think it's strange that we're here too? It was an excuse to keep us away."

"She really should have known better than to assume we'd go along with that order," Ruse agreed with a teasing cluck of his tongue.

Why wouldn't she have wanted us to see the bar? Maybe I'd asked too many questions at the market earlier today. There were just so many things to experience that I didn't understand but wanted to.

Like the young man who was tossing coins into the circle of water to our left. I peered at him and then the coins, the metal discs glinting as they caught the tiny underwater lights. "That's money he's throwing away, isn't it? Why would they put it in the water? Is that how they pay for those relaxing courage drinks?"

"They pay for the drinks at the counter," Ruse said. "And mostly with paper bills or plastic cards. The coins don't buy much. They throw them into the water for fun and to pretend it'll give them the power to get whatever they want."

My gaze jerked back to the coins. "Does that work?" So far I hadn't met mortals who could work magic of any kind, let alone on that scale.

"Of course not. They just enjoy the pretending."

Mortals were rather strange about a lot of things. Before I could puzzle any longer about that, Thorn moved forward. I looked in the same direction.

Sorsha was stepping away from her friend with the

swishy clothes and hair. She was smiling, but tension wound through her posture. A twinge shot through my gut. "Where's she going? Is something wrong?"

"She seems to think it is." I could feel more than see the flex of Thorn's considerable strength. "Four men came in together a minute ago. Their movements appear very purposeful. She may have had past dealings with them or seen some other warning sign."

"She's heading for the back door," Ruse pointed out. "We'd better keep up, don't you think?"

Thorn glanced toward the front of the room again, but then he turned to stride after Sorsha, leaping between shadows as need be. Ruse and I traveled along behind him. If any of the newcomers tried to harm her, we were between her and them now. It must have been a good thing we'd come along.

The incubus had been right about the door. Sorsha twisted the handle, murmuring a faint tune to herself, and pushed outside. We leapt after her into the thicker darkness of an alley.

A totally different combination of sensations washed over me: the faint chill of the night, the contrast between the dark, narrow space we'd come out into and the yellow glow of streetlamps at the opening a few buildings away, and a dank, definitely rotten smell seeping from the trash bin Sorsha darted around. It took me a moment to adjust —and to notice the figure that had already been out here in the alley.

The man looked so scruffy I might have taken him for

a werewolf in mid-shift if everything else about him hadn't screamed *mortal*. He'd been standing farther down the alley, but at Sorsha's exit, he turned and headed toward her with steps that both lurched and swayed. A bottle of that sour-smelling liquid dangled from one of his hands. He didn't seem relaxed or brave to me, though, only unsteady. And intent on catching up with our rescuer.

"What's he do—" I started to ask, and sucked in the rest of the sentence and my breath at the gleam of a knife he'd pulled from his pocket.

He was going to hurt her. We had to stop him. Those thoughts blared through my mind clearer than anything— and my body went rigid. A sickly chill congealed in my stomach, so dense it erased even my memories of the treats I'd snacked on at the market and later at dinner.

I *could* stop him. I could—like that other time—but to do that again— Despite my urge to protect the woman who'd saved us, every particle in me flinched away from the thought with a smack of horror.

It was a good thing I wasn't the warrior among us. As I froze, Thorn hurled himself forward.

14

Sorsha

I paused in the short hallway that led to the bar's back door just long enough to glance over my shoulder. None of the guys who'd set off my warning bells appeared to have clocked me as a target. As far as I could tell, they were still circulating through the front half of the bar, not yet looking or coming my way. Good.

In my bar-wear, I felt unnervingly vulnerable. The badge pinned to my bra might protect me from shadowkind powers, but it'd do nothing at all against human means of combat. After the mixed martial arts classes Luna had insisted I take in my early teens —*Because you never know if you might encounter some enemy that prefers brute force over hocus pocus,* she'd said —I could handle myself all right, but four against one wasn't great odds.

"Oh, girls just wanna have guh-uns," I sang under my breath as I slipped out into the back alley, not that I knew how to fire a gun anyway.

The alley was dark and dank, and a homeless dude was loitering outside the building next door, swigging from a bottle of vodka I could smell from seven feet away. Thankfully, it'd be just a short jog to the lights of the street. Once I was watching from outside where any searchers wouldn't expect to find me, I'd be much more in control of the situation.

I hurried toward the sidewalk, that sense of control already settling comfortably in my chest, and uneven footsteps scraped the pavement behind me. The drunk guy was heading this way too. I picked up my pace so I could keep well ahead of both him and his stink—and he lunged at me with a speed I hadn't expected.

The vodka bottle tumbled to the ground with a crackle of breaking glass. The second the guy's hand closed around my wrist—firmer and steadier than made any sense given his supposed inebriation—my fighting instincts kicked into gear. My body twisted, and my leg shot up for that most basic of self-defence maneuvers: a knee to the balls.

I'd say one good thing about him: he did have his private parts exactly where I needed them to be. My knee connected with his most sensitive appendage, and the air shot out of him with a pained grunt. He stumbled backward, flailing to keep his balance. A knife flashed through the air in his other hand.

Holy mother of mincemeat, what exactly had he been planning on doing to me with that thing? Drunk homeless dude, my ass. This guy had just put on a front while he waited for a target.

Had he been waiting for me specifically, or had I just gotten extra lucky tonight?

I didn't have the chance to ask him about it. I shifted my weight back, my fists coming up, ready to give him a lesson in why you don't attempt to knife random women, and the air between us split with a sizzling sound that raised the hairs on my arms. A huge, brawny form wavered into view in mid punch.

Thorn's fist slammed into my attacker's face just as the "drunk" guy had lurched back toward me. His crystalline knuckles raked through the flesh of the guy's cheek and nose down to a gleam of bone. A cry of pain had just started to break from the asshole's mouth when the shadowkind warrior *literally* broke his throat with a slash of his other hand. He gouged straight through the guy's neck, cutting off the cry into a gurgle and a spray of blood.

My attacker crumpled into a heap, blood puddling around him. Thorn stepped back with a satisfied swipe of his knuckles against his palm, and—holy mother of magnificence.

I stared, briefly distracted from the carnage. Specks of the guy's blood had spattered across the warrior's chest... His bare chest, with bulging muscles on full, glorious display. In fact, he was bare all the way down.

When shadowkind moved through their realm or through the shadows in ours, they dropped their physical forms, including any clothes they'd been wearing. It appeared Thorn had been too focused on leaping into the fray to remember to bring into being more than the essentials of his body, modesty be damned. And, wow, the equipment he was packing between *his* legs definitely lived up to the rest of his impressive form.

I jerked my gaze away after just a moment of gaping, but that was enough for Thorn to notice. He looked down at himself and let out a noise of consternation. At the edge of my gaze, I saw his typical tunic and trousers blink into being, covering all that deliciousness. It was almost a shame.

What was definitely a shame: the mangled body I was now staring at again, just a few feet away from me. My stomach flipped over. I sidestepped to avoid a rivulet of blood that trickled toward me. "What the hell was that?" I demanded, my heart thumping from the fight— and maybe a little from the eye candy I'd gotten right after, despite my revulsion at the rest of the scene.

Two other figures I should have realized would be along for the ride shifted in the darkness. Ruse tilted his head to one side as he regarded the dead man. He brought his hands together in a light clap. "Excellent smiting. A+ for technique. Maybe a little overboard in the nakedness department, but I'm really not one to criticize that."

Thorn glared at him with a twist of his mouth that

might have been a little embarrassed. He turned to me. "My apologies that I didn't intervene sooner, m'lady. And for the... unfortunate oversight when I first arrived."

"I'm not complaining about *that* part," I said, and shot my own glare at Ruse when he smirked. "None of you should be here at all—you were supposed to stay at my apartment! And you—you massacred this guy." There really wasn't any better word for it.

"He was attempting to harm you," Thorn said, completely ignoring my first point. "He had a weapon. I was simply preventing him from using it." He frowned at me as if upset that I hadn't thanked him yet.

I supposed I did sort of owe him some gratitude. All the same... "Thanks, but I was handling it just fine by myself. You can't go around *killing* people left and right, even if they seem like real jerks. Unless someone's actually on the verge of killing me, you can stick to beating their ass and sending them running. Or rather, let *me* beat their ass and send them running."

Thorn's forehead furrowed. "I can hardly wait to see if an attacker will get to the point of a mortal blow. He was a miscreant of some sort. What does his death matter?"

I stared at him for several seconds while I tried to construct an answer his shadowkind worldview would understand. He clearly didn't subscribe to the idea that life was sacred regardless of what the living thing was doing with that life. Truthfully, I wasn't exactly *sad* that the asshole was dead, even if the sight of his battered body horrified me.

I'd never seen anyone die except Auntie Luna, and her departure had been more sparkly than bloody.

"On this side of the divide, we don't go around killing anyone who pisses us off," I said finally. "There are laws, and a certain mortal sense of morality... You might not agree with it, but it'll be easier for all of us if you try to respect it at least a little."

"I respect what keeps you and us alive," Thorn said. "That matters more than mortal laws or your qualms about our presence."

I resisted the urge to reiterate the fact that I probably would have been just fine even if he hadn't jumped to my rescue. One guy with a knife vs. my martial arts skills shouldn't have been a problem. Of course, who knew if my attacker had more than a knife? Bloody mess and all, I might find it in me to be a bit touched that Thorn was so dedicated to my safety.

They *all* were. Snap eased up beside Ruse and looked me over with a worried air. "You *are* all right, aren't you? He came at you very quickly."

"I'm totally fine." I brushed off my arms as if to demonstrate.

"If it makes you feel any better, this was no great loss." Ruse motioned to the bashed body. "I got a read on him before our fist-happy friend here took care of the matter. You aren't the first woman he's attacked—and if he'd had his way, you'd have been pinned up against the wall while he forced himself on you." He grimaced as he spoke those words as if it disgusted him to even voice that possibility out loud.

My skin crawled at that revelation. But the way the guy had gone after me, the pretense of being drunk and all, hadn't felt like some random rape attempt. "Is that all you picked up on?" I asked.

"I didn't have a whole lot of time to rummage around in his emotions and motivations before he and they ceased to be."

"Why did you come out through the back to begin with?" Thorn said. "Did you see a reason to be wary when you were inside?"

Oh, shit. I'd totally forgotten my original goal. "There were four men who came in—not part of Jade's usual crowd. I got the impression they were searching for someone. Considering what you three have gotten me mixed up in and your idea that we were followed this afternoon, I thought that someone might be me. I was going to double around and keep an eye on them from outside at the window."

I hesitated with a glance at the body and then hustled the rest of the way to the street. When I reached the front of the bar, I held myself to the side of the window and peeked inside.

I couldn't make out every corner of the place from here, but it only took a quick skim over the patrons to determine that none of the preppy guys I'd slipped out on were in view. Which meant they probably weren't in there at all anymore—it wasn't likely all four of them had squeezed into one of the nooks I couldn't see. My jaw clenched.

My shadowkind trio had gathered behind me. "It looks like they left while we were busy dealing with the jerk in the alley," I said. "Now there's no way of telling what they were up to." I might have been glad that my uninvited protectors had joined me if Ruse could have taken a read on *those* dudes. "I'm not sure they were looking for me—it just seemed better to be careful."

Snap peered past me into the bar. "Yes, that's why we came. To be careful with your safety."

It was hard to be mad at him when he put it like that with his sweetly melodic voice.

I headed back toward the alley with a sigh. "All right. We'll just all be extra careful until we find out how much attention we've already drawn. And if we want to make sure we don't stir up even more trouble, you'd better clean up the mess you left here." I shot a look at Thorn. "I hope you're as good at getting rid of dead bodies as you are at creating them."

15

Sorsha

By the time we made it back to my apartment, it was just shy of midnight. Normally after a night out with Vivi, I'd have returned pleasantly exhausted and ready to crash into bed. After this evening's events, uneasiness was still jittering through my veins. I couldn't imagine drifting off into dreamland anytime soon.

The clean-up itself hadn't been all that horrific. Living mortal beings couldn't travel into the shadows, but inanimate objects could, and my attacker had definitely been lacking in animation after Thorn's brutal defense. While the warrior had "given the body to the dark," whatever exactly that entailed, Ruse and Snap had spirited over a few buckets of water from somewhere or other. Based on the chlorine smell, I suspected it'd been a nearby public pool.

Splashing the water over the pavement had washed the remaining traces of blood down a storm drain. And voila! It was as if the dude had never set foot in the alley, let alone attempted to bring a knife to my throat there.

That didn't mean I was totally at ease with how callously Thorn had dispatched him in the first place... or with the attack and what had propelled me into the alley beforehand. Either I was simply having a very bad day topped with a sprinkling of some paranoia of my own, or someone had taken notice of the investigating we'd already been doing. I wasn't sure which was more likely, but the fact that the latter was even a possibility itched at me.

Luna would have said it was time to run. Hell, Luna would have been out the door with emergency bags grabbed the second these three had turned up in the kitchen. She was shadowkind, sure, but that meant her warnings about the rest of her kind had held even more weight. *Most of them won't see you as anything more than an inconvenience or dinner*, she'd told me. *I don't trust any of them I don't already know deserve it, so neither should you.*

But as questionable as I might find their methods, I thought the trio had proven that they did care about my well-being... and I didn't even have an emergency bag anymore. I hadn't needed one in the past eleven years—hadn't ever needed one except that night when the hunters came for Luna. As I meandered down the hall now, I found myself clutching my purse strap as if holding onto it would ensure everything was okay.

Snap leaned in to examine my face, his own divine visage so close that my skin flushed in spite of everything. The heat didn't reach my cheeks, apparently, because he knit his brow with concern. "You look a little pale. Should you eat something?"

Of course that would be his answer to the problem. I considered pointing out that there might not be anything to eat in my kitchen anymore, after the way the three of them—especially him—kept pillaging it, but I didn't want to make him feel guilty.

"No, it's not that." I flopped down on the sofa. "I'm just tense after... everything. If I put on some mindless TV and zone out for a bit, I'll start to unwind." At least, I hoped so.

Ruse hummed to himself as he sauntered into the room after us. "I think we can do a little better than *that* to raise your spirits." He ran his fingers over the shelves by the TV and plucked out a CD case. With deft fingers, he set the disc in the old boombox that sat on one of the end tables.

The buoyant beats of an '80s song careened from the speakers. Ruse came over to me and held out his hand to help me up. "You missed out on most of your dancing time—not that the bar was an ideal venue for it. This is more the music that'll liven you up, isn't it?"

I let him pull me to my feet, but I gave him a wary

look. "Have you been peeking inside my head? I *told* you—"

He waved me off with a chuckle. "Miss Blaze, I don't need to read your mind to pick up on your taste in music. Your CD collection speaks for itself."

He had a point there. Considering CDs had been defunct for years now, I only had a few albums other than the ones from Luna's original essential stash. He'd picked the Top Dance Hits one—she'd owned every year from '80 to '89, but only '86 had made it into the emergency bag set. As the Bangles encouraged us all to "walk like an Egyptian," I had to admit she'd made the right choice.

"Okay, fair," I said, only grumbling a little.

He smirked at me. "Who has CDs anymore anyway? Are you as committed to the technology of times past as you are to the music?"

However much my spirits might have lifted with the beat, they sank again at that question. "They were my aunt's—I mean, they belonged to the shadowkind woman who raised me."

From the flicker of Ruse's eyes, he recognized that he'd stumbled onto delicate ground. He twined one hand around mine and tugged me into the middle of the room. His tone gentled but kept the same playful quality. "So that's where your obsession began. You honor her well by enjoying the era as much as she did."

I liked that way of looking at it. "I grew up listening to these songs," I said in my defense. "And they *are* catchier than a lot of newer stuff."

"I'm not going to argue. You're just lucky I even knew how to work that player." He gestured toward the boombox. "It's your good fortune that I happened to spend a decent amount of time in the mortal realm during the years those machines were popular."

He'd been passing over to seduce and feed at least a few decades ago. To look at him, I'd have placed him in his early thirties, but with shadowkind, that didn't mean much.

I gave him a sharp look. "Exactly how old *are* you?"

"A gentleman never tells." He winked. "Let's just say that on one of my first excursions across the divide, I shared pork rinds with Leonardo Da Vinci."

My eyebrows shot up of their own accord. "So, you've got several centuries on me, then. I never thought I'd be one to go for men quite that much older."

"I've made it worth your while, haven't I? Besides, age is more a mortal concern. In the shadow realm, we barely notice that time exists. If you calculated based on my visits into your world, it wouldn't add up to more than a few years."

I gave him a shove with my free hand. "In that case, I've been hooking up with a preschooler. *So* much better."

The next song was just starting. The incubus swayed my hand in time with its beat. "What does any of that matter? Humor me. You wouldn't want me to have to resort to dancing with the mannequin, would you?"

Actually, I'd have kind of liked to see that, but the

rhythm was starting to work its way into my limbs. He'd waited awfully patiently. "I suppose I could give you this dance. Let's see what you've got."

Ruse grinned and spun me around, the motion taking my breath away for a moment. When he pulled me back to him, my free hand came to rest on his well-built chest. Gazing up into his roguishly handsome face with that dimple in his cheek made it hard for me to get my breath back.

I forced myself to step away from him, letting the beat carry my feet. It worked its way through me from toes to head. My arms lifted into the air, my waist twisted as I shimmied, and Ruse let out a little whoop of encouragement as he got down to boogie too.

We faced off against each other, sidled over to bump hips, and circled around each other as that song faded into the next. I was starting to work up a sweat, but the incubus didn't look the slightest bit affected by the exertion. He grasped my hand again to draw me closer and dipped me like he had the mannequin earlier in the evening. A laugh spilled out of me.

Snap had been watching from the sidelines, but something about that moment appeared to spur him to action. He stepped away from the doorway and started to sway with the music too, his golden curls glinting under the overhead light. He didn't know any dance moves I'd ever seen, but his body caught the rhythm with such fluid motion that it was hard not to watch him. His sinuous style came to him naturally enough to look graceful rather than awkward.

Ruse pumped his fist. "Now it's a party!"

As if in agreement, Pickle scampered into the room. The little dragon hopped and flapped his clipped wings in a dance of his own as he darted around my feet. I scooped him up to set him on his favorite perch, keeping my hand by my shoulder to steady him as I twirled.

Thorn stood in the doorway as if on guard. His gaze followed us as we danced, but the typically grim set of his mouth suggested he didn't approve of this kind of frivolity. But it wasn't as if we had any leads we could be chasing down in the middle of the night, and frankly, I was a lot more likely to figure out this mystery if I wasn't all tangled up with tension. A gal had to let loose every now and then to stay sane.

I swiveled, dipped, and sashayed around Ruse again. Pickle bobbed his head in time with the rhythm. Ruse caught me by the waist for a moment, tipping his head to press a quick kiss to the other side of my neck, and heat shot through my body that had nothing to do with the workout.

He let me go, and I turned toward Snap, mimicking his motions as well as I could. I probably looked like an idiot next to his godly form, but what the hell. The heat kept flowing through me—along with a weird tingling that was seeping into my mind. I'd have blamed it on desire if it hadn't seemed to muddy my senses rather than heighten them.

I shook my head in an attempt to clear it, and a wave of dizziness washed over me. As my feet stumbled under me, Ruse caught me from behind. "Careful there," he said in that chocolate tone, but my pulse had hiccupped for reasons that had nothing to do with his sex appeal.

"I think—" My tongue was stumbling too. A chill prickled through me under the haze. Something was definitely not right.

The room was spinning now—or was that me? I pressed the heel of my hand to my head, but the dizziness kept washing through me, the fog closing in on my thoughts. My stomach listed as if I were standing in a boat on rough waters.

"I don't feel so good," I managed to say, and then I lurched right over to hit the floor on my hands and knees.

16

Sorsha

The smack of my fall radiated through my hands and legs. My stomach heaved, and I almost lost whatever remained of my Jack and Coke onto the living-room floorboards. My head drooped toward the ground.

Hands caught me before I could completely collapse. The music switched off. Ruse's voice reached me through the fog that had enveloped my mind. "Sorsha? What's going on?"

Then came Snap's softer but clear tone. "There's something in the air. I can't pick up any larger impressions from it, but I don't like the way it tastes. It's thicker over by—I think it's coming from the hall."

I couldn't find my tongue to offer any insight. Heavy steps I knew must be Thorn's thumped away.

Ruse stroked his hand over my hair soothingly.

"Sorsha, something's affecting you—some kind of drug? I should be able to partly clear your mind so it doesn't knock you out completely, but I have to get in there first. Your little brooch blocks too much of my power for me to help all that effectively. Can you manage to take it off?"

A breath hitched out of me. My little brooch—my badge. He couldn't touch it himself—none of them could —at least not without it doing who knew what damage to them. The only way *he* could remove the badge would be by stripping my dress and bra right off.

I could do this, couldn't I? Just focus on that one thing. Move my hand off the floor to my chest. Under the fabric of my dress. Yank the badge off. Simple.

It should have been, but I wobbled when I lifted my hand. Even after Ruse steadied me, it took a few fumbles before my fingers caught on my neckline, and by then I'd half-forgotten why I was groping myself in the first place.

A metallic crash sounded from far away. Thorn's footsteps thumped back toward us. "There was a device at the door propelling some sort of gas underneath. I bashed it down the stairs. No sign of the person who placed it there—" He cut himself off. "Someone's coming."

"Watch for their shadowkind weapons," Ruse warned him. His grip tightened on my shoulder, maybe readying to get on with the stripping if I couldn't manage the task myself. "The brooch, Sorsha. You can do it."

Right. Right. I shoved my hand toward my bra. My

fingers fumbled over the metal badge and snagged around its edges. There was a clip right... *there.*

It popped off the fabric cup with a click. I tossed it across the floor with a clumsy flick of my hand, and an instant later a warm tingling spread across my scalp. The sensation seeped through my skull and into my clouded mind.

Within seconds, the floor under me felt more solid, the sounds around me clearer. I raised my head, blinking. Ruse was crouched beside me, his gaze intent. Snap stood braced by the doorway, his eyes flicking between us and the hall, where I assumed Thorn was staked out by the front door.

The door slammed shut. "They're coming up," our warrior called back to us. "There are a lot of them—I can't tell what kind of weapons they have. I can take them on—"

"No," Ruse snapped, his voice gone ragged. I had enough awareness now to wonder how much the voodoo he'd worked on me had worn him out. That couldn't be a typical use of his cubi powers. "It's got to be the same people who came for Omen. You know they were prepared enough to take any of us down. And Sorsha's still out of it." His tone softened when he returned his attention to me. "Let's get you up."

He hadn't been able to drive all of the drug out of my system. My limbs still swayed as he helped me to my feet; my vision doubled for a moment before steadying again.

My thoughts were clearer, but they jumbled every time I turned my head.

Something banged against the door so hard the hinges creaked. My pulse stuttered at the sound. Ruse gripped my arm tightly. "I don't think you're in any condition to stand and fight, Miss Blaze. Do we have any good routes out of here other than that door?"

I could think well enough to answer that question. "Fire escape. Outside my bedroom window."

"Got it. We're going to make a run for it."

He nodded to Snap, who slipped out ahead of us. I snatched the strap of my purse where I'd left it on the sofa. Pickle scuttled alongside me, his head weaving through the air anxiously.

In the hall, Thorn was braced in front of the door. It shuddered again, and his fists clenched where he'd raised them level with his chest. Determination shone in his dark eyes, but when he glanced toward us, taking in my near-stumble as Ruse helped me along, his expression shifted from severe to startled and back again in an instant.

"What have they done to her?" he demanded, and swung toward the door again as if he could pummel the attackers on the other side with the force of his glare alone.

"Some type of drug—meant to knock her out, I think. Either they figured it works on shadowkind too, or they didn't know we'd be here." Ruse hustled me to the bedroom. "Come on."

"If they don't know we're here, they might not have—"

"*Come*," Ruse insisted. "We can't know either way. Is it worth risking us all ending up in cages again—or dead? Remember who was right the last time we got overwhelmed?"

Thorn let out an extended curse under his breath and swiveled toward us. At the same second, one final blow to the door burst the hinges if not the deadbolt. As it bowed into the hall, Ruse yanked me through the bedroom doorway.

"Open the window," he ordered Snap.

Snap shoved at the pane, which slid upward with a grating sound. My gaze caught on the curve of my backpack peeking from beneath the bed, and a cold shot of panic surged through me.

"There's evidence here—if they see it, they'll know for sure—I have to—"

My sentences broke with my colliding thoughts so many times I decided I was better off just acting rather than trying to explain myself. I grabbed the backpack, slung it over my shoulder, and then cast a frantic look around the room.

What else might I have lying around that would tell the invaders I was not just interested in Omen but had freed and destroyed the possessions of at least a dozen major collectors across the past few years? Shit, shit, shit.

If word got out that I was the sticky-fingered, monster-emancipating fire-starter, every hunter and collector in the state, possibly the country, would be looking to come at me the way they'd murdered my parents. I wouldn't be able to turn to the Fund either—they'd probably disown me.

The door clattered all the way to the floor, and shouts rang out from the hall. Thorn let out a wordless rumble, and there was an impact that sounded like his knuckles meeting flesh, but his own grunt of pain followed it. They had something that could hurt him.

There wasn't time to come up with a five-point plan of carefully considered action. My mind latched onto the strategy that had been my saving grace every other time I'd needed to cover my tracks.

As Ruse dragged me to the open window, a rush of warm summer air washing away the air-conditioned cool, I dug my bottle of kerosene and my lighter out of the backpack. My arm jerked, splattering the fluid in an arc across vanity, bookcase, and bed. "Thorn!" I yelled, and flicked on the lighter.

With a lurch of my heart, the flame seemed to leap from the tool I was clutching to my target before my hand had even reached the vanity. It licked across the polished surface with a waft of sharper heat and coursed along the trail of kerosene—over the floor, up my mussed sheets.

Ruse let out a hoarse chuckle. I snatched Pickle up, stuffed him into my purse as far as he'd go, and scrambled out the window after the incubus. Snap had already disappeared somewhere below.

More hollers, thuds, and grunts carried from behind

us. The flames hissed, flaring higher—and then Thorn was charging through them, his fists bloody, a black mark slashed across his jaw where I guessed he was going to add another scar to his collection.

He spun just as he reached the window and exhaled a massive breath with the force of bellows at a forge. The flames whipped up all across the floor, crawling the walls toward the ceiling. A few figures I could only hazily make out through the flashes of light and the clotting smoke yanked themselves to a halt on the threshold. I tore my gaze away and dashed for the ladder.

The fire would only hold them off for so long. If they decided they couldn't charge through it, they'd race down to try to cut us off on the street.

A shout from below told me our attackers had been one step ahead. Someone had staked out the fire escape too. I wavered where I'd started down the rickety metal ladder, and Thorn burst through the window.

He sprang over me. Before I could so much as blink, he'd dropped from the second-floor platform to the ground with only a huff and a smack of his feet against the pavement.

Flesh mashed. Bone crunched. I fled down the ladder as fast as my limbs would allow, Ruse following just as speedily. Thorn let out a strangled noise, and there was a *thwack* that I would bet was a smaller body slamming into the wall below.

The second my feet touched down, the warrior grabbed my wrist and hauled me toward the street. He was limping—a jagged tear gaped open in his trousers just below his knee.

Shadowkind didn't bleed the way we did, as Thorn was demonstrating very vividly right now. Rather than liquid spurting, wisps of black smoke unfurled from the wound hidden by the fabric. The thicker darkness of the night swallowed them up.

I caught a glimpse of two bodies, one slumped by the wall spilling a lumpy mess of brains from its head, another sprawled nearby with its back wrenched to an angle that made my stomach churn. The smoke alarms were wailing above, gray billows streaming out the open window.

It wouldn't be only our attackers descending on this place soon. I ran with the shadowkind toward the street, thanking the heavens that I'd worn flats with this dress.

Get out of here—now, now, now. The urgent cry in my own head propelled me onward. Could I really outpace these hunters—or whatever they were—in my current state?

We sprinted down the street, my stomach roiling as much from the drug still in my system as the gruesome scene Thorn had left behind. My backpack battered my side. Then up ahead I spotted a veritable gift from the gods: a bike leaning against the fence outside a house on the other side of the street, not even chained.

I might not be licensed to drive, but I could sure as hell pedal with the best of them. I veered across the road, yanked it from the fence, and hopped on.

A startled yelp reached my ears—the bike's owner must have had it in view—but I was already flying along the sidewalk, the wheels whirring. My mind had narrowed down to one thing amid the lingering haze: get as far away from the attackers at my apartment as was humanly possible.

The buildings and streets whipped past me in a blur. My thighs burned, but I kept pumping my legs as fast as they could go, even as my balance wobbled. This late, hardly anyone was out and about. When a stream of traffic lights showed up ahead, I swerved down one side street and another until a perfectly timed green light gave me a chance to bolt across the busy road.

I'd lost all track of my supernatural companions, but at this hour, the city was more shadow than not. They might not be able to match a truck's speed, but I hoped they were keeping up with my bike by the means only they could use. Better they traveled in ways no mortals could see them anyway.

Every now and then, I shot down an alley or cut across a parking lot—taking routes no larger vehicle could use in case I'd picked up less welcome followers. After several of those and an ache that had expanded all through my legs, my panic eased off. I pedaled on for at least another ten minutes before I finally coasted to a stop at the corner of a block of low-rise apartment buildings.

The back of my dress clung to my skin, damp with sweat. The night air stung as I sucked it down my raw throat. My breaths and my pulse gradually evened out. In my purse, Pickle squirmed and let out a mournful-sounding squeak.

I still had him. I had my wallet and my phone and other purse essentials—I had my cat-burglar-esque equipment in my backpack. Everything else...

Three forms emerged from the shadows around me. As the last of the adrenaline drained away, the full impact of what I'd left behind—left behind in *flames*—hit me too hard for me to acknowledge the trio.

Luna's CD collection. Her fairy dust shoes and her scrunchie. I didn't give a shit about my own clothes—those I could replace—but the few fragments of her life I'd been able to hold onto...

The pearly box with my parents' letter. That realization came like a punch to the gut. I nearly doubled over as I clung to the handlebars.

I'd stuck the box back on the shelf in the closet. I hadn't even thought of it, I'd been in such a rush. The fire would have consumed everything in that room, if not the entire apartment. The one gift my parents had left for me was utterly gone, and I had no way of ever replacing it.

My guts felt as if they'd knotted into a solid mass of mourning. I hadn't been ready, not for any of this. More than a decade in the same city, three years in the same apartment—I'd gotten complacent. So fucking stupid. Luna had taught me better than that.

"Sorsha?" Snap said tentatively. He brushed a gentle hand over my shoulder.

I inhaled sharply and forced myself to straighten up.

The ache in my weary legs was nothing compared to the stab of loss in my chest, but these three wouldn't understand why I cared so much about those things. I'd just have to swallow the grief down like I had Luna's death and the other losses since...

As I dismounted the bike, Thorn stepped closer. The tear remained in his trousers, but his calf had stopped leaking the smoke of his essence. That seemed like a good sign. Shadowkind did usually heal quickly.

"You should probably hold onto this," he said, holding out one of his brawny hands. "It seems rather... delicate. It didn't entirely survive the fighting I've already had to do—I apologize."

He was offering me the box I'd just been mourning. A crack ran through the pearly lid, and one of the corners was chipped, but it was *here*. Whole and unburned.

I snatched it from him much more hastily than was really polite and popped it open. The letter was still nestled inside, my mother's spiky handwriting scrawled across the notepaper. I snapped the box shut again with the irrational terror that a sudden wind might steal that treasure from me after all.

A lump filled my throat. I stared up at Thorn's face. "When did you take this?" And the bigger question: *Why?*

His rugged features revealed no more than his usual grimness. "I noticed it in your closet as I was coming into the bedroom. It appeared, before, that it was important to you. I thought you would want it saved from the flames."

I hadn't realized he'd been paying any attention when I'd talked to Snap about it, let alone that he'd recognized the depth of my connection to what must have looked to him like a fairly mundane object. He'd risked a few seconds in the battle to rescue it for me. That was worth a heck of a lot more than any heads he'd bashed in on my behalf.

"Thank you," I said, swallowing hard. "I would have hated to lose it. Honestly, I don't know how to thank you enough."

As I searched his face for the compassion he must have acted on, his expression tensed under my scrutiny.

"It was nothing," he said brusquely. "Certainly not compared to the debt I'm still repaying. We shouldn't linger out here in the open for much longer, should we?"

I winced inwardly at the curt dismissal. Maybe that was all he'd been thinking of—how he owed me for getting him and the others out of those cages. However he felt about me, he obviously didn't want to waste any time accepting my gratitude.

I slipped the box into a safe compartment of my backpack. "You're right. We've got to hole up somewhere for the night. I'm totally wiped—we can take stock and make bigger plans in the morning."

Ruse cocked his head toward the apartment buildings beside us. "It looks like we have an extensive spread of possible hideouts. Let's see which ones we can use."

17

Sorsha

As we reached the apartment building, I started rummaging through my backpack for my lockpicking tools. Before I'd even set my hands on them, Ruse had slipped through the shadows into that of a potted plant on the other side of the lobby door. He opened it for us with a flourish. "Gentlemen, madam."

Right. Breaking and entering was a hell of a lot easier when you had supernatural powers on your side. For a second, my skills seemed to pale in comparison.

On the other hand, I couldn't be defeated by a spotlight and a few pieces of iron and silver, so maybe it was fairest to say we simply had different strengths.

Getting inside the building didn't solve all our problems. "We can't waltz into any old apartment," I whispered. "The current tenants aren't going to be as welcoming to uninvited guests as I was to you three."

"I can check to see which are unoccupied," Ruse said, and tipped his head to Snap. "If you take a taste of the doors for those, you might be able to tell how soon the residents were planning on coming back."

Snap nodded, eager as always to contribute to our plans.

As we checked out the hall of apartments that branched off from the dingy lobby, Thorn kept scanning ahead and behind, his stance tensed, as if expecting another attack. Based on the threadbare carpet and its faintly musty smell, this clearly wasn't a five-star residence—but that was better for us as far as security went. All the same, the atmosphere combined with the scene I'd just fled set my skin crawling.

With my next breath, I quietly sang a lyric I'd mangled into pure nonsense. "Til now, I always got pie on my own—I never really dared until I met brew." Ruse raised an eyebrow at me, and I grimaced back at him. "It makes me feel better. And I could use a whole lot of better right now."

"Whatever makes you happy, Miss Blaze," he said with a grin, and slipped through the shadows around the first door. He emerged seconds later shaking his head, and we moved on to the next.

"How many people know of your involvement with this 'Fund' and where you live?" Thorn asked, managing to keep his own voice quiet to fit our current stealth mode.

"No one outside of the Fund knows about the Fund," I said. "Well, other than some of the higher shadowkind who live mortal-side, like Jade—and the hunters and collectors are at least vaguely aware that we're around. I haven't had anyone over at my place since I adopted Pickle." I reached into my purse to scratch the dragon's back between his wings, and he let out a hum that was almost a purr. "Even the Fund people wouldn't really approve of me keeping him, despite the circumstances."

"But someone who'd visited you there before might have remembered."

"Possibly. That's still a very limited number of people —and no one I can think of would have given my address to a stranger." I sucked my lower lip under my teeth to worry at it as Ruse returned from the fifth apartment. He motioned to Snap, and we stopped while the godly shadowkind worked his powers.

"Whoever's decided they need to bring me in—or shut me up—wouldn't need to drag the information out of my friends anyway," I said. "If someone saw us at the bridge or the market, or realized I was at the bar asking questions, it wouldn't be hard for them to find out my name. Which is unfortunately a pretty distinctive name. Anyone who can orchestrate some kind of conspiracy against the higher shadowkind should be able to dig up my address from that no problem." My black market contacts did the same with collectors using less definitive information.

Snap drew back after several flicks of his tongue around the doorknob. "They expected to return in the morning," he said. We needed longer than that.

"The real question," Ruse said as we moved on, "is what made our enemies so sure you were going to cause trouble for them."

"They could be monitoring Fund activities—could know I've been involved with that. And then seeing me poking around at all made them nervous." Which made *me* even more glad that I'd kept Vivi out of this mess. If she'd come along on our earlier investigations, would they have stormed her apartment too? She wouldn't have had three shadowkind guards ready to jump in and protect her.

No, I couldn't let my best friend hear a peep about this, not while the assholes who'd come for me tonight were still on the loose.

"The sword-star people are very powerful," Thorn said darkly. "We can't know everything they're capable of finding out—or doing." He glanced over his shoulder again.

"There's no way they could predict we'd come *here*," I reminded him. "I don't even know where here is."

"We weren't truly prepared for them to launch an attack at your apartment. It could have gone much worse. I won't be caught off-guard again."

I wasn't going to argue with him there. As irritated as

I'd been with my unexpected—and stubborn—houseguests, I was awfully grateful that they'd been around tonight.

"Next time," the warrior added, "if there's a chance that doesn't risk our escaping unscathed, I'll take one of the attackers for questioning. Ruse can persuade them to talk."

"You bring me the guy, and I'll work my magic," the incubus agreed as he wisped from the last first-floor apartment. "Looks like we're heading upstairs."

Uneasiness itched at my skin as we tramped up the steps, but after a few more unworkable apartments, Ruse found another that was currently empty. "There was a calendar on the fridge with the next week marked off as a vacation," he said. "We may have our jackpot! Snap, do the honors?"

Snap leaned in to sample the impressions that floated around the door. He straightened up with a brilliant smile. "They were imagining a plane ride and beaches on the other side. One of them asked the other if they'd remembered to have the mail held until they got back."

"Then they're not expecting anyone else to be dropping by either. Perfect." Ruse clapped his hands and vanished through the shadows again. A second later, he was opening the apartment door for us from the inside.

Crashing in some stranger's apartment had sounded like a sensible enough option when it'd only been in theory. Going to anyone I knew was way too risky, and I hadn't seen any hotels around here we could check in to.

Stepping over the threshold into someone else's home, though, sent an uncomfortable prickle down my spine.

Everywhere I looked, my gaze caught on remnants of the people who lived here. A bright pink jacket with rabbit fur trim on the hood hung on one of the hooks in the front hall next to a scuffed-up leather duster. They must have eaten bacon for breakfast the morning before they'd left, because a hint of that salty, greasy scent lingered by the kitchen. The living room held an old record player and a stack of cardboard sleeves way more ancient than my CDs.

Standing in the living room doorway, the sense of mourning crept over me again. Those CDs were gone— melted in the fire, most likely. So were all my clothes except what I wore on my back. The pieces of furniture that might not have matched but that I'd picked out based on comfiness. My laptop, which had been lying on my unmade bed where I'd last been using it. The goofy hand-painted mug Vivi had given me several Christmases ago.

Everything I'd owned that I wasn't carrying, from the practical to the sentimental, had been burned away. Even if the fire hadn't reached every corner of the apartment, it'd be too dangerous to go back to scavenge. The thoroughness with which I'd thrown the life I'd built there away hit me at full force for the first time. I gripped the doorframe, riding out the wave of loss.

I'd picked up the pieces of my life before with nothing but a single duffel bag's worth of possessions and strength of will. I could do it again. And I couldn't say I regretted the actions that must have brought on tonight's attack. I'd rather get to the bottom of Luna's death than have all that *stuff*.

But still. It'd been *my* stuff. It'd been my home, the first one that had really felt totally mine after bouncing from one Fund member's house to another and then shacking up with the one serious boyfriend of my early twenties. I inhaled and exhaled, groping for my self-control, willing back the tears that had started to burn at the corners of my eyes.

Before my shadowkind trio could notice my momentary fragility—or at least, before they could ask any questions about it that might break open the floodgates—I pushed myself onward down the hall.

Mercifully, there were two bedrooms. The first one I peeked into, a small, windowless space that was probably meant to be a den, had just enough room for a double bed and a tiny birch table beside it, both of which might have come straight from Ikea.

I guessed that one served as a guest bedroom, because the master bedroom next door blared personality. A pink shag rug, flower decals all over the walls, lava lamp on the dresser, orange-and-pink patterned bedspread framed by velvet cushions—it was a '60s-style dream.

"Well, I can't possibly sleep in there," I said, grateful for the excuse. Slipping into a bed someone else had clearly made their own gave me even more creeps than simply entering their apartment. "My sensibilities are fully offended."

"It does have plenty of character," Ruse said, his tone amused.

Thorn shifted his weight on his feet. "I'm going to take a circuit of the neighborhood," he announced. "Ensure there are no additional dangers lurking that we should be aware of."

He strode off without waiting for a response. Snap had already bounded off into the kitchen, the cabinet doors squeaking as he opened each to ogle the contents. I should probably have felt guilty about the food that wasn't ours he was going to be chowing down on, but I couldn't quite bring myself to care in that moment. I'd just lost the majority of my worldly possessions. Mr. and Mrs. '60s fanatics could spare a little grub.

I crossed the hall to the other bedroom and set down my purse. Pickle sprang out, shook himself with a huff, and trotted down the hall to join Snap, maybe pursuing a late dinner of his own.

Ruse had lingered at my side. When I turned to face him, his warm hazel eyes searched mine. "I expect you could use some rest. If you need anything, you know where to find us."

"Yeah," I said, and my throat tightened for a different reason. The incubus had worked awfully hard to lighten my spirits tonight—and then had his efforts ruined by that unexpected assault on the apartment. He hadn't needed to try to cheer me up.

All at once, I was sure that I didn't want to be alone

right now. I wanted to be with someone who cared about my happiness.

He bobbed his head to press a light kiss to my forehead, his fingers grazing the side of my face with a trace of heat, and then he was swiveling on his heel to go. I caught his hand before he'd taken more than one step. He shot me a questioning look.

"There are a few things I wouldn't mind doing in that bed before I get to the resting part," I said.

Ruse offered me a crooked smile. "A generous offer, but there's no need. After our last interlude, I should be in tip-top shape for at least a few weeks."

Oh. Had the other night's encounter really been about nothing more than feeding for him? Embarrassment constricted my chest.

It'd been ridiculous for me to think anything else, hadn't it? He was an incubus—that was what sex meant to him. Just because he'd had fun setting up the impromptu dance party didn't mean he was interested in more intimate activities for nothing but the pleasure of it.

I dropped his hand, pulling back into the doorway. "Of course. If you don't want to—"

Something flickered in Ruse's eyes as he took in my expression, and then he was reaching for me, his hand teasing along my arm to grasp my elbow. His head bowed close to mine again. My pulse stuttered with desire I couldn't suppress, but maybe I didn't have to.

"I can't think of any way I'd rather spend my time more than sparking a different sort of fire with you, Miss

Blaze," he said, his voice dropping low. "The only thing I don't want is for you to feel obligated."

All right then. I found myself grinning at him, maybe a little goofily, but really, can you blame me? It was about time I got a little good news.

I rested my hand on his firm chest. "You promised me the best sex I've ever had, and you delivered, and we haven't even really had sex yet. I promise you my proposition has exactly zilch to do with any sense of obligation."

"In that case..." He nudged me backward into the room, kicking the door shut behind us.

In the cramped space next to the bed, he cupped my face and dipped his to claim a proper kiss. The press of his mouth, hot and determined yet tender, woke up every inch of my body.

It'd been a long, hazardous night, but I definitely wasn't too tired to welcome this escape.

And I didn't want this time to be all about me. I intended to get the full incubus experience—well, emotional meddling aside.

As I kissed him back, my fingers sped down the front of his shirt to unbutton it. When the muscular planes were bared, I couldn't resist dropping my head to kiss him just below his shoulder, drinking in his bittersweet cocoa scent. Yum.

Ruse trailed his fingers over my hair. As soon as I eased back, he tilted my chin up to recapture my mouth. As his tongue twined with mine, he found the zipper at the back of my dress and slid it downward torturously slowly.

With each inch, his thumb stroked over the naked skin he'd uncovered. By the time he'd reached the bottom, a hair's breadth from my ass, my body was swaying toward his, wanting more: more closeness, more heat, more of that tantalizing touch.

"This looked exquisite on you," he murmured as the fabric slid down my thighs to pool at my feet, "but I think I like it even better off."

"I think I'd like everything *you're* wearing off," I informed him, tugging at his shirt.

He chuckled and shed it in a second. When he tipped me back on the bed, I reached for the fly of his slacks, and tonight he didn't stop me. He obviously understood that I was in this for the entire act now.

And he was clearly into it too. The length I encountered through the fabric of his underthings—an incubus wearing briefs; who'd have thought?—was rigidly erect. A pleased thrum emanated from Ruse's throat as I teased my fingers over it. He bent closer to jerk the cup of my bra down with his teeth, and gods above, I'd never seen anything hotter.

He sucked my nipple into his mouth, and for a few minutes, the pleasure he was conjuring in my breasts distracted me from my own mission. My head leaned back onto the pillow, a gasp slipping out of me. As he slicked his tongue around one stiffening peak and then tested his teeth against it, I dug my fingers into his hair, finding his horns.

Ruse rumbled again, low in his chest. He tossed my bra aside and turned his attentions to my other breast.

Every swivel of his tongue sent me soaring higher, but I didn't lose sight of my goals completely. When he traced his hand down my side to remove my panties, I sat up to make sure the rest of his clothes came off too. He drew back to slide out of his slacks and briefs, and then he knelt before me in all his leanly carved glory. His cock jutted so solidly aloft, I had the urge to down it like a shot at the bar.

One of the benefits of sex with the shadowkind—one I'd never needed to consider before—was that they didn't produce children. They simply sprang into being rather than being born, and there was no record of any human involvement resulting in pregnancy on either side. Which was a very good thing, because I hadn't exactly thought to pack condoms.

The mouth-watering visage I was taking in wasn't his *real* glory, though. This was only the human appearance he put on to blend in. I hauled my gaze from the parts I hoped to have penetrating me soon to his face.

"Like what you see?" he said with one of those typical smirks.

I ran my fingers down his chest, following the grooves of his muscles, until I reached his cock. I couldn't resist giving the silky skin that covered the rigid length an eager stroke, but I held his gaze.

"I do," I said. "But I'd like even more to see you as you really are."

Ruse tensed—just slightly, but his nudity made it hard to hide. He opened his mouth with an intake of breath that already sounded like a protest.

Before he could speak, I held up my hand to stop him. "I've seen a hell of a lot more than I'd bet any woman you've been with before had. If they could handle it while high on your seductive vibes, I'm pretty sure I can while sober. And I *am* totally sober now to make that call." Any lingering effects of the drug had dissipated during my frantic bike ride.

Ruse peered at me for a long moment. "Why?" he said finally.

I shrugged. "You can see me exactly as I am. It'll feel more equal if I can say the same about you. Besides, it'll make a much better story if I can say I got it on with a fully-fledged incubus rather than just a dude with horns." I knocked his hip with my knee playfully.

Something about my explanation appeared to make up his mind. His smile returned. "All right," he said. "Don't say I didn't warn you."

He closed his eyes, and a shimmer ran over his body. Ran over it—and stayed, a hazy golden glow emanating from his skin as if he were part firefly. His little horns lengthened, curving in a full loop and pointing toward the ceiling again. His cock curved too, his pubic bone protruding farther out at the same time. When he opened his eyes again, the pupils had dilated, but the irises had expanded as well, nearly filling the whites. They gleamed a gold as bright as if the brilliant summer sun were reflecting off them.

"Well?" he said, with a new smoky quality to his voice that seemed to wind around me in its own embrace.

Sweet shiny sugar-puffs, a story for the ages indeed. Had he really thought I'd run scared from *this*?

I raised my hand to touch his glowing cheek. "You were handsome before. Now you're fucking magnificent."

His smile stretched wider. He bowed his head to kiss me hard, the tingling heat of his lips spreading into mine and all through my body. "Let's get on with the fucking then," he murmured against my mouth.

He gave me a gentle shove to lie down, joining me as I did. Everywhere our skin touched, little shocks of bliss quivered into me. He wasn't even inside me yet, and the rush of my release was already building to a peak.

We kissed again and again, until the scorching pleasure of it blurred my thoughts together. His hand dipped between my legs, his thumb flicking over my clit, and just like that, I did come, with a shaky moan that had me thanking all that was good in the world for the existence of incubi and their soundproofing magic.

The sound had hardly finished leaving my lips when Ruse delved his fingers right inside me. With a few quick pulses, I was coming again on the heels of my first orgasm, my body trembling with the combined force. "Oh my God," I gasped out.

Ruse stole another kiss with a chuckle that vibrated into me. "I'd prefer you give me the credit."

I let out a laugh that turned into another moan as he rubbed the head of his cock over my slit and plunged inside. My fingers dug into his shoulders as if the ecstasy might wash me away if I didn't hold on tight. The next sound that leaked out of me was embarrassingly close to a whine of need.

"I've got you," Ruse murmured in the smoky tone that set me even more ablaze. He rocked deeper into me, and I discovered exactly what was so special about his official incubus equipment. The curve of his cock veered perfectly to press the hot button of bliss deep inside me. With each thrust, the bulge of his pubic bone stroked my clit. Pulses of a pleasure I'd never even imagined raced through me, faster and more searing by the moment.

I arched up to meet him, wanting to pay him back as well as I could with my more limited human means. Remembering how he'd reacted to the caressing of his horns before, I lifted my hands to his head. My fingers tangled in his hair and then found the enlarged points with their graceful spiral.

When I squeezed them, Ruse groaned and drove into me even harder. Another orgasm crashed through me, sending me flying and then dragging me down into depths like a blissful undertow. And once I started coming, I couldn't stop. Each thrust of his cock into me tossed me up and under all over again with just enough time to gasp for air. My entire existence became a gale of pleasure.

Through the storm of ecstasy, I had just enough awareness to realize that the incubus hadn't joined me, not with his own release. I managed to raise my jellified legs to his waist, welcoming him even deeper as I gripped one horn and ran my fingernails down the muscles of his back.

"Come," I mumbled. "Come with me."

Ruse's next groan shuddered as it fell from his lips. His mouth crashed into mine. With a roll of his hips, bliss tossed me up and over once more. A flood of tingling heat filled me as he followed.

As he eased to a stop over me, I couldn't help thinking that everything considered, this hadn't been such a bad night after all.

18

Ruse

There was nothing quite as gorgeous as a woman basking in the afterglow of ecstasy—an ecstasy *I'd* brought her to. Possibly it was even more satisfying seeing that release in Sorsha than any woman before. She was the first I'd taken to those heights while she was fully aware of what I was, and she'd welcomed everything I could offer all the same.

She sprawled out on the bed, her cheeks flushed with a rosy hue that might have been even more lovely than the waves of her red hair spread across the pillow. Her chest rose and fell where my arm lay just below her breasts. I stroked my fingers over her side just for the pleasure of touching that warm, smooth skin once more. Warm and smooth—and layered with toned muscle underneath. I appreciated a woman who could be both soft and strong. Her fiery sweet scent lingered in my nose, equally delicious.

My own skin still hummed with the aftermath of my orgasm. I'd drawn the glow back into it, returning to my more subtle mortal guise, since it wasn't wise for any of us to get used to walking around in this realm au naturel. I'd worn these trappings of humanity often enough that this false body felt more comfortable than my own in mortal-side air, other than when I was employing my powers.

I had enjoyed *my* release quite a lot. Watching Sorsha give herself over so completely to the act, hearing her beg me to join her just as completely, knowing she'd wanted this interlude as much as I had—I didn't think I'd ever come so hard.

But the moment was over, and I really ought to leave her to the rest her mortal body would be craving after the extended, chaotic night. I kissed one of those rosy cheeks and moved to push myself upright.

As I shifted on the bed, Sorsha's hand came up to touch my arm, as if she were beckoning me to stay. My gaze shot to her face, a quiver of uncertainty prickling through me—and before I had a chance to catch myself, I'd peeked into her mind.

The emotions at the forefront were easy to read once I let myself: a pleasantly drowsy haze and a longing to keep my warmth next to her as she drifted off.

I jerked my awareness back, a twinge fluttering through my chest. She really did get some sort of contentment from my presence even now that the act I was most skilled at was over. That knowledge sparked a little more contentment in *me* than I was comfortable with. And as I relaxed back down next to her, the twinge sharpened into a pang of guilt.

I'd promised her I wouldn't violate the privacy of her mind. She'd made it very clear that this one term was non-negotiable, no matter what physical intimacies we shared. If she knew I'd broken my word...

My first instinct—and, really, my second and third as well—was to dismiss that secret into the shadows where she never needed to find out. Why tell her something that would upset her if I didn't need to? But when she stirred and rolled onto her side, catching my gaze with a dreamy little smile, the pang stabbed too deeply for me to ignore.

She'd been genuine and open with me. She'd cared enough to let me feed despite her reservations—offered me more trust than apparently she should have. Hell, she'd literally rescued me from captivity and the slow starvation I'd faced there.

I was man enough to give her the respect she'd earned, wasn't I? Even if the consequences wouldn't work to my favor.

"Sorsha," I said carefully. "I—just now—I read your emotions. Only for a moment, only a few."

Before I could go on, she jerked back from me and sat up. Her hair spilled over her shoulders like rivulets of flame—or blood. From the look on her face, I might as well have cut her. "What?"

I sat up too, groping for an acceptable explanation. "I

didn't intend to—it's second nature at this point, and I slipped, and as soon as I realized I pulled back. It won't happen again."

Her arms crossed over her chest, hiding the lovely slopes of her breasts. Her voice came out taut. "If you did it without meaning to, how can you be sure you won't accidentally trip into my head again?"

A reasonable question. "I'll be more on guard now. I'll—"

"No." She scooted farther away on the bed and motioned to the door. Her expression had tightened, shutting me out as fully as that brooch of hers once had. "I don't want to hear it. Just get out. I—" Her hand fumbled across the bedcovers for a second before clenching. Realizing she'd left the brooch and its protections behind in her burning apartment like she had so much else? Somehow that small gesture wrenched me more than anything before had.

I was already springing off the bed as I'd been planning to in the beginning, if more hastily than before. With a blink and an ounce of concentration, the clothes I'd shed in our encounter vanished from their disarray around the room and reassembled themselves on my body. I risked glancing at Sorsha one more time. "I'm sorry."

"Just go," she said, her voice firm but hollow, as if my confession had drained away all the pleasure I'd given her.

I winced, the guilt expanding like a vise around my lungs, but I went.

When the bedroom door was shut between her and me, I paused in the hall to catch my breath. Nicely done. Very smooth. I'd better hope I never needed her for more sustenance, because she sure as hell wasn't getting it on with me ever again.

She might not ever share another dance with me or laugh at my banter or, fuck, even smile at me.

None of those things should have mattered. I didn't require any of them to survive. As I slunk to the kitchen, I reminded myself of that over and over until I was almost convinced. Almost. Well, a little chatter with Snap might cheer me up.

It wasn't our naïve devourer I found in the kitchen, though, but Thorn, back from his patrol and looking about as grim as usual, which I assumed meant it was good news.

I dropped into the chair across from him at the stubby Formica island that protruded from the wall. "No sign of this sword-star crew?"

"Not so far," he said in a tone that suggested he expected they'd appear to wreak more havoc on our existence any minute now. You could hand this man a glass that was full nearly to the brim, and he'd still mutter about the smidge it was empty.

A little china bowl filled with hard candies sat in the middle of the island. I plucked one up and then simply turned it between my fingers, the cellophane crinkling.

Physical food didn't do anything for me except perhaps offer a pleasant flavor, and I wasn't sure I was in the mood to actually stick anything in my mouth. Not after I'd already stuck my foot in there so badly with the woman down the hall.

Thorn glanced past me as if he knew where my thoughts had headed. His fathomless gaze came back to rest on my face.

Not for the first time, I wished I knew what in the realms *he* was. He'd never shown his full form where I could see it, and his presence in the shadows didn't offer any qualities distinctive enough for me to match him to other beings I'd encountered. The powers I knew of—his strength and alertness to aggression—could have belonged to any number of kind.

I'd never met a devourer before Snap, only heard rumors of them. Quite possibly Thorn was some rare creature that few of us ever encountered as well. Which meant I had no clue what other powers he might be hiding behind that scarred exterior.

Omen had wanted the best of the best, at least from the shadowkind willing to take up his cause. He'd trusted Thorn. I trusted Omen... about as much as I trusted anyone. Better to leave it at that than to worry.

"You've been getting rather close with the mortal one," Thorn said, with a tip of his head toward the hall.

I raised my eyebrows at him. "That *is* sort of my thing, as you well know. Have you got a problem with it?"

He stared right back at me, unshaken by my implied

challenge. "I don't think such involvement will make it easier to protect her. If it affects your concentration, it may bring about the opposite result instead."

"My concentration is just fine. We cubi deal in bodily intimacies, not emotional connection—we make no secret about that."

"So, you have no interest in her beyond physical satisfaction."

He didn't say it like a question, but I felt the need to answer it anyway. "I like her well enough, but I'm hardly going to get attached in any way that would throw me off my game. Omen picked *me* for good reason too. Everything is under control."

And besides, it wasn't likely I'd have any more involvement with Sorsha at all after tonight, not that I wanted to mention that to Thorn. Not that, or the fact that Omen might not have picked me if he'd been aware of one particular past lapse.

No one needed to know about *that*. I knew better now.

"As long as it stays that way," Thorn said, getting up. He left me on my own in the kitchen, grappling with a rekindled uneasiness I couldn't quite shake.

19

Sorsha

I'd never felt nervous about heading into a Fund meeting before. Never had any reason to believe the act of walking into a low-rent movie theater might be seen as suspicious. But now, given recent events, I was waiting in a dim alleyway four blocks away, shuffling my feet against the rain-damp concrete and praying that the clouds still clotted overhead didn't decide to open up again while I was out here. My umbrella: another casualty of last night's apartment fire.

The afternoon's rain had brought out a mildew-y scent that made my nose itch. Every time footsteps sounded on the sidewalk, I shrank back into the thicker darkness by the brick wall beside me. None of the people who passed through the evening looked like a possible threat to me, but then, I hadn't been prepared for a band of organized attackers to crash into my apartment either.

I'd been working with the Fund in this city for eleven years, and none of the members had ever even been so much as harassed, except maybe now and then by the mortal-side shadowkind who didn't appreciate our attempts to help. No one in this group had even known a member who'd been hurt in the line of duty. Only more proof that whoever had decided I needed to be eliminated from the equation, they obviously weren't your typical hunters.

Finally, Thorn wavered out of a dark patch in front of me. "I picked up on no sign of enemy presence nearby," he said. "I believe you can safely enter the building for your meeting. But I *will* be accompanying you through the shadows."

He'd already emphasized that point before we'd left our temporary new home. I nodded, gazing up into his rugged face for a few seconds. Searching for a hint of humanity in those coal-dark eyes and hardened features —something to reassure me that this was at least a little more than a cold transaction of favors owed.

There'd been passion in his voice, if a solemn kind, when he'd talked about defending me and his companions and finding his boss. He'd thought to rescue my one token from my parents for me. There had to be something other than steely chill behind all the brawn.

I couldn't pick it out right now, though. Well, at least

steel was reliable. It'd turned out I couldn't say that for much else.

"All right," I said. "Off I go."

As I moved to stalk past him, he vanished, but I knew he was staying with me unseen. The evening was full of shadows for ease of travel.

The smell of buttered popcorn laced with mint and—was that *toffee?*—met me at the door to the Fund's private theater room. Only a few people had shown up so far, the Saturday meetings being less popular than the weekday ones, but Ellen and Huyen were over by the screen, and that was all I needed.

Unfortunately, Vivi had also turned up early. Before I could get one of our leaders' ears, my best friend had moseyed down the aisle to join me.

"Hey!" she said, and gave me a once-over. "I love that blouse. It's new, right? Where'd you get it?"

I tugged at the hem of the silky purple halter top self-consciously. It was new, but I hadn't been the one to get it. The entire outfit had been sitting outside my bedroom door when I'd gotten up this morning. Any of the trio could have realized that I couldn't wear my bar dress for days on end and swiped some clothes in the shadows of a shop, but from the hint of cacao smell that had lingered on them, I suspected they were an apology offering from Ruse.

Otherwise, he'd given me plenty of distance, which worked just fine for me. I couldn't remember any of the spectacular parts of our encounter last night without a flash of panic at the thought of him rummaging through my thoughts and feelings. How could I be sure he'd even admitted his full transgression, that he hadn't been using his powers on me the whole time?

It was going to take more than some pretty clothes to smooth things over, even if I did look pretty fantastic in them.

If I told Vivi it'd been a gift, she'd want to know who from, and I'd just tangle myself in a whole lot of bigger lies. So I stuck to a smaller one. "You know, I don't even remember. Somewhere at the mall."

"Well, it was a good choice." She bumped her shoulder against mine. "Good to see you got home all right after the bar. I was a little worried, the way you took off."

Ha. Yes, I'd gotten home all right. Getting *out* of the apartment had been much less okay. "It was no big deal," I said, feeling as if each new lie was adding to a heavy lump in my stomach. "I wish I could have stayed longer."

"No news on the tip Jade gave you?"

"Nope, I haven't had much chance to see what I can make of it yet."

Ellen left the conversation she and Huyen had been in with one of the older members and headed our way. I made an apologetic gesture to Vivi. "I've got to talk to the lady in charge. Grab me some of tonight's popcorn?"

Vivi hesitated for a second as if balking at the idea of missing what I'd say to Ellen, but then she shot me a smile and a thumbs-up. As she walked away, I hustled to meet Ellen.

Despite her love of flavors, our co-leader was thin as a rail, with frizzy, graying hair that was perpetually escaping from her loose buns. On meeting nights, stains on her fingertips often gave away her latest popcorn ingredients—today's greenish tint confirmed the mint.

I didn't have much time before my best friend would return and hear something that would make her even more curious what was going on with me. "Hey, Ellen," I said, cutting right to the chase. "Do you have a spare badge around? I seem to have misplaced mine." I wasn't giving Ruse any more chances to exercise his self-control —or not.

"Sure," the petite woman said, with a note of surprise. I'd managed not to misplace the first badge she'd given me in the past eleven years, but it could happen to any of us. She dug into her purse—of course Ellen the ever-prepared would have a little stash of those always on hand.

"Is everything else all right?" she asked as she handed it to me.

Maybe my general agitation was showing more than I'd meant it to. I pushed my mouth into a sheepish grin and pocketed the protective badge. "Yeah, I just seem to be having kind of a scattered week. I was also hoping—I wanted to get in touch with the group that monitors talk about the shadowkind for us online, but my computer's hard drive died." The whole thing had died a sad, fiery death. "Could I grab his contact info from you again? I knew better than to write it down somewhere not totally secure, but that means I'm out of luck."

I spread my hands in an attempt to look cluelessly innocent rather than like a lying liar who lied. From the weight in my gut, I might as well have swallowed a boulder. Ellen didn't appear fazed by the request, thank shimmering seal pups. She gave me a motherly pat on the shoulder.

"I'll send it to you by a secure link. You're still at the same email as before?"

"Yeah," I said with a rush of relief.

"FYI, they're looking for payment in organic kombucha these days—they take it by the crate."

Crates of kombucha it was, then.

As Ellen moved on, Vivi came up beside me. She handed me a bag of popcorn and cocked her head with a swish of her hair. "What'd I miss?"

I gave her a smile in thanks. "Nothing." One more lie to add to the pile.

My best friend's gaze turned unusually serious. She paused for a second and then said, "No matter what you find out, I'll be here if you need me. You'll remember that, right?"

The emphatic plea made my gut twist all over again. "Yeah," I said. "Of course I'll remember." I just wouldn't be taking her up on the offer, not after I'd seen just how brutal my newfound enemies could be.

* * *

Maybe the love the apartment's true owners had for the '60s explained why they hadn't demanded the landlord replace their kitchen appliances, because the stove certainly behaved like it was several decades old. After an hour of slowly turning up the heat under the frozen stir fry I'd liberated from the freezer and watching the ice crystals barely melt, all at once half of the bits had burned to the pan.

I growled at the meal as if I could intimidate it into uncharring itself. Before I could decide whether to make the best of it or toss it and start over, the shiny new laptop my shadowkind friends had obtained for me chimed with an inbox alert.

Screw dinner. I plopped myself down at the kitchen island and let out a cry of victory. "We've got it!"

Thorn, who'd been skulking by the kitchen doorway in his usual glum way, stepped only a little closer, as if it would pain him to show any more enthusiasm than that. Snap, who last I'd seen had been sprawled on the master bedroom floor tipping the lava lamp this way and that with pure joy, came gliding over a second later.

"You have the information that'll tell us where to find Omen?" he asked, his eyes bright.

"Maybe," I cautioned. Pickle hopped onto my lap from where he'd been sitting on the other chair and peeked over the top of the island. I gave his chin a scratch as I considered the screen. "Jade said that someone's put a call out for 'potent' shadowkind, and that sounds like the M.O. of the bunch that ambushed him. Our contacts on the dark web are pretty good at digging up useful communications that were meant to be private."

Hunters and collectors had their own areas of the internet's black market where they operated, of course. As secure as they tried to keep those channels, the cabal of hackers who worked for the Fund for pay managed to crack their codes on a regular basis. Usually they could trace the usernames to the actual people behind the sales, purchases, and other posts.

As I opened the file my contact had sent me, Ruse slunk into the room too. He leaned against the counter at the farthest point in the kitchen from me, his stance casual but careful.

He was giving me distance for my sake, not his, I knew. Now and then he'd tossed out a joke or teasing comment, watching my reaction intently as if a laugh would tell him he was forgiven. If he thought he was going to win me over a second time that easily, he was kidding himself.

My hand rose to my chest of its own accord, taking a momentary comfort from brushing my fingertips over the edges of the new silver-and-iron badge pinned under my blouse. I leaned closer to the screen. My other forefinger skimmed over the touchpad as I scanned the list of names and summaries of what the hacker had found.

I almost scrolled right past it. My eyes slid over the letters, continued another half a screen down, and then recognition pinged in my head. Wait a second. I leapt back to that previous entry.

Looking at it, a chuckle slipped from my mouth. Son of a biscuit eater. We'd been barking up the altogether wrong tree, but I could see how the mistake had happened.

I pointed at the name that had caught my eye. "It's not Merry Den we're looking for, and it's not a place. It's a person. John Meriden. He's behind one of the aliases that's posted at least a couple of messages over the last few months, looking to confer with collectors about their shadowkind."

Snap's spirits visibly deflated. "I told you the wrong information."

I patted his arm reassuringly. Oh, the guy did pack plenty of compact muscle onto those slender limbs.

Focus, Sorsha.

"It was an easy mistake to make," I said. "You picked up on the sounds in a way that formed words you know. It could have happened to any of us. And hey, it still helped us find our man in the end."

Thorn loomed over me, scowling at the computer as if preparing to reach into the screen and grab our target by the throat through cyberspace. "Where is this 'John Meriden'?"

"Let's see what my contact found..." As I read through the entry, my own spirits sank a little. "He only made a small slip that allowed the hackers to find his real name, they don't say what exactly—probably logging in somewhere he shouldn't have with the same IP address. But the address itself was some kind of front. They couldn't trace it back to an actual location that connects to the guy."

"With his name, it shouldn't be difficult to track down more details, should it?" Ruse put in. Pickle let out a chirp as if agreeing with the incubus.

"Yeah, I can ask them to investigate more about him specifically. They wouldn't have gone on a full-blown search for any of the names yet—this is more a summary..." I paused. "Except if he's connected to the same people who barged into my apartment last night, who knows how closely they're keeping an eye on anyone poking around in his business."

Ruse tsked. "You don't think your hackers can avoid getting noticed?"

"No, it's more that we can't be sure none of them are paid off by other parties too. They work for whoever fronts the moola—they don't have any specific loyalty to the Fund." I leaned back in my chair, rubbing the top of Pickle's head and frowning.

I'd given the cabal a general enough brief that it shouldn't have set off any major alarm bells. If the sword-star bunch sicced the same hackers on me, they could probably figure out where I was working from in five seconds flat. The black-market-savvy skills I'd picked up over the years were nothing compared to theirs.

"Let's see how much we can find out on our own without getting anyone else involved," I said. "It's safer that way. And if we can't find out anything ourselves, then we can take a gamble. We're definitely not finding Omen if the assholes who took him find us first, and they're better prepared than last time."

I opened up a regular search window and started my online game of hide and seek with Mr. John Meriden. Unfortunately, there seemed to be a few dudes with that name. Fortunately, only one of them turned up when I included the city name in my search.

The pickings were pretty sparse. Whoever the man was, he kept a very low internet profile. But I did manage to turn up a mention of a J. Meriden in connection to an address on the outskirts of the city. Checking the street view from the map, it looked like an office building—but with no sign and no other features that would tell me what went on in there. How very suspicious.

"Should have known better than those deets to send," I sang in triumph. "Jackpot!"

"We've got him?" Thorn said with gruff enthusiasm.

"We're one step closer, anyway." I waved toward the online map. "Update your calendars—we've got plans for tomorrow."

20

Sorsha

If I'd hoped I might saunter into Meriden's office building and have a receptionist point me right to him, one up-close look at the current state of the place killed that dream. Obviously it would have been ridiculous to march right in demanding to speak to him anyway, but the dreary dimness that showed in gaps through the papered-over windows didn't inspire much confidence that we'd find anything at all.

Thorn had already patrolled several blocks around the place, watching for any hint of our previous attackers. Now, as the other two shadowkind and I waited in a coffee shop down the street after a brisk walk past, he'd gone to prowl through the building itself.

Ruse sipped the espresso he'd charmed the barista

into giving him, not looking as though he was enjoying it very much. Even Snap was too restless to make more than a few half-hearted exclamations over the whipped-cream-topped hot chocolate the incubus had gotten for him.

I'd decided to forgo caffeine altogether, since I didn't need my nerves on any higher alert than they already were, but I was starting to regret leaving my hands empty. As I fidgeted with the napkin I'd pulled out of the dispenser, slowly tearing one corner, our hardened warrior stepped out of the shadows across the room as if he'd emerged from the bathroom rather than the darkness. I was pretty sure Ruse had coached him on that move.

"The way is clear," he said when he reached us, his voice low but formal as always. "There is an entrance at the back I believe it would be wisest for us to make use of. M'lady, my companions and I will travel unseen and meet you there."

I guessed that made sense. Still, I couldn't help feeling I had a target on my back as I ambled outside like I was just enjoying this lovely summer day. I'd committed plenty of crimes, snuck into plenty of buildings I wasn't meant to be in, but always with the cover of night. Under the blazing sun without my cat burglar get-up, I might as well have had a spotlight pointed at me.

If the place was empty anyway, there was no reason to poke around during the day. No employees to listen in on or even question if we'd dared. But we were here now. Thorn was even tenser about the situation than I was—if he thought we could go ahead, I was probably safer here than lounging on a beach in the Bahamas.

I just wouldn't think about the fact that he'd missed the hunters who'd shipped him off to that cage I'd rescued him from.

I strolled around the block and down the driveway beside the used furniture store next door. Cutting across the parking lot took me straight to a rather imposing steel door at the back of Meriden's apparently former workplace. Thank galloping gremlins that something about the process of melding iron into steel seemed to diffuse its repulsive effect on most shadowkind.

I glanced around to make sure no one was hanging out nearby to see me, pulled on my gloves, and tried the handle. It didn't budge.

Huh. I'd expected the trio to make it there before me. An uneasy quiver ran down through my gut. I looked around again, bracing myself to run—and the handle jerked over with a metallic crunching sound from the other side.

Before I could bolt, the door swung open to reveal Thorn's own imposing visage. The handle from the other side of the door, broken and twisted, dangled from his brawny hand.

"The place has some fancy-pants locks we couldn't manage to open without a certain amount of destruction,"

Ruse said with a baleful look toward the taller guy. "I *tried* to suggest to this lunk that we make sure you thought it was wise to literally break our way in before going ahead."

Thorn was already motioning me in with an urgent sweep of his arm. "We'd have drawn much more attention standing around outside discussing the matter— or leaving her out there wondering what had befallen us. She's in now."

Snap peered around the storage room I'd joined them in. "It doesn't look as if anyone's come by here in a long time."

The shelving units that filled the space were mostly empty, the few bedraggled cardboard boxes that remained holding nothing that revealed more than what type of printer paper the business had used. The date on a shipping label informed me that particular package had been delivered five years ago.

Had this place been empty that long? My hopes sank even further.

The storage room opened up to a hallway lined with interior windows. The rooms on the other side appeared to be labs with gleaming metal tables and fridges next to open spaces that held nothing more than scuffs on the floor suggesting there'd once been other equipment there. Only muted light filtered through the tiny, high outer windows set with frosted glass. A bitter chemical odor hung in the air.

Thorn got us into one of those rooms with a similar trick with the lock—if you could call brute strength a "trick." Inside, Snap crouched down by the scuff marks. The first flick of his tongue provoked a wince that echoed through his entire slim body.

"Silver and iron," he said, his voice gone tight. "There were cages here."

The kinds of cages that would only be used to hold shadowkind. The sword-star bunch had removed the obvious evidence, but they hadn't counted on a being with Snap's skills checking out the place.

"Can you pick up anything else about them—what sort of shadowkind they were keeping?" Ruse asked.

Snap took another tentative taste and shook his head with a shudder. He moved on, sampling the air over and around the table and then the fridge. His beautiful face tensed with a frown it was painful to see.

"I can't taste much about the people who used this room," he said quietly. "But they were doing something with—something *to*—shadowkind creatures. Something that hurt."

Thorn's hands clenched at his sides. My own fingers had curled into my palms. It wasn't as if we couldn't have guessed that whoever had taken their boss—and probably come for my Auntie Luna as well—had nefarious purposes, but if they'd operated out of this building, there was no doubting their intentions now.

We checked each of the lab rooms in turn, even though my stomach knotted at the growing strain that showed in Snap's demeanor. The impressions of whatever awful experiments he was having to glean became worth it when he straightened up from a cabinet in the last room with a brilliant grin.

"I saw it! Someone who opened this recently—however recently they were last working here—had that star symbol with the swords on the folder he was holding."

"We're definitely in the right place, then." I glanced at the pale walls around us with another shiver of uneasiness. "Meriden must be our guy." But so far we hadn't seen anything here that could lead us closer to him.

"The front of the building had more... debris," Thorn said. "Something there might give us a sense of where to continue our investigation."

I wasn't at all sorry to leave the vacant labs behind. We passed another steel door to reach the front half of the building, which opened up into a pretty typical office layout.

A maze of dividers wove across the floor, separating out a couple dozen cubicles other than where a few had toppled over. The plain steel desks remained, but weirdly none of the chairs. A water cooler without its jug stood next to a dust-coated coffee maker just outside a small kitchen area. Doors along the opposite wall led into private offices, but the name plaques had been removed from their brass holders.

Snap immediately set off to sample all the

impressions he could find. I veered in another direction, picking through the crumpled papers, long-dried pens, and other garbage the employees had left behind in case any of it held an identifying clue that didn't require supernatural voodoo to discern.

Ruse followed the same course I did, inspecting the cubicles on the other side of the aisle. As Snap and Thorn drifted farther away, he glanced at me. I was bent over a desk, struggling to reach a paper that had fallen between it and the divider wall it appeared to be bolted to.

I half expected him to make a cheeky comment about my waving ass, but instead he blinked out of sight. The paper vanished into the shadows, and a second later the incubus was standing next to me, holding it out.

"Oh. Thank you." I couldn't stop my posture from stiffening a little at the warmth of his body right next to mine.

I took the paper, which turned out to have nothing but a couple of obscene dick doodles on it. Such amazing productivity.

Ruse stepped back, his mouth twisting into a grimace. His lips parted, and then he hesitated. "Sorsha," he said finally when I started to turn.

"What?" The word came out terser than I'd intended, but I hadn't been going for friendly either.

"I—" He let out a huff of breath, but from his expression, I got the sense he was frustrated with himself, not with me. "You can be angry with me forever if you want. I'm not telling you I didn't fuck up. But I do want you to know I didn't break your trust for kicks or to manipulate you in any way."

"No? Why did you, then?"

Despite my still-terse tone, he looked relieved that I'd even asked. "I know what value I generally bring to the table where mortals are concerned—or rather, to the bed. When the act is over, I haven't been in the habit of sticking around. No one's ever complained about my leaving. When it seemed as if you meant for me to stay with you, I wasn't sure whether I was only making assumptions or— I didn't like the idea of overstaying my welcome inadvertently. So I looked before I could catch the impulse, just to make sure that really was what you wanted."

The only thing I don't want is for you to feel obligated, he'd told me the other night when I'd invited him into my bed in the first place. Remembering that and seeing the remorse that sat so awkwardly on his roguishly handsome face, some of the betrayal I'd been feeling crumbled away.

What must it feel like, being treated as if you had no worth other than your sexual prowess for centuries on end? Maybe it didn't matter to him as much as it might to a human being, but shadowkind could still experience loss and loneliness. To have all the pleasure but none of the closeness and connection of falling asleep in each other's arms afterward... Even the months when I'd been hooking up with Leland, the lack of actual intimacy had started to dull the fun parts of our agreement.

Ruse's skills might have knocked my socks off, almost literally, but I'd take the full experience of human intimacy over supernaturally powerful passion alone any day. If *I* ever got a chance to have that for real, that was.

"Okay," I said. "I can see why you might have slipped up. I still don't want you slipping *ever* again."

I looked down at my hands braced against the desk and decided that if he'd opened up, I could give him a little honesty in return. "Having my mind messed with is a particularly sore spot for me. There was this time— when I was seven, heading home one evening with Luna, another higher shadowkind spotted us together and started mocking her for taking care of a mortal. When we tried to simply walk away from him, he used his powers on me."

"He was an incubus?" Ruse asked softly, but his eyes flashed with a golden blaze of anger.

"I don't think so, but he had some kind of charm ability. He called out to me, told me to jump around and crawl on my hands and knees and would have ordered me to walk into traffic if Luna hadn't launched herself at him then."

A lump filled my throat with the memory. "It was awful, wanting to resist, terrified of what he was making me do, but being trapped in my body that was following his commands no matter how much I tried to stop it. I know that tormenting people isn't your thing, but the thought of anyone using their influence on my mind brings back that terror."

If I hadn't been completely sure of Ruse's remorse before, there would have been no mistaking it etched in his expression now. "I hate that I reminded you of that time—that you'd need to associate me at all with that dumpster fire of a being. If I can't manage to keep the promise of never slipping up again, you're welcome to light *me* on fire and cheer while I burn."

My lips couldn't help twitching upward at the vehemence with which he made that offer. "I think I can manage without burning anyone alive. Let's just see how it goes. And don't push your luck."

"Duly noted," the incubus said with a playful salute, though his eyes were still serious. I was just venturing onward to resume my search when a joyful voice rang out from the office kitchen. Of course Snap would have ended up in there sooner rather than later.

"I have something!" He loped out with his face beaming as bright as his curly hair. With one hand, he held up a mug that had a jagged shard missing from its side. "This cup belonged to Meriden. He brought it in from his house, and I can see the house in the impressions that've stuck to it."

Excitement raced through me. I hurried over. "Are you sure it's his?"

He tipped the mug to show us the base, looking so breathtakingly pleased with himself I had to restrain the urge to kiss him. "I can hear someone saying the name while he was holding it—and look. This is for John Meriden, isn't it?"

Marked on the mug's base in black sharpie were the initials J.M.

I laughed and settled for squeezing Snap's shoulder in a fragment of an embrace. "You did it. He'd better watch out now—we're coming for him where he lives."

21

Sorsha

Helpfully, the residents of the apartment we'd borrowed had left the keys to their vehicle in a bowl near the door. When Ruse pressed the unlock button in the parking lot at the back of the building, a shiny silver SUV beeped.

We'd treat it well, I told myself as we walked over. We'd even leave them with a full tank of gas as a thank you present.

Then I opened the passenger side door, and my eyebrows shot up. "Oh, for the love of sweet potato fries."

It'd looked like a perfectly normal SUV from the outside. The inside stunk of the '60s. Literally. A waft of musky, earthy patchouli washed over me. As I wrinkled my nose, I took in the bright pink mini shag rugs on the floor in front of each seat and the bejeweled peace sign glittering where it hung from the rear-view mirror.

Maybe walking would be better.

But no, given the house Snap had described from the impressions on Meriden's mug, we were heading out to the posh suburbs at the north end of town, and that was a hell of a hike even for me. So I clambered into the back of the car with Snap while Ruse took the driver's seat and Thorn stretched out his expansive legs next to the incubus.

I wasn't going to let this assault of decades past go unchallenged, though. Tapping at my phone's screen, I connected it to the SUV's sound system and started Tina Turner's *Private Dancer* album playing. Take that, flower children.

As the opening notes of "I Might Have Been Queen" spilled from the speakers, Ruse gave a knowing laugh. He backed the SUV out of its parking spot more smoothly than I'd have expected from a guy who'd probably only needed to use his driving skills about once a decade, and we were off.

We were looking for a big colonial style place: white walls, gable windows, and columns on either side of the double front door. A wide lawn with a tree that shaded the driveway. And, most importantly—because there were probably a thousand houses in the suburbs that fit the rest of the description—Snap had also caught a glimpse of a bronze statue of a rearing horse poised next to the front steps. We just had to hope it was still there after however many years it'd been since Meriden had last worked in the office building.

I opened up my map app. "Keep going north on this street until I tell you otherwise," I ordered Ruse. "We've got a ways to go."

"Navigate away, Miss Blaze!"

Receiving only a couple of honks—Ruse wasn't so smooth at the whole changing lanes thing—we made it around the edges of downtown and up into the wealthier district where I'd set more than one collector's home on fire. I got the incubus weaving up and down the streets while the rest of us scanned the houses beyond our windows.

After a couple of hours, my vision was starting to blur from staring so long. Snap made a soft hissing sound against his teeth. "I'm not seeing the same one—not the way I tasted it from the mug. I don't know for sure it was in this city."

"He might live farther out of town," I admitted with a grimace. It would take days to scour the entire greater metropolitan area—if even that got us what we wanted. Maybe I'd have to put our fates in the hands of a black-market hacker cabal after all.

"We're here now—might as well give it our best shot," Ruse said with good cheer. I guessed he enjoyed driving.

We continued on until my stomach started to grumble that it needed something more substantial than the bag of barbeque chips and mug of coffee I'd already downed as a sort of lunch. At a particularly loud gurgle,

Thorn turned in his seat with a questioning look. With the final notes of *The Joshua Tree* fading from the speakers, I admitted defeat. We definitely still hadn't found what we were looking for.

"Let's head back and grab some dinner, and I'll try to figure out how to reach out to my internet associates in a way that won't get us killed."

"I approve of that plan," Ruse said. Even he was starting to sound a bit weary.

We cruised down one last residential street, heading south. Just as the houses started shrinking and the lawns were getting scruffier, Snap jerked toward his window.

"Stop! There, on that street we just passed. Turn around!"

We got five honks for Ruse's next maneuver, pulling a U-ey and then a left on the heels of his companion's urgent plea. Snap gestured to a house three from the corner: white walls gone a bit dingy, paint flaking from the columns on either side of the door, a rather bedraggled oak tree by the driveway. The late afternoon sunlight glinted off a tarnished statue of a rearing horse next to the front steps.

Ruse let out a low whistle. "Nice job."

He had enough sense of stealth to drive a little farther before parking outside a house on the other side of the street. I squinted at the building Snap had indicated, noting a key feature he hadn't picked up on from his vision.

"Meriden doesn't live in the whole place. It's divided

into apartments. There are three different mailboxes beside the door."

Ruse motioned toward the driveway that ran alongside the house to a garage farther back. "And another around the side there." Another door stood atop a couple of concrete steps with its own mailbox, maybe a separate entrance to the basement or a back apartment.

"It seems we can be reasonably confident that the object of our interest resides somewhere in that place," Thorn said. He glanced at me. "We should investigate while you stay here, m'lady. We don't know how closely Meriden's home might be monitored. You can keep watch in case he leaves while we're conducting our search."

"I don't even know what he looks like," I protested. Like hell did I want to hang back in the car like a kid waiting for her parents to run an errand. Sure, the shadowkind could slink around unseen and I couldn't, but this guy had been working with—or on?—shadowkind for years. He might be able to detect them anyway. They shouldn't have to take all the risk, especially when investigating on our own had been my idea.

"Make note of any male who leaves the premises, then."

"But—"

Thorn's dark eyes turned hard as obsidian. "You're staying here. There's nothing you can do inside to help our investigation that we can't do ourselves."

That statement stung. I stiffened, groping for an

argument in response that I thought he'd accept. "He's not likely to have left any obvious evidence of where he works just lying around, considering how careful the sword-star bunch are obviously being. I know the city—I know mortals. I might realize something is significant that you wouldn't."

"If we turn nothing up, then we'll consider it."

"He may be home," Ruse pointed out with an apologetic note in his voice. "You couldn't go waltzing into his apartment while he's there anyway."

I sighed. "Fine." As I sank back against the patchouli-scented seat, the reminder prompted a question I hadn't thought to ask before. I turned to Snap. "If Meriden is in there... can you test *him* and pick up impressions of other places he's gone, or—"

At the flinch that tightened the shadowkind's heavenly face, I cut myself off. His whole body had tensed, his green eyes going momentarily dark and distant, as if he was seeing something a long ways away that he wished he'd never had to see at all. Then he was looking to his companions, still rigid in his seat.

"No," he said, a quiver running through his clear voice. "I won't. Omen said— We agreed—"

"Hey," Ruse said in the same warm, gentle tone he'd used with me when I'd been reeling from the drugged air the other night. He reached over to grasp Snap's hand. "We're not asking anything like that of you. Don't worry about it. She was just curious—she didn't know."

I glanced between the two of them. "*What* don't I know?"

Snap's shoulders had come down at the incubus's reassurance, but he still looked haunted, as if a different sort of shadow had risen up through his usual brightness. He exhaled sharply and appeared to get a grip on whatever emotions my question had dredged up. "It's different with living things. It isn't something I would ever want to do."

I could hear an unspoken *again* in the resistance that wound through his voice and the way his gaze darted away from me. Something about his abilities... horrified him? Sweet harping Hades, how bad could it be for him to react like this?

Under all that joyful innocence, this god of sunshine had scars of his own. Scars and secrets.

I had the urge to touch him like Ruse had, to tell him that I knew what it was like to swallow down pain—that whatever haunted him, I wasn't going to judge him for it. But now wasn't the time for uncovering those secrets. We'd delayed here long enough.

I let myself give his arm a quick squeeze. "I'm sorry I brought it up. I had no idea. I'm sure you can dig up all kinds of useful dirt your regular way. You're the one who brought us here, after all."

Snap blinked at me, and a glimmer of his usual curious demeanor returned. He turned to Ruse. "Why would we want dirt?"

The incubus cracked a smile. "Another one of those

silly mortal expressions. Come on. If we don't get moving soon, Thorn's likely to explode with his impatience."

"I'm hardly that limited in self-control," our warrior muttered, but he did vanish into the shadows around his seat awfully quickly after Ruse's remark. The other two slipped away a second later.

I refused to let myself slump. Although maybe it would have been a good tactic to avoid anyone wondering why I was sitting out here on my own. I settled for fiddling with my phone instead, as if I just *had* to finish this level of Whatever The Hot New Game Was before I could haul ass to wherever I was going.

Every few seconds, I glanced toward Meriden's house and all around, but no one emerged from either door, and of course I couldn't see my shadowy friends. "Just a small town girl, living in a lonely world," I muttered to myself.

As if on cue, the phone in my hands vibrated. Vivi's number came up on the display. My throat tightened as I answered it, even though I should have welcomed the distraction.

"Hey!" I said with as much normal enthusiasm as I could feign. "What's up?"

"I was calling to ask you that, girl. You seem to be making all kinds of mysterious plans lately."

Her tone was teasing, but I winced inwardly all the same. "Not really. Honestly, all I'm doing right now is hanging out on my own." Not a lie! Somehow I couldn't feel all that victorious about it.

"No exciting news, then?"

"Still nothing. I promise, when I've got anything to tell, you'll be the first to know." I just wasn't going to tell anyone at all until I knew men with gas and guns wouldn't be coming for every person in the know.

Vivi laughed, which didn't really make sense—I hadn't told a joke. Something about the sound was a little forced. Apprehension pricked at me.

"We should get together for a proper hangout sometime," she said before I could go on. "Come over to my place, pick another movie off our watchlist, order in Thai. We could both use some time to unwind, don't you think?"

"Yeah," I said. "You know I'm always up for a movie-and-Thai night." I paused. "Is everything okay with you, Vivi?" The bastards hadn't harassed her in some way simply because they'd found out about our friendship, had they?

"What? Of course! Just missing that one-on-one time with my bestie. Hey, can you remind me how to get to that thrift shop on the east end you were telling me about? I was thinking of doing a little shopping after work tomorrow."

It wasn't an odd request, and I didn't see how it could have been prompted by nefarious villains, but her jump from one subject to the next still struck me as awkward. Was she grasping at straws to keep us talking? As I gave her the directions, I listened carefully for any hint of background noise that might reveal more than she was saying, but my ears didn't catch a thing.

"Okay, perfect," she said when I finished, and let out another giggle. "So, you're at home right now?"

I couldn't easily explain where I actually was, so... "Yep. Just finishing up dinner, actually, so I should get going." Save me from having to lie to my best friend even more. "Let's say Friday for movie night?" If my life was still precarious by then, I could always cancel.

"Sounds good to me. Is there anything else I can pitch in with in the meantime? You really shouldn't have to go it alone with, well, anything."

Her voice had taken on that concerned tone. I winced —but I wasn't actually alone in this mission, was I? "I know, Vivi. Thank you."

"Well, I guess I'll see you at the next meeting!"

She hung up without her usual "Ditto!" Of course, she didn't *always* say that when we were signing off, maybe not even half the time, so it didn't necessarily mean anything. Nothing about the conversation had been overtly weird. The tension of the past few days might simply be bleeding into all of my perceptions.

Still, a deeper restlessness gripped me as I returned my attention to Meriden's house. Had the guys found anything? Had we walked into a trap somehow? Why the hell was I sitting uselessly out here with no clue what was going on with anyone who mattered?

My hand came to rest on the door. I knew that walking over there was a bad idea, but—if they *had* gotten into some kind of trouble—

I was still wavering between common sense and

impatience when the trio shimmered into being around me as if they'd never left. None of them looked exactly happy, but they appeared to have returned in one piece.

"Well?" I demanded before they'd had a chance to speak of their own accord.

"He's definitely living there," Ruse announced.

Thorn's mouth was set in its usual solemn line. "The back apartment. We have plenty of evidence of that, but nothing that points to where he might be spending his time otherwise—and he wasn't currently there."

Snap made a face as if that was his fault. "We do know what he looks like now. The impressions I picked up were mostly mornings and late at night. He might be wherever Omen is the rest of the time." He glanced toward the others as if to confirm.

Thorn nodded. "We'll come back tomorrow and see where he goes after he completes his morning routine. Then we'll discover where this Meriden is carrying out his wretched work now."

22

Sorsha

By the time we made it back to the apartment after picking up a drive-through dinner, night had fallen. The only light was the glow from the posts at the corners of the parking lot. The warm breeze carried a hint of smoke—from the flavor of it, it was a trash can fire. Great neighborhood we'd ended up in.

Since we had the pilfered keys now, I went in through the lobby as if I belonged in the building while the trio followed via the shadows. No point in drawing attention to ourselves with the guys' striking good looks and Thorn's nearly inhuman physique.

A middle-aged woman in turquoise scrubs was looking through a few envelopes by the mailboxes. She didn't even glance my way as I breezed past her to the stairs. I didn't think anything of her, or of the fact that she ended up ambling along several steps behind me. Only when she came out into the second floor after me did I realize I could have a problem. She might be familiar enough with her neighbors on the same floor to know I didn't belong in the apartment I was heading to.

It only took a small trick. I stopped and muttered a curse to myself as if I'd remembered something that frustrated me. Then I stepped closer to the wall to rummage through my purse. The woman walked by... and kept going all the way to the stairwell at the far end of the hall.

That was odd. Maybe she'd taken a longer route to her own floor to get some exercise? My skin prickled as I hustled the last short distance to the apartment door and ducked inside.

The guys took a few more seconds to appear, and when they did, it was in mid argument.

"How could they already know we're here?" Ruse was saying. "We only just got back from Meriden's house, and she was already in the lobby."

"They could have followed us from the office building," Thorn said, and spun toward me. "We have to leave. That woman who followed you—she stopped and watched to see which apartment you went into, and then she immediately took out her communication device. She must have been waiting for us. And if our enemies know we're in this building, the rest of them will be waiting nearby."

My pulse stuttered with a jolt of adrenaline. Fucking

hell. Thankfully I'd brought my backpack along for the drive, so I had almost all of my things. But I couldn't take off without—

"Pickle!" I called, pitching my voice low but urgent. "Pickle, come, we've got to go."

The little dragon dashed out of the room I'd slept in, tufts of feathers clinging to his scales and floating into the air in his wake. He must have found a down pillow to nest in, damn it.

There wasn't time to make amends for our unwitting hosts' destroyed property. I bent down with my purse open and motioned for him to jump in. He balked for a second and then made the leap. My jerk of the zipper, closing it to hide him, was met with a snort of protest.

While I'd gathered him, Thorn had slipped away into the shadows again. He wavered back into the front hall with an expression even graver than before.

"They're just coming out from the stairs at both ends of the hall," he said. "More than a dozen of them—and this time they're fully equipped like the ones who took Omen."

I yanked the dangling strap of my backpack over my other shoulder and held my purse close. "There's no fire escape this time. Do you think we have any chance of making it past them in the hall?"

"The three of us could take a shadow route, but you —" Thorn's head jerked to the side as if he'd heard something from the hall. His expression set with resolve. He swiveled on his feet. "The vehicles are... that way."

Grabbing my wrist to tug me with him, he sprinted down the hall toward the bedrooms.

"What—?" I managed to get out as Ruse and Snap dashed with us. Before I could complete that question, Thorn had let go of me to charge straight through the bedroom door. It burst off its hinges with a crackle of splintering wood... and Thorn kept going, his fists rising in front of him, straight at the far wall.

He slammed into it arms first and drove straight through, plaster and plywood crumbling around him to rain down on the floor. As my feet jarred to a stop in the middle of the room, I gaped at the Thorn-sized passage he'd opened up between this apartment and the one next door. Oh my freaky stars, the guy didn't do things by halves, did he? We had a whole lot more than a pillow to apologize for now.

If I'd had any doubts about racing after him, they were resolved in an instant by the *boom* of our apartment door exploding open behind me. Yeah, we had *definitely* overstayed our welcome here. I hurled myself through the smashed opening after Thorn.

He'd already barreled right through the neighbor's apartment and out the other end, leaving another gaping hole in the kitchen wall. Shrieks spilled from the living room. As we ran by, I saw a young woman frantically hopping up and down where she'd jumped onto her couch, as if she thought she were dealing with a very large mouse that might come scurrying up her leg.

Add another person to the list of apology letters I was never going to send.

Shouts rang out behind us. I pushed myself faster, through the kitchen's hole and past an elderly couple sitting frozen in shock with their dinner forks halfway to their mouths. "Really sorry!" I managed to toss out to them as I raced by.

"Send the bill to the bunch coming after us," Ruse suggested with a breathless laugh.

A waft of outside air swept in from the hole in the couple's bedroom. Jagged edges of cinder block and brick protruded around it, framing the night and the parking lot lights. As I reached it, I gulped. I'd known Thorn was strong, but—fuck, he was a demolition machine. Was there anything he couldn't bash through?

I already knew the answer to that: silver or iron or both. Which the villains chasing after us would no doubt be carrying plenty of.

Thorn stood on the ground two stories down. He held out his arms. "Leap! I'll catch you."

He meant me, obviously. Snap disappeared into the shadows and emerged next to him a moment later. Ruse gave me an encouraging nudge.

"I've never seen him do this before, but I think you can count on him being *very* invested in making sure you don't go splat," he said with a wink, and then glanced behind us. "Unlike our tenacious fan club."

My sense of self-preservation was torn between fear of the twelve-foot drop and fear of the weapons the enemies charging after us might be carrying. At least, like Ruse had said, the guy below *wanted* me to survive. I sucked in a breath, clutched my purse to my chest, and sprang into the open air.

My stomach flew to my throat and my hair whipped up from my head. I had only a second for terror to burst through me before my body smacked into two incredibly strong arms.

Thorn caught me with just enough give that the impact left only a fleeting ache in my back. He didn't put me down, though, but sprinted with me toward the SUV. My head jostled against his expansive chest. The smell of him filled my nose, musky with a smoky edge like coals that had just stopped glowing: warmth and a warning wrapped together.

Ruse had whipped past us through the shadows and was starting the engine. Snap peered at us through the rear window from the back seat. Thorn wrenched open the door on the other side, tossed me in beside Snap with a slam behind me, and dove into the front passenger spot.

I landed in the middle of the seat, my hip jarring against one of the buckles, but I couldn't really complain about the warrior's haste. Yells and thumping footsteps carried from far too close behind us.

The second Thorn materialized inside the vehicle, Ruse hit the gas. The SUV tore backward and around. I tumbled farther to the side, bumping into Snap's slender frame. He grasped my arm to steady me as Ruse burned rubber, roaring down the drive and out into the streets.

"Sorry," I said to Snap, fumbling with my bags. I tucked my purse in the far corner on the floor's shag rug where I figured Pickle was least likely to get crushed.

"It's all right," Snap said softly. The light of the streetlamps passing by glinted off his eyes. As the roar of several other engines reached us, they opened wider. "Will they be able to catch us, do you think?"

Ruse let out a rough chuckle. "I swear on my libido, I'm going to do everything I can to make sure they don't."

"We can't stay in this vehicle," Thorn said. "They'll be familiar with it now. As soon as we can, we must abandon it and continue by other means."

"No kidding. I think I'd better lose the homicidal maniacs behind us first, though—don't you?"

Thorn gave a wordless mutter of assent, and Ruse jerked the wheel, spinning us in an abrupt ninety-degree turn—and then, an instant later, another. I still hadn't gotten the chance to fasten any of the seatbelts around me. The momentum threw me into Snap again, the second lurch landing me right on his lap.

I guessed I'd just have to resign myself to being a ping-pong ball for this ride. It beat whatever the sword-star bunch wanted to turn me into. "Sorry," I said to Snap again as his buffering arm came up to support me. He shook his head with a smile as if to say he didn't need any apology.

As the SUV jostled back and forth with more of Ruse's quick maneuvers, I swayed and gripped Snap's knee. The moment we stopped rocking around, I attempted to squirm off him to give him at least a little personal space. My shoulder knocked his chest, and all at once Snap's body went rigid against mine.

I held myself still, my gaze darting to him to check if I'd inadvertently hurt him. I'd never been quite this close to his divinely handsome face before, just inches between us. His chest hitched against my arm with a stuttered breath, and his moss-green eyes stared at me, as bewildered as if I'd suddenly transformed into a polka-dotted caribou.

Something was obviously not okay. I shifted my weight to get off him, and another swerve of the car sent me sliding back into his lap. My ass pressed into Snap's groin—into a solid form that was even more rigid than the rest of him.

Oh. *Oh.* My eyes caught his again, just as they flashed with a glimmer of brighter green, like that glimpse of neon I'd gotten in the collector's room. His hand braced against my thigh and then pulled back as if he wasn't sure where to put it. Heat seeped between us everywhere our bodies touched, which at this point was quite a lot of territory.

So he did have it in him to get turned on. From the uncertainty in his expression, he hadn't been any more aware of that fact than I'd been. But now that I'd noticed it, there was no mistaking the bulge of his erection.

His pupils had dilated slightly, his breath coming shallower and faster than usual. A tingle quivered through my lungs and down to the apex of my thighs in response. He'd gotten this turned on, probably for the first time in his existence, because of me. And every part of me was totally on board with that. I just couldn't tell how on board *he* was.

It wasn't as if we were in any position to explore the possibilities further. The awkward intensity of the moment broke with a screech of the tires. Ruse hauled the SUV in the other direction, and I flew off Snap onto my back, just barely catching myself before my head banged into the opposite door.

After one more burst of speed, the incubus slammed on the brake and cut the engine. "They're not going to find us here for at least a little while. Now we just have to figure out where we're taking off to next."

We'd stopped in a laneway so tight I could barely squeeze out of the SUV. Good thing the shadowkind, especially Thorn, didn't have to bother with the doors. The backs of brick buildings loomed on either side of us; the glint of streetlamps shone only faintly in the far distance. I had no idea where we'd ended up, but it definitely didn't look like an easy spot to stumble on.

"We'll want another vehicle." Thorn motioned to Ruse. "Why don't you slink around and see what you can turn up that couldn't be easily linked to us? I'll patrol the area to ensure our enemies haven't followed us too closely." He glanced at me and Snap. "You two get ready to flee if we need to, but stay here for now in case we don't find another vehicle in time. I won't be long. Ruse had better not be either."

"I can take a hint," the incubus said. They both slipped away into the darkness, leaving Snap and I in silence.

In the tight space that was as much as I could open the door, I picked my purse off the floor and gave Pickle a comforting pat through the fabric. He murmured his displeasure.

Snap flitted into the shadows and out again by the back of the SUV. I leaned against the trunk at the opposite end from him, giving him the space I hadn't been able to offer in the car. Snap gazed down the lane toward that distant haze of artificial light. In the dimness, I thought I could tell his cheeks had flushed, but a glance at his nether regions showed that he was no longer, er, standing at attention.

We stood there in silence for a few minutes. Then words spilled out of me before I could second-guess the impulse. "It doesn't have to be a big deal, you know. It's a totally natural reaction that anyone could have in close contact like that. Just a little friction, stirring things up."

His head swiveled with its serpentine grace to consider me. "Just a little friction," he repeated, in a tone I couldn't read. "Is that all it means to you?"

I opened my mouth and closed it again, abruptly unsure how to respond. "Not always," I said finally. "But I can look at it that way if that's what you'd prefer."

He looked away from me with a flick of his tongue over his lips. "I don't know. I—" He paused, apparently grappling with his words as much as I had. "It's not a sensation I'm used to. It was... unexpected. As it was happening, I wanted very much for it to be over with, but I also wanted more. I'm not sure which preference was stronger."

I found myself wetting my lips too. I sure as hell wasn't going to push him, but— "Well, if you end up deciding on more, just let me know."

He shifted against the trunk with an audible inhalation, but before either of us could say anything else, Ruse appeared in front of us. He jabbed his thumb toward the end of the lane. "I've got a cab waiting that-a-way, with a very agreeable driver who won't mark down the pick-up. Where's the lunk?"

"Right here." Thorn stepped out of the shadows just as the incubus finished speaking. "Our pursuers haven't made it this far yet, but we should move on with all haste. We can't shelter for the night in one of those taxis."

An idea clicked in my head, so fitting I could have laughed if tension hadn't still been knotted through my chest. "I know the perfect place for us to go."

23

Sorsha

Even though there was no denying Ruse's seductive charms, we had the taxi drop us off a five-minute walk from our actual destination. The incubus gave the driver a jaunty salute and said in a cajoling tone, "Thank you, my friend. You'll drive back downtown and forget you ever came out here."

As the cab pulled away, Thorn glanced at me. "What is this spot you wanted us to come to?"

I started walking, pointing to the glowing motel sign ahead of us, the letters distorted where half of the bulbs had burnt out. "This is a place people go to specifically when they don't want anyone to know where they've gone."

Every time Vivi had driven us to the outlet stores farther down this strip, we'd passed the motel with its weather-worn sign offering hourly rates. It'd become a running joke, making up stories about who would be so desperate for anonymity they'd take a room in a place that looked straight out of a slasher flick. A dude having an affair with his wife's sister—who was also his kid's teacher and his brother's girlfriend. A mafia foot-soldier on the run from both the mob and the cops after a catastrophic incident involving a thrown plate of cannelloni. And so on.

Now I was getting to experience that desperation firsthand. Lucky me.

The sign also declared that the management only accepted payment in cash, because they were just that classy. My hand settled on my purse as we approached the front office, but Ruse waved his hand at me dismissively. "I've got this."

In the last few days, my criminal activities had multiplied like rabbits. After yet another tight escape and looking up at the dingy shingles lining the motel's roof, I couldn't quite bring myself to care about this latest con. "Be my guest."

As we'd agreed in hushed discussion in the cab, Snap and Thorn lurked in the shadows while Ruse and I went in. I took one look at the sputtering fluorescent light mounted on the ceiling, the board of nails dangling tarnished keys with numbered fobs, and the faded floral curtains that must have been at least a few decades old, and swallowed a slightly hysterical giggle. I was standing in the middle of a real live cliché. The only thing missing was getting murdered in my sleep, but who knew—there was still time for that.

Ruse strolled up to the reception desk with its patchy varnish and shot one of his smooth grins at the woman there, who had bags under her eyes big enough to hold spare change. "Hello there, darling," he said in the same voice he'd used on the cab driver.

The woman gave us a look of utter boredom, but as Ruse drew out the companionable chitchat, a friendly warmth came into her eyes. By the time he asked her for "two rooms, side-by-side, with an adjoining door if you've got that," she was so happy to help that she handed him two keys off the wall without the slightest hint of skepticism about a young couple asking for completely separate rooms.

"We could have made do with one," I said to him after we'd stepped back outside. "It's not as if the three of you need beds."

Ruse clucked his tongue at me. "I was respecting your privacy. Besides, I need to get my fix of late night cable TV, and I wouldn't want to keep you up."

I rolled my eyes at him, but the truth was, I did feel better having a little space that the shadowkind weren't invading. And even if the incubus and I were on better terms now, I wasn't interested in doing anything *other* than sleeping tonight. As we reached our rooms, a yawn stretched my jaw.

"Let's have a look at them before I decide which is mine," I said.

There wasn't exactly much to choose between. Both boasted similar flower-print curtains that were more gray than any other color now, moth-bitten carpets, and bed covers dappled with faint stains bleach hadn't quite eliminated. A chlorine-y scent clung to them, but at least that meant they should be somewhat sanitary if not pretty to look at.

The first room had a slightly larger TV, so I left that one to Ruse and set my bags down on the bed in the other room. Thorn followed me in through the adjoining doorway. He closed the door and studied the knob.

"We should leave this unlocked on both sides," he said. "None of us will disturb you unless there's urgent need—but if we should have to escape in a rush..."

"No argument here." I sat down on the end of the bed and eased open my purse. Pickle sprang out with a distressed but ineffectual flapping of his clipped wings. He shot a steely glare at the purse, as if it were to blame for his troubles, and bounded into the bathroom to put as much distance between it and him as he could.

Thorn prowled through the room, eyeing every wall, corner, and piece of furniture for signs of danger, going as far as swatting at a spiderweb so tattered I suspected the spider had abandoned it months ago.

"I'm pretty sure there aren't any actual serial killers hiding under the bed," I teased, but that only prompted him to actually check under the bed just in case.

While he occupied himself with that, I slid the deadbolt on the outer door into place and went into the bathroom to fill up a glass of water for Pickle. The little dragon took a sip, allowed me to stroke his neck a few times, and then tugged one of the towels into the tub to make a fuzzy nest for himself.

When I came back out, Thorn was still there, now standing near the door between our rooms. As I flopped down where I'd been sitting before, he stayed in place, his pose oddly hesitant.

"M'lady," he said, and paused. When I lifted my head to meet his gaze, he cleared his throat and glanced briefly at the floor before continuing.

"When we first came to you, I intended to keep you out of danger. I didn't anticipate that our presence would propel you so much further into it. You have lost your home, most of your belongings, been drugged once and nearly captured twice in a span of three days..."

"I do remember all that," I said when he trailed off. "I was there."

He made a frustrated sound, his hands clenching. His voice came out even gruffer than usual. "I'm trying to say that I apologize for misjudging the threat—and that you may have been right to wish us gone in the beginning. I can't make up for what's already come to pass, but I can avoid dragging you into further peril. We're closing in on Omen's captors even as they attempt to close in on us. You've assisted us far beyond what I ever would have asked, so I can't possibly ask for more. When we continue on Meriden's trail tomorrow, you can go your own way, apart from us."

Understanding sunk in slowly and then hit me in its final burst like a slap to the face. "What?" I sputtered. "You're telling me to take off?"

Thorn grimaced. "We would see to it you have everything we can provide that you might need—Ruse should be able to supply you with money and perhaps other resources—and we would ensure that we draw our enemies' attention to us to give you time to make a clean escape. If that isn't enough—"

"It's not about whether it's *enough*." I pushed myself off the bed to face him on my feet, my hands balling into fists at my sides. "Are you fucking kidding me? I lost my apartment, yeah, and lied to my only friends and now have run all over this city with bad guys at my heels, and you think after all that I'm going to throw in the towel and say it was all for nothing?"

The warrior's expression turned puzzled. "You never intended to find yourself in such treacherous waters."

"Maybe I didn't expect exactly this, but I knew there were risks. I saw what happened to Luna because of these sword-star assholes. So what if things have gotten 'treacherous'? When exactly did I give you the impression that I'm the type to run off with my tail between my legs when the going gets hard?"

Thorn was silent for a moment. "You're offended," he said. "You're angry with me."

"Yes, I'm fucking angry." Was there anything nearby I could throw at his somberly stoic face? The lumpy pillow wouldn't be at all satisfying. "I committed to finding out what the hell is going on, and I'm going to see that through. It isn't just for you, you blockhead. It's because of these pricks that Luna is dead. They might have killed my parents too. Who knows how many other people and shadowkind they've hurt before then and since? And you really think I'd take the chance to shrug it off and walk away?"

I'd obviously rubbed him the wrong way now and then—it wasn't as if his attitude hadn't irritated me often enough too—but I would have thought that by this point he'd believe they could count on me just a little. I'd run when the hunters came for Luna, when it was too late to help her anyway, and it'd killed me doing that. No way in hell was I letting the bastards off the hook now that we had them in our sights.

But he'd really thought I'd accept his offer that I leave. Possibly even expected me to be *grateful* for it. My teeth gritted.

"That wasn't how I saw it," the warrior said stiffly. "I merely was concerned for your well-being and the strain we've put on it."

Since I couldn't throw anything at him, I set my hands on my hips instead. "Stuff your concern up your ass. I'm not looking the other way while someone's out there still sticking beings like you in cages and who knows what other horrors, so you can just forget about keeping me out of it. I *have* helped, and a lot, haven't I, as inconvenient as this mortal body might be to you all?"

"I would never deny that. We would not have

accomplished anywhere near as much in our quest without your assistance."

"All right. Then assume I'm going to keep assisting, and keep your ideas about what kind of 'strain' I can handle to yourself unless I ask for your opinion. Agreed?"

Thorn bowed his head. When he raised it, his lips were twisted at a more pained angle than before. "M'lady," he said, and seemed to struggle before adding my name. "Sorsha. I apologize. I promise I didn't intend to insult you, although I see now how insulting my proposition was. I hope you will accept that my misstep was made out of lack of consideration and not contempt for your courage and resilience."

The flare of my anger simmered down, although I couldn't tell how much he meant those words and how much he was simply placating me. It was hard to read that ever-solemn voice.

"All right then," I said. "Apology accepted. And listen, I can promise you this—once we find Omen and whatever other shadowkind these assholes have trapped, I'm going to burn everything that belongs to *them* to the ground just like I did your collector's house. That's the least they'll deserve."

The corner of Thorn's mouth quirked up, just for a second, into what might have almost been a smile. "I look forward to that day," he said in the same sober tone. "I'll take my leave of you so you can rest and prepare for tomorrow's plans."

"You do that," I said, but my grumble was half-hearted. He stepped out, closing the door behind him with a click. I sank down on the bed, my heart suddenly heavy.

I was in this 'til the end. I hadn't the slightest doubt about that. The only question was how much of my life from before would end up in tatters before this mission was over—if I was left with any life at all.

24

Snap

T horn came striding into our room from Sorsha's looking oddly irritated and invigorated at the same time. His jaw was tightly set, his eyes as dark as ever, but he moved with an almost eager purposefulness.

Ruse looked up from the sagging armchair where he was mashing buttons on the little box that controlled the bigger box of the TV and raised his eyebrows at our companion.

"Have a nice chat?" he asked, managing with the lilt of his voice to imply that they might have engaged in all sorts of intimacies other than talking. I supposed that was part of his particular talent. It made me want to squirm where I'd been sitting on the edge of the bed, even though he hadn't directed it at me.

Thorn glowered at him. "We did, actually. And

someone had to confirm her room contained no hazards. We've brought enough woe down on her head already."

"But you have to admit she's handled herself just fine."

Thorn paused for a moment. "Yes. She has." He swiveled on his heel abruptly. "I'm going to keep up a patrol of the nearby streets until we can leave in the morning. Stay alert and ready to defend yourselves and the mortal one if need be. And *you*, figure out how we can safely follow Meriden without our former vehicle."

That last bit was clearly aimed at Ruse. If I'd had more experience with the mortal realm, perhaps I could have helped more with making plans, but as it was, I wouldn't be of much use to any of them until we were right at the scene.

That was all right. I'd contributed my share, just as Omen had expected I would. I hoped when we found him he was in well enough condition to be pleased with his choices.

It did mean that at the moment I was left with little to do but stew in my thoughts. After Ruse had given Thorn a coy wave good-bye, the incubus's gaze traveled to me. Another itch traveled over my skin. He was an expert in all things to do with bodily pleasure. Had he already picked up on a change in the energies between me and Sorsha?

I'd rather not give him time to notice if he hadn't yet. I got up from the bed, shaking out my limbs as if stiff from staying in place too long, and said, "I think I'll retire to the shadows."

Ruse shrugged. "Up to you, but you're about to miss some very excellent TV." He gestured at it. "Late at night is when you get to observe all the things mortals think no one will want to see but feel the need to put on the air anyway."

True or not, there was something I wanted to observe more. Or rather, someone. The strange vibe with which Thorn had left Sorsha's room niggled at me. He'd been hard on her before—he was hard in general. Had his spirits been lifted because this time he'd managed to affect her with his criticisms?

I slipped into the shadows that lay here and there across the room, but then I hesitated. I'd gotten more of an eyeful than I'd been looking for the last time I'd peeked in on our mortal companion. But I knew where my two colleagues were now. I could retreat in an instant if need be.

With a tingle through my being, I leapt from the foot of the bed to the darkness that framed the adjoining door. Then I was peering from that space into Sorsha's room, so much like ours.

She was lying on her back on the bed on top of the covers, one hand behind her head and the other resting on her stomach. Her coppery eyes were open, contemplating the ceiling with that haze I'd come to recognize meant a person was thinking of something farther away. She didn't look upset, at least, only thoughtful. A crease had formed between her eyebrows.

Nothing about her appearance had changed that I could pinpoint. I'd always found her enjoyable to take in with that ruddy hair against her creamy skin and the vibrant glint that so often lit in her eyes. Much more interesting than a peach, as delicious as the fruit might be. But now, ever since that unexpected development during our hasty getaway...

My gaze veered across her body, over the curves of her chest and hips that drew my attention much more intensely than they ever had before. She shifted up on one elbow, and I couldn't help following the sway of her breasts. Then the way her thighs slid against each other as she stirred again.

A strange, heated sensation unfurled through my being with the urge to find out if those parts beneath her clothes would be as soft to the touch as her hair was. To discover how her expression might change if I gave in to that urge.

I turned my awareness away, back to my own room. It was easier to master the emotions flowing through me when I couldn't see her. Beneath the heat of the impulse, a chill shivered through my nerves.

Somewhere in the longing I could taste the start of a headlong fall. Would I be able to pull back from it if I let myself tumble?

If I couldn't... The one time I'd careened past the point of control before...

My mind shuttered against the memories.

The new feelings hadn't emerged out of nowhere. They'd risen from the physical body that let me interact with this realm. If I understood why, how it all connected, what it *meant*, maybe it wouldn't be so unnerving.

Our bathroom door was already closed. I pulled myself out from the shadows there, the air settling more solidly around my form. Only a little city glow carried through the small window beside the sink, but I didn't want to turn on the light and make Ruse wonder what I was doing in here.

The appendage between my legs lay flaccid in my pants now. I let one hand drop to it, but it didn't stir at the contact. I hadn't thought much about that particular part since we'd first passed over to this realm with Omen, other than the occasions when I'd spent enough time outside the shadows that I needed to relieve myself using it—and during Thorn's initial, stern reminder that if we got into a physical fight, I should be careful not to take a blow there, or the pain would be temporarily disabling.

It had never become so taut before, or lifted the way it had in the car, even though Sorsha's bottom had been pressing down against it—

The memory of that firm yet pliant roundness, of my arm around her back and her hair grazing my cheek, rushed through my mind like the scent of her had filled my nose. And what a scent it was: sweet like the honey I'd sampled at the market but with a sharpness as biting as the flames she'd lit in the wake of our first escape. I wondered if I flicked my tongue against her cheek, not with any power but just to taste in the physical sense, would her flavor be as intoxicating?

And then that appendage, what I'd heard Ruse refer to as his "cock," had twitched and stiffened with a flood of pleasure totally different from any I'd felt before, hot and hungry and unsettlingly forceful.

Like it was stiffening against my hand right now in response to those memories. I swallowed hard and ran my fingers over it experimentally. Thinking back to Sorsha lying on the bed as I'd seen her just now...

It rose even higher, straining against the fly of my pants. With each brush of my fingertips, ripples of pleasure and the hunger that came with it radiated through the rest of my body. I closed my eyes, caught again between the longing for more and the terror that quivered up from deeper within me.

There had been a sort of pleasure in my first—and only—devouring. A cold, bottomless hunger that sucked in and shredded, and a tight, icy bliss as that hunger was satisfied bit by bit. The two together had driven me on and on...

Nausea coiled through my stomach at the memory.

That wasn't the worst of it, though. The devouring had been horrible and horrifying... and the part of me that had sunk in its ethereal jaws clamored to sate itself all over again.

My fingers had stilled over my erect member. With

the thought of other acts, it was starting to wilt. I gave it another stroke, willing the distant past away.

This sensation wasn't the same kind of pleasure. It wasn't the same hunger. What I wanted when the heated tingles spread through my groin was not to satisfy myself so much as to create a pleasure that would satisfy her too.

She hadn't been disturbed by the idea. Recalling her offer that I should come to her if I decided to pursue my desire brought an eager flush into my chest and cheeks.

I wasn't sure I could control this sensation. I wasn't sure where tumbling into it would lead me. But it felt like a kindling rather than an obliterating. It was possible, wasn't it, that this unraveling could be different in that way too? That it might take us someplace good?

I could wait and see how things seemed by the light of day. Proceed with caution—until I couldn't be cautious anymore, if I took that route.

My thoughts slipped back to Sorsha: to the warmth she'd shown me, to her laugh, to her enduring strength through all the danger we'd faced. If I did dive in, it would be with her. I knew already there was no one else who'd make it worth the risk.

25

Sorsha

"I should have brought a pair of binoculars," I grumbled, slouching against the leather seat with new-car smell prickling in my nose.

Ruse tsked teasingly at me from the driver's seat. "Patience, Miss Blaze. Our job is to be ready to drive when the Incredible Hulk gives the word."

He meant Thorn, who was stationed in the shadows somewhere down the road where he *could* make out what was going on at Meriden's house. Those of us keeping our physical bodies were staked out in a driveway a couple of blocks away. Ruse had even made a show of getting out of the car and walking around to the back of the house in case anyone was watching all the way over here and would have thought our arrival odd otherwise.

He'd slipped back through the shadows after, and the

sedan's tinted windows ensured no one was going to be IDing me or my shadowkind friends through the glass. I appeared to have stumbled straight from a slasher flick into a spy caper.

It was a pretty posh car all around. I peered at Ruse from where I was still hunkered down in my seat. "Are you sure the salesman isn't going to snap out of your little charm spell and realize he's lost a major chunk of change, plus commission?"

"First off, I assure you there's nothing 'little' about any part of my prowess," Ruse said. "And yes, you can rest easy. He thinks *he* got the better end of the deal."

"But he didn't. Someone at the dealership is going to notice eventually."

"Your mortal conscience is so adorable." Ruse's smirk softened around the edges with a hint of affection. "If all goes well, we won't need to keep this lovely piece of machinery for more than a few days, and then I'll drop it off in the lot. No harm done!"

Other than the potential harm of whatever wear and tear we put it through, which considering how the past few days had gone might be a lot, but since the alternative had been sitting around in the horror-movie motel with my thumb up my ass, I shut up.

I suspected the only reason Thorn had agreed to my coming along at all, yesterday's apologies about misjudging my commitment aside, was because he'd be *more* worried leaving me on my own than having me where he could keep an eye on me. As annoying as his own commitment could be, he did take the whole protection racket very seriously.

Across from me, Snap turned his head, following the path of a gray minivan that was cruising by.

"Wrong direction for that to be Meriden," I said. "And much more the kind of car the white-picket-fence families around here would be driving than a conspiracy of shadowkind hunters."

He nodded as if taking my observations in stride. If last night's awkwardness was still affecting him, he hadn't let it show in any way I'd noticed so far. Maybe he'd decided pretending his momentary arousal had never happened and praying it never did again was the better course of action.

I was allowed to feel a *tad* disappointed about that, don't you think?

"Perhaps I don't understand because I haven't spent enough time in this realm," he said, "but I can't see what those people would want with us. With higher shadowkind in general. What are they *doing* with Omen and whoever else they've taken, and why?"

"The collector who had us felt awfully proud of the power he had over us, keeping us locked up," Ruse said. "Remember how often he'd come around to gloat? Mortals can be just as addicted to a sense of power as shadowkind can—maybe more so."

Snap hummed. "It didn't seem as if that building we searched before was for just holding and displaying the shadowkind they'd captured. They were going much farther than that."

"Everybody wants to rule the world," I said carelessly.

The godly shadowkind blinked at me. "Do they? I don't."

"No, it's just— It's words from a song. Never mind." I gave a vague wave of my hand. "Whoever these people are, they're probably power-hungry too, just for a different kind of power. The hunter M.O. has evolved before, right? From what I've heard, way back in the day, all they were interested in was tracking down and slaughtering any of you they could find. It took a while before they found out that they could actually make money from the hunt—mostly if they kept the beings they captured alive."

"There were always collectors," Ruse said. "Just like there were always sorcerers." He glanced at Snap. "Those are the mortals who've developed a system for manipulating shadowkind into using their powers for the sorcerer's benefit. But I remember hearing of collectors in my early days... There were only a few of them, and it was harder for them to arrange the purchases without the internet and all, I'd guess. And mortals in general were much more bloodthirsty about anything remotely supernatural back then."

"At least when the creatures are in cages, I can let them out again." I kicked the back of Thorn's vacant seat and scowled at the street outside. "These sword-star people are definitely something else, though. So many of them and so organized, plus they're trying to get shadowkind *from* the collectors instead of for them. And from what you said about the impressions you picked up in that lab, Snap—I don't like it; that's for sure."

The incubus opened his mouth as if he were going to add something else—and the gray minivan that had passed us just a few minutes ago drove back into view, turning toward Meriden's house at the intersection between him and us. I sat up straighter, studying it. Why would they have come back around?

The minivan slowed to a stop toward the end of the next block, and a figure hustled over to it from one of the driveways I could barely distinguish at this distance. I tensed even more. "Start the engine," I told Ruse on instinct, a second before Thorn flickered in and out of view in his signal to us to pick him up.

"Thorn's calling us!" Snap said.

Ruse peeled out of the driveway but rumbled on down the street at just a smidge over the speed limit, despite the urgency he must be feeling as much as I was. If we *looked* like we were chasing the minivan, we'd blow all the care we'd put into this cover.

I gripped the door, my heart thumping. A baby blue compact had pulled away from the curb behind us. Great, now we had two sets of spectators to worry about, not counting anyone who glanced out their house's windows.

The incubus didn't even slow down as we passed

Thorn's post. The warrior must have sprung into the sedan from one shadow to another. With a blink, he was sitting in the passenger seat as if he'd never left.

He jabbed his hand toward the windshield. "Meriden got into that van. Don't lose it. But make sure they don't know we're tracking them."

"I remember the plan," Ruse said mildly. At a stop sign, he drummed his fingers against the steering wheel, the only outward sign of his own impatience. The minivan turned out of view up ahead, and I stifled a growl.

Now that the people in the van couldn't see us either, Ruse gunned the engine a little faster. When he took the same turn, the vehicle was still in view, the gunmetal-gray paint shining in the mid-morning sunlight a little more than a block ahead of us.

I let out my breath, and it snagged in my throat on my next inhale at a flash of color in the side mirror. Craning my neck, I spotted that baby blue compact taking the turn after us. Uneasiness itched at me. "I think someone might be tracking *us*."

Thorn glanced back, his lips slanting into a deeper frown. "It appears to be just a driver, no passengers. I could deal with them if need be."

I squinted at the figure, but between the light reflecting off the windshield and the pale hood pulled low over the driver's forehead, I couldn't even tell whether it was a man or a woman. "It only took one person to bring a whole squad down on us last night," I reminded him.

"Let's not jump to any conclusions yet," Ruse suggested. The minivan veered right, and several seconds later he copied the maneuver. I exhaled slowly—and here came that blue car, following us again.

The incubus's mouth twisted. "Okay, maybe we should start jumping now."

"We can't keep following the van with someone else following us," I said. "No one's seen who we are yet, but the more obvious it becomes what we're doing, the more likely they'll sound the alarm."

Ruse gave the wheel another beat of his fingers and made a pleased sound at the sight of the van's turn signal going on. We were coming up on a major throughway, four lanes with plenty of traffic as commuters headed to work. The incubus ignored the left turn lane the minivan had pulled into and drove straight ahead.

Thorn grunted in dismay. "What are you doing?"

"Just watch. Ah, here he comes."

The blue car stayed on our tail. Ruse sailed through the intersection and halfway down the next block, and then swerved with a jerk of the wheel into a gas station.

"Ooof." My chest jarred against the seatbelt I thankfully had on this time. Not that my ribs were thanking it.

I clutched the edge of the seat as Ruse tore through the gas station between the rows of pumps and out onto a different street. The engine roaring now, he careened into the next right, cut across the parking lot outside a print shop, and flung us around through a couple more hasty turns. Then, with one final squeak of the tires, we flew out onto the large street the minivan had turned onto.

And wouldn't you know it, there was the damned thing still only a block ahead.

Ruse chuckled. "Thank the dark for rush-hour traffic. Any sign of our hanger-on?"

I studied the view beyond the back window for several seconds as we cruised after the minivan. The baby blue sheen should have stood out in the sea of black and silver, but I didn't spot it. A weird choice for a stealth mission, really. Knitting my brow, I swiveled toward the front again.

"You lost them—but maybe they just happened to be taking the same route and weren't after us anyway. They didn't seem all that on the ball."

"Doesn't really matter as long as they're not behind us now. Let's see where Meriden is off to."

We skirted the edge of downtown, coming within ten blocks of the apartment building we'd crashed in—and then crashed through—not long ago. The minivan took a few more turns before ending up in the docklands, where aging factories loomed on either side of the streets and the smell of algae seeped into the air conditioning. The river that wove through the east end of town used to be a major shipping route before the manufacturing industries had started moving overseas.

With much less traffic on these streets, Ruse had

dropped back to a couple of blocks behind the minivan. I stirred restlessly in my seat. How long a road trip were we on, exactly? And why hadn't I brought more snacks to—

The minivan jerked to a halt by the curb. A skinny figure topped with gleaming black hair scrambled out and darted out of sight between two of the buildings.

Thorn cursed. "Go! We have to see where he went."

The second the minivan had pulled away, Ruse hit the gas. We jolted back in our seats as he sped over. When he passed the last side-street before the drop-off spot, Thorn vanished, presumably rushing off through the shadows to track the man where the car couldn't follow.

"He might need me to test the area," Snap said, and wavered away an instant later.

As Ruse drove by the alley I thought Meriden had taken, I peered down it, but he'd disappeared as effectively as the shadowkind had. The incubus eased to a stop at the end of the block and idled there.

The minivan was long gone. As far as I could tell, there was no one around to make note of us. But I'd thought that before and been wrong.

I twisted to scan the street. "Do we just wait for Thorn and Snap? Should we be searching for Meriden too?"

Ruse appeared to make a quick deliberation. "Let's keep driving—it'll look less suspicious if anyone is monitoring the area, and maybe we'll spot our target somewhere around the block."

He circled around, and I leaned closer to the window, studying every doorway, window, and alley. The gloomy structures showed no sign of life at all, like giant, rotting carcasses of beasts slain long ago. An engine thrummed in the distance, but whatever vehicle the sound came from, we never saw it.

Ruse continued on a block farther, to where a rusty crane creaked in the wind over the river. He looped back around with a rough sigh. "Hopefully the Hulk had better luck."

We were just coming up on the street where we'd left Thorn and Snap when both of them slipped out of the shadows into their seats with a shudder through the air. Ruse eased over to the curb and cut the engine.

Thorn didn't wait to be asked. His voice came out taut with frustration. "We lost him. No trail to pick up. Snap couldn't tell where he passed by."

"If he didn't touch anything closely enough with his body, it wouldn't have left an impression I could connect to him," Snap said in a mournful tone. "Many shoes walked over that ground; I couldn't taste any that were definitely his."

"Quite the system this group has worked out," Ruse said. "I'd be impressed if it wasn't so irritating of them."

Thorn's shoulders tensed. "It's more than irritating. It's unacceptable. At every turn, they get the better of us, foil every measure we've taken. We fumble along while

Omen faces who knows what torment—" He stiffened even more at the sound of footsteps outside.

An older man came into view, heading into our street from down by the river behind us. Not Meriden—his hair a mix of mouse-brown and silver, his shorter frame slightly slumped. But without a word, Thorn whipped open the door, sprang out of the car, and charged past my window.

A sound of protest burst from my throat. I jerked around to see the massive shadowkind barreling toward the man as if he meant to knock him right off his feet. For the love of little baby elephants, what was he thinking?

I hesitated for just a second, and then I leapt out after him.

The man had halted in mid-step at the sight of the colossus closing in on him, but Thorn didn't so much as slow down. He slammed his hand into the man's chest and yanked the front of his polo shirt up to his chin. The man swayed backward, scrambling on tippy-toe to keep his feet on the ground.

"What do you know about the man who got out here?" Thorn demanded.

"What?" his victim said in a reedy voice. "What man? When? I—I don't know what you mean."

"You must know *some*thing."

"I swear, I was only walking by—there's a shop down the street where they sell the only coffee my wife will drink." He jerked his hand, and the plastic bag dangling from it rustled. "Please. I'd help you if I could."

"Thorn!" I stopped on the sidewalk next to him, my throat constricting. "He's just some random guy walking by. He wasn't even near the drop-off spot."

"That's what they'd want us to think." Thorn shook the man. "Whatever you've seen, whatever you know, you'll tell me, *now*." His voice had gone hard and cold as a winter freeze.

The guy was trembling, his toes barely scraping the ground. He couldn't make anything more than a choked squeak now. I didn't think Thorn was trying to kill him— but he might with that incredible strength, if he was too distracted by his need for answers to notice the full effect he was having on that mortal body.

I wasn't completely sure the warrior wouldn't turn that strength on me if I crossed him in this moment, despite debts owed. The breath left my lungs, but I forced myself to grasp his arm.

"Thorn," I said, vaguely aware of the other two shadowkind reaching us. "He doesn't have any answers. I know you've been beating yourself up for not protecting Omen, for not finding him sooner, but this isn't going to make it right. It wasn't your fault anyway."

Finally, Thorn's gaze shifted to me. In that moment, the anguish in his eyes was so stark that my throat clenched up again for a different reason. It resonated through me, stirring up echoes of the guilt that wrenched me so often in the first years after Luna's death —the unpredictable flashes back to the attack, the incessant attempts to piece together some way I could have saved her, as if it could have made a difference by then.

"How can you know that?" Thorn asked in a raw voice.

I made myself hold his gaze, even though the tension radiating off him set all my nerves jittering with alarm. I knew where that agonizing frustration came from. It wasn't aimed at me or even the man he was holding, not really. And I could tell him this with more certainty than I'd ever been able to absolve myself.

"Because I've seen just how far you'll go to keep the people under your watch safe, and it's *really* fucking far. I'd probably be dead at least twice over if it wasn't for you. We're going to figure this out. I know that much. Just... not this way. Please."

Gradually, the warrior's arm relaxed. The man's feet touched down. He sagged with a rasp for breath that brought Thorn's gaze jerking back to his victim. He took in the man's quivering form before glancing back at me, and a flicker of an expression that might have been distraught crossed the warrior's face.

Oh, there were feelings buried under that hardened exterior—plenty of them. The thought of the overwhelming loyalty that drove his guilt sent a shiver through me, one not entirely unpleasant.

"I only wanted to find out what he knew," he said.

I squeezed his arm where my hand still rested on it. "And now that's done."

Ruse sauntered over to the man and helped him

gather himself with a grip of his elbow and a friendly pat to the back. "He's confused and terrified, and the confusion is real," the incubus said to us. "He really doesn't have any idea what this is about. And I think I'd better make sure he doesn't give it any more thought, hmm?"

He eased the man off to the side to talk to him in soothing, persuasive tones. I let my hand fall from Thorn's forearm. He watched it drop to my side as if he wasn't sure how it'd ended up on him in the first place.

"What do we do now?" Snap asked.

"Well..." I looked around. "We know where Meriden gets dropped off. They probably stick to a similar schedule every day—it'd get complicated constantly switching locations with no reason to."

Thorn picked up the thread of my thoughts. "We'll come straight here tomorrow morning. Be ready to follow him as soon as he gets out. Pick up the next part of the trail." He raised his head, his usual cool determination returning.

I found myself smiling at him—this brutally devoted monster. "Exactly. I'd call that a plan."

26

Sorsha

I could tell Pickle wasn't feeling so comfortable with our current situation from the massive nest-build he'd undertaken. The motel bathroom tub now held two bath towels, one hand towel, and at least four rolls worth of shredded toilet paper. He looked a little ridiculous curled up in one corner, his small green body taking up barely a tenth of the space, but I wasn't going to pick a fight with him over it. At least, not until I needed to take another shower.

"Sleep tight," I told him with a pat on the head. By the time I'd finished brushing my teeth, he was snoring with raspy little hiccups. I held back a laugh and shut the door to muffle the sound.

Like that, the intermittent rumble of passing traffic drowned him out. The yellow light of the parking lot security lamps streaked through the thin fabric of the curtains. I padded through the glow to the bed, sprayed the air with another puff of the lavender-scented freshener I'd bought, and settled down under the covers, hoping I was tired enough to tune out the lumps in the mattress. The padded surface did a pretty good imitation of the Sahara dunes.

I'd closed my eyes but not yet drifted off when a faint shift in the air made me suddenly certain I was no longer alone. One of my shadowkind friends had slipped into the room in their supernatural way. Ruse, I assumed, but as I started to roll over, it wasn't his languid voice that reached my ears.

"Sorsha?"

Snap was standing in front of the door between our rooms, as if trying to do the best approximation of having entered the normal way without actually having opened the door. In the dim light, his curls darkened from gold to bronze, but the smooth planes of his face still managed to catch a little glow.

As I sat up, he kept totally still. I couldn't tell whether that was because he wanted the distance or he thought I might.

My pulse stuttered. Had our enemies tracked us down yet again despite all our precautions? "What's going on? Is something wrong?"

"No. I mean, I don't think so." His tongue flitted over his lips. "You said, yesterday, that if I decided I wanted more, I should tell you."

His gaze dipped—just for a moment, but obviously enough that the warmth of his attention grazed my breasts through my undershirt. I'd only worn that and panties to bed, where the sheet was now pooled around my waist.

As his meaning sank in, the warmth drifted lower to settle between my legs. All at once, my whole body felt flushed.

"I did say that," I agreed. "So... you do?"

He hesitated, and then the smile that transformed him from handsome to heavenly spread across his face. "Yes. Very much."

I found I wasn't totally sure what to do next. With Ruse, it'd been easy. He'd known exactly what he wanted and what he could offer. Snap was clearly discovering all this for the first time. It was thrilling to think I'd been the one to stir up that sort of desire in him... but also a little intimidating.

I didn't have the best track record with men. Somehow I always seemed to end up disappointing them in the end. It'd be an awful shame if I inadvertently traumatized the guy so badly he fled back to the monk way of life.

We didn't have to rush into anything. I needed to figure out how far *I* wanted this to go. Obviously given who and what we were, it couldn't be anything more than a fling—like with Ruse, enjoying what we had in the moment—but it was hard to see taking any shadowkind as a lover as a totally casual act.

For now, we could simply explore the possibilities. I scooted over on the bed to make room. "Why don't you come here, then, and we'll see where the moment takes us?"

Snap crossed the floor as swiftly as he'd been still before and sank down next to me. As he gazed into my eyes, his lit with an eager shine. His hand came up to trace across my cheek and into the fall of my hair. His smile faded.

"I want you to know I'd never hurt you. My abilities —I have to focus to use them; it doesn't happen automatically. I wouldn't put you in any danger."

His voice held so much resolve that my heart wrenched. He really thought I might be afraid of him, of what he could do. Hell, I didn't even know what that *was*, and I still didn't have the slightest concern that he'd ever inflict it on me, not after the way he'd reacted the other day when we'd talked about using his powers on living things.

I reached up to wrap my hand around his with a gentle squeeze. "I know. I'm not worried."

"Good." His smile returned like the sun emerging from behind a passing cloud.

He leaned closer, his nose nearly brushing my temple. His breath painted heat down the side of my face. The scent that rose from his skin was fresh and bright as spring clover, with a darker mossy undertone like a reminder that there was more lurking beneath the surface.

"There's so much I want to do," he murmured. "I don't know where to start. I don't know what you'd like."

The desire that had settled low in my belly tightened into something sharper. At this point I suspected I'd be all for whatever he went with. "Why don't you start with what *you'd* like, and I'll let you know if we need a change in direction?"

He responded with a pleased hum that sent a tingle over my skin and dipped his head as he inhaled deeply. Drinking in *my* scent, I realized. Holy mother of pearl, he'd barely touched me and I was already soaking through my panties.

His hand drifted down to my neck, his fingers stroking across my collarbone. His lips pressed lightly against my cheek, charting a path across it to the crook of my jaw. At every point of contact, my body lit up with quivers of bliss. A shaky breath spilled out of me.

Snap paused. "Is this all right?"

"Oh, yes," I said. "That was a good sigh. You know, there is one thing most people find they like a lot…"

I'd meant to let him lead this exploration, but I couldn't help myself—so shoot me. I tipped the angle of his jaw and guided his mouth to mine.

His breath caught as our lips met, and then he was kissing me as if the understanding of how to perform that act were written into his soul. My fingers twined in the silky curls at the back of his head. The heat of his mouth was so hungry yet tender it drew a whimper from my throat.

With the parting of my lips, he deepened the kiss. His forked tongue teased over the seam of my mouth, sparking pleasure. Oh, yes, I'd like some more of that, please.

His hand had slipped farther down, following the curve of my breasts—and stopping with a flinch I could tell he'd tried to suppress, just shy of the protective badge I'd left pinned to my undershirt. Shit, I'd forgotten about that.

"Sorry," I mumbled against his mouth, and drew back just far enough to tug the undershirt off. I did trust him—enough to go without that small ward tonight.

Snap took in the sway of my breasts as I bared them, neon brilliance gleaming in his eyes. He cupped one, carefully but with more confidence than when he'd started, and seemed to study the shape of it, the point of my nipple, the way that nub pebbled with a tingle of pleasure at a swipe of his thumb over it.

His smile widened. He kept his hand there, caressing the curve of my breast and the peak at equal measures, and brought his mouth back to mine. I could have drowned in the sweetness of that kiss.

He lingered on my mouth before taking his kisses lower: past my jaw, down my neck, over my collarbone, setting me alight everywhere his lips touched. When he reached my chest, he raised my breast as if it were one of the mortal delicacies he so enjoyed savoring. As he sucked the peak into his mouth, I couldn't help gasping. The flick of his tongue over my nipple, the forked tips encircling it with a slight tug, brought an even headier rush of pleasure.

"I know what Ruse meant now," Snap murmured. "About how you'd taste. He was right. You're better than any peach."

"Considering how much you enjoyed the peach, that's a pretty high compliment."

He chuckled and pressed a peck to the curve of my breast. "He has tasted you—everywhere. Hasn't he?"

The heated flush that had taken me over deepened. "Why, has he been talking about it?"

"No. I only—" Snap pulled back so he could look me in the eyes, his expression turning slightly apologetic. "The first night, you told us to leave you alone, but Ruse didn't come away with us. After a little while, I went looking for him. I slipped into your bedroom in the shadows, and I saw— He was down here." His fingers glided down to my lap, and a flush colored his own cheeks. "I didn't mean to spy. I left right away."

At least he had some small sense of privacy. But the thought of him watching the incubus with me in the act, even for a moment, spurred on my desire.

"Ruse can be... very appealing," I said.

"It's in his nature to be." Snap eased down the sheet to uncover my thighs. "I saw how much you enjoyed what he was doing to you." He kissed my cheek and then my mouth again, long and harder than before. I'd almost lost the thread of our conversation, caught up in the press of his supple lips, when he slid them away to speak again.

"I want to make you feel as good as he did. I want to bring you that kind of pleasure. And even more."

Well, I certainly wouldn't complain about that. But I did feel the need to say— "You know, Ruse has centuries of experience perfecting his technique, plus powers and a form specifically designed for seduction. I'm not saying you shouldn't be ambitious, but maybe we should focus on one step at a—*oh*."

His hand had skimmed over my panties, grazing my clit at the perfect angle to provoke another gasp. Snap gave me a grin that might have had a hint of the incubus's smirk to it and repeated the motion. Then his long, lithe fingers dipped lower, and curiosity came back into his expression. "You're wet."

"Yeah," I said. "That means you're already doing an excellent job of making good on your ambitions."

He pressed between my legs more firmly, setting off a pulse of pleasure, and I bit my lip. I ran my hand down his chest to make my own exploration of his lean frame. This shirt definitely needed to go. As I pulled at it, he released me just long enough to help remove it.

With all that divinely toned muscle bared, Snap leaned toward me. He hummed happily at the sweep of my fingers over that terrain and returned his attention to my sex.

The unmistakable evidence of his own arousal showed in the bulge below the waist of his pants. There was the involuntary response that had started us down this unexpected path. It shouldn't go untended to.

I teased my fingers over the bulge, and this time it was Snap who sighed. His hips shifted nearer to me, seeking out that contact. I stroked him again, harder, and he burrowed his face into the crook of my neck. His teeth nicked the sensitive skin there with a shudder of breath.

"That sensation... makes it very hard to think," he said.

I laughed lightly. "The point of doing this isn't to think. It's to feel. And you can feel a hell of a lot more than this, if you'll let me show you."

He nodded into my hair and then raised his head to claim my mouth. The roughness of his kiss and the friction of his hand still fondling me through my panties left my head spinning. I managed to focus enough to curl my fingers around his erection through the fabric for a better grip.

He swayed into my hand with each pump up and down, chasing the pleasure I was paying him back with. At my nudge, he tipped with me so we lay on the bed next to each other. I squirmed even closer into his kiss and his touch.

Maybe it was best if we stuck to hands for this first spin around the block. Much simpler than navigating the mechanics of full-on sex, especially when Snap could hardly be prepared for the intensity of *those* sensations. I could already tell he'd get me off just fine like this. Hell, I wasn't sure how much longer I'd last as it was.

I found the wherewithal to jerk the zipper of his pants down and discovered Thorn wasn't the only one for whom dressing didn't come automatically. Snap hadn't bothered with any kind of underwear. He probably hadn't realized they were a standard part of a mortal outfit. How would a shadowkind know, after all, if no one had happened to mention it? It wasn't as if he'd had to consider clothes at all where he'd come from.

For now, it only made my intentions easier to carry out. I closed my fingers around his naked cock, reveling in the smoothness of the skin over his rigid member, and Snap let out a guttural sound. His tongue flicked right into my mouth to twine with mine, provoking a giddy shiver. I kissed him back just as enthusiastically as I swiped my thumb over the head of his erection and spread the precum forming there down its length.

Snap yanked at my panties and delved his hand beneath them. My chest hitched in delight at the stroke of his fingers right across my clit. The same instinct that must have guided his first kiss brought his touch down to my opening, testing the slickness there and then slipping inside me. He began a gentle pumping motion that became more blissfully forceful with each repetition.

I moaned, bucking toward him in pursuit of release. "That's good. So good."

He brought his other hand to the side of my face, watching me as the motions of his fingers built me up to that ecstatic shattering apart. Pleasure had flushed his face a deeper shade than before, and his breath came raggedly, but his attention never left me.

The swivel of his thumb over my clit and one final

thrust inside me sent me reeling with the burst of my orgasm. My eyes rolled up, stars sparkling behind them while my body clenched around his fingers.

Snap caressed my cheek even as he rocked inside me through the aftershock. His voice came out soft and fierce at the same time. "My peach. My Sorsha. *Mine.*"

I wasn't in any state to argue that sentiment, if I'd even wanted to. It was all I could do to keep my hold on his cock and stroke him faster to bring him with me.

As the rest of my body sagged with satisfaction, he let his eyes haze, giving himself over to the pleasure now that he'd fulfilled my end. A groan reverberated from his chest. His hips jerked.

He tugged me to him suddenly, his mouth crashing into mine. A tremor raced through his body as the hot gush of his release spurted across my hand.

"Oh," he mumbled. "That—"

He cut himself off with a breathless laugh and kissed me once more. This one lit me up from head to toes even in my sated state. I nestled closer to him instinctively, resting my hands against the warmth of his chest.

When the kiss ended, I glanced at him coyly through my eyelashes. "So, was 'more' the right choice?"

"Yes. Yes. And for you too."

Apparently my enjoyment had been so clearly on display that he didn't feel the need to ask. I was okay with that.

As I tipped my head to rest it on the pillow, Snap

gazed down at me. A hint of uncertainty crossed his face. "What usually happens now?"

Ah. Yeah, I guessed in some ways that was a trickier subject than the sex act itself.

I skimmed my fingers up and down the taut planes of his stomach. "Sometimes people like to consider it done and leave. Sometimes they'd rather be close for a while longer, so they stay together while they sleep."

"Then I will stay," Snap said decidedly. He wrapped one arm around my shoulders and lay his cheek down by me on the pillow, tucking my head under his chin. His mix of bright and dark scents enveloped me. I relaxed into his embrace with only a small pang of regret that for all I knew, this might be the only interlude we'd get before our lives went even more to hell.

27

Sorsha

The computerized interface in Ruse's snazzy car was so complicated I couldn't figure out how to connect my phone, so I settled for making my own soundtrack. "Don't stop deceivin'," I sang as the four of us cruised into the docklands, hidden behind our tinted windows. "Hold on, send 'em reeling."

Ruse shot me an amused smile as he took a turn. "You're lucky you don't get arrested, messing with the words that badly."

I stuck my tongue out at him, because I was just that mature, and leaned my arm against the window ledge. The faded factories along the river looked even drearier today with a haze of clouds graying the sky. There was no rush hour out in this part of town. The growl of our engine was the only sound on the street.

Of course, that'd be exactly how Meriden and his co-conspirators liked it.

We'd already decided that parking right by the drop-off spot was too risky. Ruse drove a few blocks farther and pulled up to the curb around a corner. The plan was that Thorn would lurk in the shadows where Meriden had gotten out yesterday, and Snap would linger close to our corner. When the minivan arrived, Snap would alert us and Thorn would give chase on foot. We were hoping either he'd discover a building here where Meriden was conducting his current work, or we'd be able to close in on whatever other vehicle picked the guy up in the area, if one had.

At the very least, we'd figure out more about his route than we'd been able to last time.

Thorn swiveled in his seat to beckon to Snap. "It's an hour earlier than yesterday's drop-off. We've got time to patrol the wider area first. Come on."

Snap balked, his gaze sliding to me for a second before he met Thorn's eyes. "I'd rather stay close to the car. Isn't Sorsha's safety the most important thing?"

"We'll be ensuring her safety by confirming none of our enemies are staked out nearby," the warrior said. "You can test the surroundings for signs of where they might have been here before as well."

"And, y'know, *I'll* be right here in the car with her," Ruse said. "You're not leaving her unprotected. Not that she's defenseless on her own either."

"Of course she's not," Snap said insistently. "But

we've seen how aggressive these people are. You're the only one who doesn't have any kind of power that's meant for combat." His hand crept across the seat to give mine a quick squeeze, his chin lifting. Apparently last night's interlude had stirred up a brand-new possessive instinct. I hadn't anticipated that.

Ruse rolled his eyes. "Are you referring to that dangerous skill of yours that gives you the shakes when you even think about using it? How many attackers could you take down at one time anyway—two? Three? I could charm them into not wanting to attack us at all."

"I don't remember that strategy getting us out of the last few attacks."

"All right, all right." I held up my hands in a time-out gesture. "I appreciate everyone's intense concern for my well-being, but for all we know, an entire militia is descending on us while you all argue about it. If anyone comes at Ruse and me, he can simply *drive away*, which so far has been the most useful power of all." I gave Snap's hand a reassuring pat in return. "I'll be fine. Go see what you can find out there. Without your other powers, we wouldn't have gotten even this far."

My touch and the reminder of his past contributions appeared to mollify my new lover. His posture loosened. He nodded in agreement and then, so suddenly I didn't see it coming, leaned in to give me a swift kiss.

His lips pressed warm against mine for all of a second. I barely had a chance to return the gesture before he'd slipped away into the shadows. Thorn let out a wordless mutter of what sounded like consternation and vanished too.

Ruse shifted in his seat to lounge sideways where he could look back at me. There was nothing surprising about his smirk or the raise of his eyebrows. "Well, *that* was certainly interesting."

"Shut up," I said, because that had worked so well before.

"I did notice that Snap wandered off for quite a while last night. Now I'm getting an inkling where he might have gone."

"Which part are you having trouble with: the shutting or the upping?"

"Who said I was criticizing?" A sly glint had lit in his eyes. "I'm impressed. I didn't know he had it in him, but you obviously woke up a sleeping dragon."

I folded my arms over my chest. "Is it going to be a problem? I *really* don't need you two arguing like that all day long."

The incubus laughed. "I'm hardly one to push for monogamy, Miss Blaze. As far as I'm concerned, you should take your pleasure wherever and from whoever suits your fancy. I'd just like to stay in the mix if that's an option." His gaze turned more heated.

I couldn't say that I wasn't imagining a repeat of our past encounter when he looked at me like that. "We'll see."

"Making me work for it. That just turns me on even more." He winked. "I could teach the newbie a few things, you know, if you ever wanted to invite me along for the ride. How to get you off, how to heighten that enjoyment..." He extended his arm to trail a finger down my leg from knee to shin. Sparks coursed from me from that line of heat.

Ruse and Snap attending to me in unison? What gods had I sacrificed goats to in some past life to be worthy of that bliss? It'd depend on Snap being okay with the idea, though...

Ruse's smirk grew. "I can see you're thinking the possibilities through."

I huffed and nudged his hand away with a playful kick. The incubus just chuckled as he withdrew. "The offer will stay on the table as long as you'd like. Or if you'd really like, we could put *you* on a table. What a lovely platter to feast on."

If he kept going, I might melt into a hot, horny puddle right here on the seat. "Maybe we should be focusing on the whole saving your boss problem right now?"

"Spoilsport," he teased, and shifted to peer out the window. "No wave of soldiers crashing toward us so far. I wonder how long we'll be able to hole up in that motel before they—"

Snap cut him off, wisping out of the shadows into his seat with a quiver through the air. "Thorn's gone to the drop-off spot already," he said without preamble. "He thinks he saw the van heading this way."

I checked our car's clock and frowned. "It's way earlier than yesterday."

"Maybe they change up the times a little every morning to throw off anyone like us," Ruse suggested.

That was totally possible, but it didn't quash the prickling of my nerves. Sucking my lip under my teeth, I leaned toward my window, even though I couldn't see much of the street the van had taken from there. If Thorn was right, we'd find out what was up soon enough.

A rumble of an engine sounded, distant but getting louder by the second. Ruse rested his hand on the ignition. Snap hastily looped his seatbelt over his chest. We knew better than to count on a smooth drive.

As I waited for the pause in that rumble when the minivan would let Meriden out, my heart pounded as if it were chasing the passing seconds. The engine sound droned louder. Any moment now—

The gunmetal-gray minivan zoomed right by us, cruising on down the street without any sign of stopping. A startled noise hitched out of me just as a second car zipped after it—the baby blue compact we'd thought might be following us yesterday.

Fudge me sideways 'til Sunday. What the hell was going on?

"Ruse?" I said.

He was already starting the engine. "If we need to get going, we'll stage that getaway, but right now I think we'd better see where they're heading."

Thorn wouldn't be able to keep pace with the vehicles on foot, even through the shadows. As Ruse swerved into the road and around, I gripped the door handle, my pulse thudding faster. Snap grasped my hand again, this time holding on tight. Despite myself, I actually did find the gesture comforting.

We'd just pulled around the corner when the minivan jerked to a halt a few blocks ahead of us. A side door flew open; a slack figure tumbled out onto the sidewalk with a thump. Before the door had even slammed shut again, the minivan was tearing away.

They *had* made a drop-off—but I didn't like the look of that crumpled body. As we drove toward it, it didn't stir.

"Do we stop?" Ruse asked. The baby blue car had, just up the block from where the minivan had made its deposit. A slim figure in a white velour tracksuit hopped out, hood pulled up, but as the driver rounded the car, the wind tugged the fabric back just enough for a jolt of recognition to shoot through me.

"Stop. Stop!" I said.

The tires squealed as Ruse hit the brake. I scrambled out and found myself face to face with my best friend.

Vivi had wobbled to a halt on the other side of the fallen body, just ten feet away from me. Her gaze caught mine for a second, wide-eyed, and then dropped to the sprawled man. A tremor ran through her shoulders.

All I could see so far was the deathly stillness of the body and a reddish tinge along his hairline, but the sickly graying of her face told me to brace myself as I stepped closer.

I was pretty sure it was Meriden. The hair was the

same color and cut as the guy I'd glimpsed exiting the minivan yesterday, his jeans and tweed suit jacket a similar style of clothing. Then his face came into view.

If you could even call it that. He barely had a face at all now. The front of his head—what I could see with it tipped toward the pavement—was a mash of splintered bone and bloody flesh. The only way you could tell it ever had been a face was its position relative to his hair and ears. His chin, nose, and forehead were caved in, his cheekbones crushed, all of it beaten in as if thwacked over and over by a baseball bat.

As my stomach lurched, a chilly realization crept through my nausea. His associates hadn't just smashed him up beyond visual recognition but shattered his jaw and teeth. Dental records wouldn't be any help. My gaze dropped to the hands that had twisted close to his skinny frame, and I flinched. Little red rivulets of blood streamed from his fingers where it looked as if they'd been shoved into a woodchipper all the way to the second knuckles. Forget fingerprinting too.

The people who'd dumped him here had ensured there'd be no definitive ID, not just for us but for any police force unless they happened to have the guy's DNA on file.

"Oh my God," Vivi was mumbling into the hand she'd clapped over her mouth. "Oh my God, oh my God, oh my God."

None of my shadowkind companions had joined us. Had they stuck to the shadows because of the additional witness? I wasn't sure whether to be grateful for that discretion or not. Their presence would raise more questions, but it wasn't as if there weren't a whole heap of those already. And I might have felt steadier with at least one of those powerful companions by my side.

I wrenched my gaze away from the mutilated man to focus on my best friend. "What are you *doing* here, Vivi? How did you— Whose car is that?" It didn't have rental plates, and she'd still been driving her long-time cherry-red Beamer when she'd picked me up for a trip out of town a couple months ago. Not that the car really mattered in the grand scheme of things, but it was the most concrete thing I had to latch onto in this crazy situation.

"My grandma's," Vivi said in a distant voice. "She let me borrow—I knew you'd recognize my regular one..." She yanked her eyes up to stare at me. "And you clearly didn't want me around. What the hell have you gotten yourself mixed up in, Sorsha? It's obviously incredibly fucking dangerous—why didn't you ask for help?"

I *had* help, but I wasn't going to mention that. "*Because* it's incredibly fucking dangerous. Obviously." I waved my hand at the body. "Do you think I want people who'd do that setting their sights on you?"

"But it's okay that they might come after *you*? You should have told me—told the Fund, if this is something to do with the shadowkind... Are these the hunters who came after Luna? Was this Meriden guy part of that somehow?"

Right, I'd told her I was looking into something to do with Luna when I was diverting her before. But— I knit my brow. "How do you know anything about Meriden?"

Her lips twisted. "I got it out of Jade after you talked to her—made it sound like we were looking into it together. Which, you know, even *she* thought had to be the case. Although I didn't realize it was *Meriden* like one word until I started asking around in his neighborhood—"

Her mouth snapped shut. She hugged herself, backing up a step from the body, but I was still staring at her. "His neighborhood?" She *had* been staked out there yesterday. "Just how much have you been spying on me, Vivi?"

"When I called you a couple days ago, I had one of the Fund's usual guys tracing it," she admitted. "And then I got him to poke around, and I did some asking—I went out there to scope it out and saw that car driving off to follow the van, and I figured it was you... Since you didn't show up today, I just followed the van."

"You realize how crazy that sounds, right? Like you're a psycho stalker."

"I just wanted to help you," she burst out. "You were shutting me out, and I could tell you were working on something big, something that made you nervous. I know you've got things you keep to yourself, and that's fine, but you don't usually lie to me, Sorsh. I was really freaking worried about you, okay?" A quaver crept into her voice. "And it looks like I was right to be. What's this all about? We'll figure it out together. You've got to tell me now."

"No, I don't." Another realization hit me, this one cold enough to freeze my gut. I'd never spoken Meriden's name to anyone outside my shadowkind trio except Jade, and then as "Merry Den" and a place. We'd kept a careful distance and a low profile when checking out his home. But Vivi— "How many people did you talk to about Meriden? Did you go right up to his house?"

Her expression twitched. "I called a few people in the Fund, and asked the guy who traced your call to look into it—he got me the address. After I lost you yesterday, I went back and talked to a few of the neighbors about him. Nothing too obvious, of course."

It didn't have to be obvious to tip off the people he worked for. My jaw clenched. "It's because of you poking around that they realized someone was onto him. That's why they killed him. That's the kind of people we're dealing with here, Vivi, and you crashed right in with this ridiculously obvious car and the questions and the following so close..."

"I didn't know—" she started to protest, but I didn't let her keep going.

"It doesn't matter. We're not working on this together. You've got to get out of town—maybe your grandma too, since they've probably looked up the car by now—lay low and hope I end up distracting them enough that they forget about you."

"No way. I'm not letting you go up against psychopaths like this on your own—"

"You're more likely to get yourself or both of us killed than to make things easier," I snapped.

Her hands balled at her sides. "I wouldn't have had to nose around if you'd just told me what you were doing in the first place!"

"I was trying to stop something like this from happening to you. For good reason, it looks like."

"Sorsha, whatever's going on, you can't handle it by yourself."

"Yes, I can." My voice came out taut. "And it'll be a hell of a lot easier if I'm not worried about what's going to happen to you while you're tagging along. Please, just leave, go somewhere no one will think to look for you. When this is over, I promise I'll tell you everything—but not until then."

Vivi wavered on her feet. Her expression tightened. But before she could keep arguing, a looming presence solidified in the air next to me.

Thorn placed a heavy hand on my shoulder. "Sorsha *isn't* alone," he said, his gravelly voice so low it was a threat in itself. "I, for one, would also prefer if you didn't make the job of ensuring she stays safe even more difficult than it already is. She told you to go. *Go.*"

My best friend gaped at the shadowkind and then at me. "You— He— You've got one of *them* working with you?"

I bristled at the way she said "them," as if all shadowkind really were the monsters that fables made them out to be, and felt Thorn's hand tense against me.

"He knows what he's doing," I said. "Like you *don't*. So please, get out of here and find someplace safe to hole up until I get in touch."

"Or I can make sure that you do," Thorn added, glowering at her.

Vivi's mouth opened and then closed again. She swallowed audibly. Her gaze dropped to Meriden and his pulverized face, and she looked as if she barely held herself back from vomiting. She shot one last, desperate glance at me, and when I didn't soften my expression, she darted for her car.

The baby blue compact puttered away, leaving us in the docklands' eerie hush to contemplate the man who could no longer lead us to our goal and the savageness with which our foes had ensured that.

Snap and Ruse emerged from the shadows beside us. Ruse clucked his tongue at the body disapprovingly, but even he appeared to be momentarily lost for words.

"Now what?" Snap said quietly.

A huge lump had formed within the queasiness in my stomach. I swallowed thickly. "I don't know." All our work, all the clues we'd uncovered and the trail we'd followed—it ended here. Everything we'd done had gotten us nothing but a ruined corpse in a stretch of hollowed-out factories.

28

Thorn

Even without leaning nearer, I could tell there was a certain expertise to the savaging of this mortal's body. Blows chosen with care for maximum impact and to destroy specific zones. The zones they'd chosen, I couldn't account for. Mortals had strange inclinations.

None of the battering had ended this one's life. When I bent down by the body, my nose caught a faint but distinctive chemical tang that no human's senses would have discerned. He'd been poisoned in some way before the savaging.

Sorsha stood beside me, motionless other than a brief shiver that passed through her stance. Her jaw was tight.

"He's dead because of us," she said with an unexpected strain in her voice.

Ruse shook his head. "We took every possible precaution. From what your friend admitted to, you were right—her clumsiness must have tipped the sword-star folks off that someone was overly interested in Meriden."

"But Vivi wouldn't have been interested in him if she hadn't noticed that I was hiding something. If I'd faked it better—or maybe if I'd told her the truth and managed to convince her to stay out of it—if that even would have worked..." She bit her lip.

I frowned at her as I straightened up. Why should this man be anything to her other than a fallen enemy? She appeared distraught by his death not just for the practical implications but for his own sake as well.

Mortals and their fickle emotions.

"What of it if *he's* dead?" I said. "The trail we were following is dead. All the answers we found centered around this man. Without him, we have no more than when we started at the bridge."

Snap stirred as if he might have argued that point, but then he grimaced. There *was* no arguing it. We'd been focused on his Merry Den from the start, narrowing in closer and closer on that target—and here we were. He'd already checked all over the bridge; that was the only distinctive detail we'd found to follow up on. We'd lost all direction.

It wouldn't have mattered if I'd been faster yesterday, if I'd managed to track Meriden's path from here to begin with. I'd lost *him* when it'd been our last chance to use him. Just as I'd lost Omen to begin with, lost our freedom when those hunters had descended on us afterward...

I had no justification for it. I'd failed again, pure and simple. While these ruthless mortals did darkness only knew what to Omen—while he might be barely clinging to life—if *he* wasn't already dead, that was. Every one of us standing around Meriden, even the lady, knew that the one we'd set out to save might have been dead before Sorsha had ever freed us from our cages.

He'd almost certainly end up dead regardless when I couldn't serve him better than this. I'd meant for this time to be different. I'd had a mere three colleagues to defend. It should have been the easiest task.

Sorsha's lips pursed, but the motion didn't change the hopelessness etched on her face. The incubus sucked in a breath and glanced down the street. He attempted to conjure a little optimism with his tone. "There is the minivan to consider."

"Do you really think they'll keep using the same vehicle after this?" Sorsha said. "Or that they'll have registered the plates in any way that would let us hunt them down? These are people who'll do this to a guy just to make sure their tracks are covered." She swept her arm toward the marred corpse.

The devourer shifted closer to her. "At least it wasn't you." His sharpened devotion showed in every inch of his posture, however that had developed.

He was right, though. I had achieved that one small victory: the mortal who'd rescued us from shameful captivity was still alive and reasonably well. For however much longer I could maintain that state of events.

"It's a long shot, but—" Ruse crouched down and checked the man's pockets, avoiding the bloody parts of the body as well as he could. Coming up empty, he sighed and straightened back up. "They thought of just about everything, like always."

As I was about to suggest we leave before our enemies also thought of sending a new pack of soldiers after us, Sorsha's chin came up. Her eyes gleamed with a ferocity that burned most of her despondency away.

"Just about, but not everything. They've never been able to predict *everything* we'd be able to do—the connections we've made, the skills we have."

She turned to Snap. "You can taste impressions off inanimate objects. I know there's something different about it with living beings, something you want to avoid— but he's not alive anymore. Can you test him and see what comes up, just like Thorn could take the drunk guy who attacked me into the shadows after he was dead?"

The devourer's eyes widened. He stared down at the corpse with a nervous flick of his tongue between his lips. "I don't know. I've never tried that before."

Ruse had brightened at the suggestion. "It certainly can't hurt to give it a shot, can it? It's not as if you could hurt him now. You certainly can't kill him any more than he's already been murdered."

I didn't know exactly what had soured Snap so thoroughly against his own greatest power, but his whole body had tensed despite the incubus's words. I squared my shoulders, preparing to order him to make the attempt with the full impact of my presence, but Sorsha spoke up first.

She touched his arm, her expression softening in a way that sent a twinge I couldn't explain through my chest. "The thought of doing it reminds you of whatever happened before, doesn't it?"

He nodded with a jerk, his gaze still fixed on the body. "I know it isn't the same. Ruse is right about everything he said. I should just—" And yet he couldn't seem to move.

"Don't think about that other time," Sorsha suggested. "Think about how it felt when you found Meriden's name or his house. Imagine how many useful impressions must be attached to him. You could get us so much closer to Omen, to stopping the people who worked in that lab."

"Yes. Yes." The devourer gathered himself, determination hardening the graceful lines of his face. He knelt by Meriden's back and leaned in.

Sorsha hovered over him, poised as if she thought she might need to leap in and steady him again, her lips curved in a gentle but elated smile. The fierceness I'd seen still shone in her eyes. Ruse watched the proceedings with eager anticipation.

The desolation that had come over our group had fallen away, just like that. *She* had defeated it, even though she'd been more affected by the death than the rest of us.

In that moment, while they all studied the body, I couldn't tear my gaze away from her—from the magnificent strength I hadn't completely perceived until just now. And not just strength. Snap might have gone through with this act under my orders out of fear, but she'd seen what he needed well enough to not just convince him but inspire him.

It shouldn't have been surprising. Our lady might be mortal, true, but she was the sort of mortal who broke into prisons and freed shadowkind from their jailors at risk of her own life and liberty. How could she be anything other than extraordinary? She'd managed to fill the gap left by our loss of Omen so surely and yet subtly it'd nearly escaped my notice.

Silly songs and flashy clothes and all, she brought something essential to our group. Something I suddenly had trouble imagining doing without, even after we had Omen leading the charge again.

But why would she want anything to do with us and the danger we'd thrust into her life once this quest was over?

The earlier twinge turned into a pang. Before I could examine it, determine just what it meant, Snap rocked back on his heels with a shaky gasp. His pupils had dilated, the brilliant green of his eyes in his true physical form glittering around them.

"I saw so much," he said breathlessly. "So many

places. The house and the streets and halls that are bright but cold. Shadowkind in little rooms with locked doors. Shiny tables like in the office we searched, computers with streams of words and numbers and wriggling lines..."

"Where?" Ruse asked. "That's got to be the place they took Omen to."

"I don't... I don't know. It all came in fragments. It's hard to piece together." Snap went still, his forehead furrowing as he must have sorted through the barrage of impressions I had to assume an entire human body would have collected. "There was a place not yet built, all steel beams and walls half attached—maybe that was from farther back. There was another house like his but with a blue door. There was a grocery store, fruit with smooth skin in his hands. A book. A building coming up out of dirt ground, with concrete walls and doors shiny like those lab tables. Music rising from a wooden platform down below where people were sitting in rows with their instruments. And another building—I think it was important—he was nervous when he walked inside."

Sorsha latched on to that comment, sinking next to him. "When he walked inside where, Snap?"

His tongue flicked again, as if he could draw more certainty out of the air. "Big glass windows. Sale. Bright boxes in the windows with little figures like people and animals and cars. I think I can see the sign." He squeezed his eyes shut. "Fun Station Depot. He went there more than one time—I see it when it's light and dark and in-between. Worried. He had to tell them something, something about his work, he wasn't sure they'd be happy enough with it."

"Did you get much sense of what that work was?" Ruse asked.

"No. Only—shadowkind. Fear and awe of them. Needing to keep them contained." Another flick. "Walking into that building, the one that made him nervous, he'd be thinking about how the way to get in was iron. I don't know what that means."

The devourer's shoulders sagged with those last words, as if drawing out so many impressions had drawn most of the energy out of his body as well.

Sorsha tapped her lips. "Iron. A key, maybe, to wherever they do their illicit dealings."

"At this Fun Station Depot?" I said. "What is *that*?" It didn't sound like a military base or hunter's den.

Our mortal had already whipped out her phone. A laugh spilled out of her. "It's a toy store," she said. "A big outlet place—not too far from where I've gone bargain hunting for clothes with Vivi." She peered at Snap. "You think he went in there a lot for something to do with his work."

"Yes. It felt that way. I don't think the shadowkind were there... but wherever *they* were, he was less nervous about that."

"And at least for this spot we have a definite location. It must be a front for some part of the sword-star bunch's operations. They'd need money for all that equipment and the people they're hiring; they'd have to set up a legitimate business to launder it through, I guess."

She nibbled at her lip in thought and then glanced up at me with a twinkle in her eyes I wished I could capture. "What do you say we go toy shopping?"

29

Sorsha

"I don't like this," Thorn said for what was approximately the one millionth time.

I restrained myself from pointing out that he appeared to dislike pretty much everything as a general rule. "It doesn't matter whether you like it or not. From what you said, you *can't* get into the room that's got to hold the important stuff. So it's up to me. No need to worry. I've been training for this moment my entire life."

That was only a slight exaggeration. I tucked my ponytail under the knit cap that now hid all of my hair. Then I stretched my arms in the thin black top that was the centerpiece of my cat burglar attire, careful not to bonk my elbows in the relatively tight space of the car's back seat. I had my pouches with all my standard equipment—sans grappling hook and rope, since the place was only one story—attached to the thin belt around my waist. Piece of cake.

I'd just keep telling myself that until I was back here with the goods.

The warrior shifted restlessly in his seat. "I could dispatch the guards."

By "dispatch," I assumed he meant "punch their throats in" as per his usual M.O. But even if he didn't— "No. Ideally, we don't want the sword-star bunch to know we ever found out about the store. If they realize we've gotten that far, they'll probably scrub every trail it could lead to before we have half a chance to follow them."

"There's got to be something major in there," Ruse said. "No business fills a few walls with silver and iron just for kicks."

"I still say I should at least go into the main building with you," Thorn grumbled. "Only the office was protected in a way I couldn't penetrate."

I leaned forward to poke his broad shoulder. "I need *you* patrolling outside the store in case reinforcements show up. It's a huge building—I can manage to avoid two security guards." The depot took up an entire block, the building sprawling across half and the rest a massive parking lot. From what Thorn had described, I'd have plenty of shelves and other displays to take shelter behind.

And I also needed to make sure he didn't get trigger-happy—knuckle-happy?—and bash up the guards even if I wasn't in serious danger.

Ruse patted the steering wheel. "I'll be ready to jet the second you get back, Miss Blaze." He gave Thorn a sly glance. "You, I'll leave behind if you're not back at the same time she is."

Thorn didn't look offended. "As you should. I can find my way to the motel through the shadows if need be."

"I can too," Snap said. "Isn't there anything I could do that would help you, Sorsha?" He gazed at me so beseechingly with those gorgeous green eyes that I wavered, though just a little and only for an instant.

I wanted my shadowkind trio out of my way so that they didn't cause unexpected problems during this heist, yeah, but that wasn't the only reason I intended on going in alone. The fact that the place even had a room protected against shadowkind showed they knew they might be dealing with beings of a monstrous sort. Who knew what kind of bullets the guards were packing in their guns—or what other weapons they might have on them? The building itself could contain other defenses that would weaken these guys.

I wasn't going to take that chance. I'd broken into plenty of buildings without getting caught. It was my specialty, really. If I went in there alone, it was only my hide on the line. If I screwed up, no one paid for it except me. I'd have been twice as nervous otherwise.

I squeezed Snap's hand. "You already found this

place for us—and I know that took a lot out of you." It'd pained me, encouraging him to go against his fears, as necessary as it'd seemed. "I'm sure you'll be able to help with whatever I bring back."

Thorn was scowling, but apparently he was done arguing. "I'll go ahead and scout out the area one last time before you head in. Wait for my signal."

"Got it." I poked him again. "And don't you *dare* follow me in. If more guards come calling, do you really want to leave me unprepared until they're already in the building? If you see anyone coming after me out there, feel free to dispatch them however you'd like." If the alarm had already been sounded, leaving bodies behind wouldn't matter, only getting out alive.

His mouth tightened, but he nodded. I thought the reminder of his responsibilities would be enough to keep him patrolling where he shouldn't be in the line of fire. If I did my job right, there'd be no alarm and no reinforcements for him to do battle with.

He vanished, and I eased out of the car, shutting the door as softly as I could. We'd parked in a lot outside a kitchen supply outlet store where the nearest security lamp was burnt out. In the thickening dusk, I'd barely be visible in my black clothes against the black car.

I stared toward Fun Station Depot, watching for Thorn's go-ahead. The cooling breeze tickled across my cheeks. Just to pass the time, I touched each piece of my gear in turn to confirm I had it where I expected it to be.

A light flashed in the distance, there and gone. Thorn

and the mini flashlight he'd helped himself to inside the store. All clear.

I gave the guys in the car a wave good-bye, unable to see through the tint if they returned it, and loped off. The soles of my sneakers made only the faintest rasp against the pavement. I veered around to the back of the kitchen supply building and crossed the street there, dashing through the lamplight.

My pulse thumped brisk but steady. I indulged in a brief spurt of song under my breath. "I can steal it, coming to your lair tonight, oh horde." The smile that came with the mangled lyric spurred me on.

As I reached the parking lot behind the toy store, I slowed. Thorn had given me a hand in one other way: he'd surreptitiously unlocked a door at the back of the store. I still had to make it through the stockroom, across the main retail floor, and into the office at the east end, but then I'd only have one lock to disable. *The way in is iron.* It didn't matter what kind of key that special room normally took—my picks would do the trick.

The parking lot was empty other than a charity donations bin the size of a small trailer in one corner. *Clothes for the Recently Deceased.* Now there was a cause if I'd ever heard one. Wouldn't want any corpses to have to wander around naked.

I slunk around the pools of security light, eased open the back door, and peeked into the dark stockroom with ears pricked. No sound reached my ears except the distant whir of traffic from somewhere behind me. Even two guards were overkill for nighttime security in a discount toy shop—reflecting the fact that the management had more they wanted to protect than just the merchandise—but neither of them hung out back here. That worked for me.

I crept between the high shelving units stacked with boxes of plushies, action figures, and Lego. Only the faintest streak of light showed beneath the door at the other end that led to the main retail area. I stopped by it, holding myself still and silent.

After a few minutes, footsteps tapped by. The guards weren't making any effort to conceal *their* movements— very helpful of them. How many months, even years, had they been on the job without ever actually needing to guard anything in here?

I smiled. Complacency was a thief's best friend.

When the footsteps had tapped away, I nudged the door open an inch to take a lay of the land. Packed shelves of playthings loomed on either side of an aisle right across from me. More stood at regular intervals to my left, but to my right, when I dared to fully emerge, I saw a cluster blocking my straight path to the spot where Thorn had said the office was.

I kept close to the end displays, peering down each aisle and then darting across the open space to make my way across the store. When footsteps tapped my way again, I ducked behind a cardboard stand of foil trading card packages. Catch 'em all—but no one would be catching me.

Slinking onward, I was feeling particularly confident for about five seconds. I slipped past the next display—and with a whir of mechanized parts, an electronic barking sound spewed out from the nearest shelf.

I flinched and barely restrained myself from smacking the thing. A little robotic puppy was stomping its feet and emitting that awful sound right by my shoulder. Because what could anyone want more than a yappy dog that couldn't even cuddle with you? Brilliant design.

Two sets of footsteps headed toward me, thudding rather than tapping now. I dashed for the nearest shelter: a life-size statue of a fashion doll poised next to rows of pink boxes containing her smaller counterpart. Thankfully, her ample chest and hips were more than wide enough to disguise my dark form behind them.

I held myself rigidly still, eyeing those curves. It'd better be true that these dolls were made in impossible proportions, because otherwise I definitely fell short.

The guards came to a stop by the yappy toy, which finally shut up. One of the men sighed. "Stupid dog. I swear all it takes is a tiny draft to set it off. I hope one of them haunts the asshole who designed those things."

"No kidding," the other said with a weary chuckle.

They poked around a bit, one ambling down my aisle, but Miss Giant Bosoms remained my savior. As I groped her butt while squashing myself farther out of view, I thought a silent *Sorry!* at her.

When the coast was clear, I edged out from behind

her and headed for the cluster of shelves between me and my goal. They turned out to circle a play area with a ball pit, train table, and a few kiddie ride-on cars. Just beyond that spot, I caught sight of the door that must lead to the office. Bingo!

Approaching it, my heart sank. Snap had said Meriden had left a strong impression that the way into this place was iron. How could that be anything other than a key—one many shadowkind couldn't even touch, so very convenient? But maybe that had been for the outer door? The one in front of me had no keyhole at all, nothing for me to pick or even pop an explosive into, just a flat unbroken panel next to a keypad to enter a code.

Shit. I had a code breaker device that might have gotten me in if I'd had the time, but it could take hours depending on the model—if it would even connect with this one. I couldn't hang around with the not-so-deadly duo that long. Even if the guards didn't pose any more of a threat than they'd presented so far, they had plenty of friends who could pick up that slack.

Standing tensed, I glared at the door. Why the hell had Meriden been obsessing about iron coming in here? It being in the walls was a way to keep shadowkind *out*, not let anyone in. It was too late to go back and ask Snap if he'd happened to also pick up on a sequence of four numbers or—

Wait a second.

My pulse kicked up a notch as I bent over the lock. Sweet kit and caboodle, let this work. I-R-O-N: 4766.

The lock beeped faintly, making my pulse hiccup, and the deadbolt slid over. Yes!

I held back a fist pump of victory and pushed the door. It swung open to admit me without a squeak. Just like that, I walked inside, met with stillness crisp with an air conditioner's artificial chill.

Not knowing whether the overhead lights would show under the door, I opted for the smaller glow of my flashlight. It caught on a steel desk mounted with a computer and monitor, a leather office chair, a couple of filing cabinets, and a bulletin board pinned with a calendar and various sales announcements.

The computer would probably contain the motherlode. I took a quick skim through the filing cabinets just in case, but they were all filled with order forms and sales reports. Sinking into the leather chair, I tapped the mouse.

The monitor blinked on—to a password request screen.

Son of a basket weaver. Of course it'd be protected, and I wasn't any hacker. I'd never had to steal data during any burglar-ing mission before.

I typed in IRON, but that luck was only good for one point of access. The password window shuddered and informed me I needed to try again. I grimaced at it. How many tries would I get before it set off some kind of alarm or locked me out completely?

The odds of me guessing the password belonging to some people I knew zilch about was about five million to one. I could gamble with the best of them, but I knew when a bet wasn't worth taking.

So... I guessed I'd better take the whole damn computer until I could find someone better at this part than I was.

There was only so much I could carry. I could find another monitor someplace else. I unhooked the computer unit from the screen and heaved it up under my arm.

Ooof, yeah, time to start doing more push-ups. My bicep was aching before I'd even taken two steps. The corner of the heavy metal block dug into my hip.

As I moved around the desk, I spotted a clear plastic box with a stack of CDs labeled in sharpie. What if some of the necessary data was on those? I shoved the box under my arm on top of the computer. Now I had sharp corners digging into my armpit too—wonderful.

I snuck out the door again and closed it with the softest of clicks. All I had to do was schlep this haul outside, and I was home free. Still a piece of cake.

I'd only crossed a few feet of floor when the damned dog burst out yapping again.

That wasn't enough to throw me off. No, I had better nerves than that. But as I dashed for cover at the sound of approaching feet, the disc case that had already been wedged precariously against my side jostled out. It hit the floor with a clatter no one could possibly mistake for a tiny draft. As I swore to myself, one of the guards yelled.

Forget cake; forget stealth. It was time to run.

30

Sorsha

I snatched up the box of CDs, jammed it back into my armpit, and bolted for the back door. Unfortunately, one of the guards came charging around the play area's shelves at the same moment, blocking my way.

What could I do but make use of what was in front of me? Clutching my loot against my body, I dove for the ball pit.

As I shoved my free arm in, the plastic spheres rattled against each other and bounced over the walls. I snatched up one and then another to pelt the guard in the face as hard as I could. He stumbled backward in a mix of pain and—probably mostly, since they were kiddie balls —shock.

The other guard was pounding toward me from somewhere behind. In a matter of seconds, they'd have me cornered. I hurled one more ball, crashed straight through the pit, and braced a foot inside one of the ride-on cars: a rather stylish red convertible.

Pushing off with my other foot as if it were a scooter, I careened past the guard down the nearest aisle, smacking him aside with my elbow for good measure. He let out an *oof* and then hurtled after me.

The hiss of the car's wheels against the tiled floor must have tipped off the other guard, because those footsteps skidded and spun to follow in the neighboring aisle. I rammed my sneaker against the floor harder, pushing the toy car as fast as its wheels would go.

"Is it one of *them*?" the second guard hollered to his colleague, in a horrified tone that told me they knew what business their employers were really in—and they weren't any more fond of the shadowkind than the rest of the sword-star bunch.

"I don't know—doesn't matter. Just stop her!" the other shouted back.

Forget that. I whipped out into the wider space between the shelves and the checkout counters. The plastic wheels made an ear-splitting squeal as I swerved sharply with a jerk of my foot. I raced the car three aisles over, wrenched it around again to zoom down the one that would lead to the store-room door—and two of the wheels popped right off.

Clearly that ride wasn't built to stand up to a proper car chase. I flung myself off it, wobbling as I caught my balance with the weight of my cargo and wincing when the edge of the computer jabbed me harder. This machine had better contain what we needed, or I was going to shove it up its owner's ass. Assuming I got the chance to find out what it contained in the first place.

As I righted myself, my own ass bumped into a display of dark-cloaked action figures at the head of the aisle. "Intruder detected!" a host of them cried out in their tinny digital voices. "Fire when ready!"

For the love of gravy, the whole store was out to get me. But as I sprinted down the aisle, it occurred to me that their suggestion wasn't such a bad one. With my free hand, I snatched a dart blaster toy off the shelves. Already loaded with five foam darts—my lucky day.

A guard had reached the end of the aisle. I glanced back just long enough to take a couple of shots behind me. One of the foam bolts bounced off his shoulder, but the other hit the edge of his glasses, knocking them askew. Score!

I was almost in good spirits again when a second set of footsteps rounded the corner. I didn't look back, firing blind as I ran on, but the click of a safety releasing reached my ears clear as anything.

These guys were taking the whole "fire when ready" idea to a much more serious level.

With a lurch of my gut, I threw myself forward even faster. My feet slammed against the tiles, the impact radiating through the soles with an expanding ache. My arm holding the computer was outright throbbing now.

"Stop right there!" one of the guards yelled as they

pelted after me—as if I were going to play nice now. I veered back and forth in an attempt to make myself a more difficult target, and I'd like to think that inspired maneuver was what saved me.

A *bang* split the air, and an instant later, a deeper agony than anything I'd experienced so far seared through my shoulder. On my right side, thank fluffy puppies, because if it'd been the left, I'd have dropped my sole reason for being here. As it was, my arm jerked with the impact, my fingers spasming with the rush of pain, and the toy gun tumbled to the floor.

Gritting my teeth, I tore onward. The door was in sight. I could make it—but I wasn't sure any more that simply leaving the building was going to guarantee my freedom.

I forced my fingers around the knob and yanked, a cry I couldn't contain breaking from my throat at the fiery sensation that stabbed through my shoulder at the effort. My head reeled, but I managed to stumble into the stockroom just as another shot rang out. The door vibrated with it.

Shit, shit, shit. My shoulder was on fire, tears prickling at my eyes. I dashed across the room for the outer door. The guards barged after me with a volley of shouts.

As I heaved the outer door open with a smack of my good shoulder that echoed into the wounded one with another flare of pain, a sharp little impulse shot up inside me.

Burn them. Burn the two of them down, right to the fucking ground. I didn't have my lighter in my hand, but the heat that pulsed through me with the frantic thrum of my heartbeat felt potent enough to leap straight from my fingers in a burst of flame.

The thought gripped me for a moment, and then I recoiled from it with a jolt of horror and the wash of the outside air over my face. Even if I *could* have done it—which obviously I couldn't have; how crazy would that have been?—burning people alive was a little beyond what I could stomach, even if they seemed intent on murdering me.

I choked down a sob at the pain now splintering right through my chest and raced into the parking lot with all the speed my legs could produce.

I could run pretty fast, even lugging heavy computer equipment under one arm, even in a haze of agony. But it was a big parking lot with no cover at all except for the *Clothes for the Recently Deceased* donation box way too far across that open stretch of asphalt. As the guards barreled out after me, it was only a matter of seconds before I became one of the intended recipients of the charity.

Pumping my legs even faster, I made for that one bit of shelter. Another gunshot crackled behind me, missing me but close enough that the tremble in the air crossed my cheek. Twenty feet left to go, my breath rasping in my throat... Fifteen... Ten...

Bang. A bullet I was instantly certain would mean

my doom exploded from the gun—and a huge, speeding body crashed into me out of nowhere, slamming me off my feet and hurling us both the last short distance to the donations box.

The burly arms that had caught me managed to turn me as we whipped through the air and around the bin. I hit the ground on my back rather than face first, although the pain that lanced through my shoulder at the impact wasn't anything to celebrate. I choked on a groan and found myself staring up into Thorn's face.

I knew it was his face because of the scars that decorated it and the white-blond hair falling in disarray on either side, not to mention the hulking body looming over me. But the planes of his features had turned even harder than before, and amid them, the eyes that stared back at me smoldered as if they were made of dying embers—no pupils, no whites, just pure, dark red.

And then there was the fact that two immense, black-feathered wings had sprouted from his brawny back, arcing over us like a shield. Holy mother of mothballs. Of all the forms he could have revealed, I'd never have expected that.

The first inane words that fell out of my mouth were, "They could have shot you."

"They *were* going to shoot you," Thorn said. His voice had the same low gravelly rumble, but with a sort of reverb to it as if it were resonating through a majestic cavern. His eyes flashed an even starker red, and his lips curled back to bare his teeth. "They already did. They would have killed you."

Was there something wrong with me that I was abruptly all kinds of heated up myself with those bulging muscles just inches from my prone body and that kind of vehemence lighting his gaze? Maybe it was just the adrenaline messing with my head.

My next words weren't all that much more sensible than the first. "And here I thought you saw me as just a nuisance."

I felt the warrior's glower as much as saw it, washing over me in another hot wave, but a touch of gentleness came through the defiance in his tone. "You are irritatingly irreverent and infuriatingly obstinate, m'lady, but I'm finding that the thought of someone hurting you makes me want to rip out their entrails and choke them with their own intestines."

It wasn't heat but warmth that fluttered inside me then. He'd practically composed a poem for me. I beamed up at him, slightly delirious from the pain, and said, "Right back at you."

Something flickered in his expression, and I half expected him to lean in and kiss me. Then thudding footsteps reached my ears over the roar of blood rushing through my head. The guards hadn't given up the chase. Had they even seen what had dragged me to safety?

Somehow Thorn's hard features managed to stiffen even more. He sprang off me and charged to meet them with a bellowed battle cry that rattled my eardrums.

One of the men let out a yelp. They'd seen now. Then all I heard was the sickening squelch of smashed flesh and the crunch of shattering bone, followed by skin and muscle rending with a meaty tearing noise. Neither they nor Thorn spoke another sound.

I'd pushed myself up into a sitting position when Thorn strode back into view around the donations box. He'd returned to the mortal-ish form I was used to, nothing otherworldly about him other than the crystalline glint of his knuckles.

Two heads, ripped from their bodies, dangled by their hair from one of his broad hands, the stumps of their necks dribbling blood and smatterings of gore. He held them up. "I didn't know which one lodged that bullet in you, so I present you with both."

My stomach churned, but I couldn't say I didn't appreciate the sentiment. "Um, thank you. I think we can leave those here, though. I'm not really a trophy type of gal." At least not the bloody body part kind of trophy. "It's not as if we can avoid the people who own this place realizing something major went down here tonight anyway."

Thorn sneered at the detached heads and tossed them behind him. "You said I could 'come after' anyone who attacked you outside the building," he reminded me.

"Yeah, I did, didn't I? Good thinking, me." I rubbed my head. It was easier not to think about the wrecked bodies that were lying farther across the lot when I didn't have to see them. Easier not to care about their deaths with my shoulder still gripped in the jaws of agony.

At this point, he'd needed to kill them. If we'd left them alive, they'd have immediately sounded the alarm so the rest of the people could start damage control. As it was... we had until shift change to make the most of the booty I'd fled with.

The *computer* booty. Get your mind out of the gutter.

The computer in question had landed on the ground next to me. I examined the metal shell and determined it was only mildly dinged. In my not-at-all expert opinion, it should still work just fine.

Thorn scooped the device up as if it weighed no more than a kitten, putting my arm strength to shame. When I reached for the box of discs, he grabbed that too.

"We should return to the others," he said, holding out a hand to help me up. He'd reverted back to his usual cool demeanor, but I was too woozy to be offended this time.

He'd saved my life in the most literal sense. He'd slaughtered men on my behalf and offered me their heads as a gift of devotion. No matter how he liked to play it, he couldn't really pretend he wasn't a teeny bit fond of me.

"Ready when you are," I said, managing not to sway. "Let's bring these bastards down."

31

Sorsha

Patching me up turned into a group effort. Ruse picked up the necessary supplies while I lay grumbling and cursing on the motel bed, the one hand towel Pickle hadn't appropriated pressed to the entry wound and the dragon himself curled up against my head in an effort to offer comfort. When the incubus returned, Thorn and Snap sat next to me. After I'd swallowed a couple of painkillers and a swig of the vodka Ruse had also deemed necessary, the warrior slowly talked the other shadowkind through the process of removing the bullet and stitching my flesh back together.

Snap shuddered when he peered at the lump of metal that was apparently visible in the wound. "It's silver."

"Good thing I'm not a werewolf," I muttered. The

guards had been at least a little prepared for supernatural intruders.

Thorn ignored my dry remark. "We wouldn't need it out otherwise. I don't want to leave anything in her that could make it harder for us to take care of her. It shouldn't cause any further trouble—no major blood vessels right there."

Snap sucked in a breath and brandished his tweezers.

His slender fingers did perform the job more gracefully than Thorn's heavy hands could have managed, although I contributed quite a bit more cursing regardless. In between the throbs of pain, I couldn't help thinking about where the warrior must have picked up his knowledge in field wounds. A long time ago and probably in countries far, far away.

Thorn didn't look particularly fazed by the wound or the bleeding that had already slowed to a trickle by the time we'd made it to the car thanks to the pressure he'd applied. Snap, for all he kept his hands steady, was much more perturbed. At my every hiss and grimace, he winced in sympathy.

"You destroyed the ones who did this?" he asked Thorn with his new possessive fierceness.

The warrior offered a rare, if grim, smile that would have been answer enough. "Oh, yes."

The lump of metal Snap plucked out didn't look large enough to have caused half of the agony I'd been experiencing. The pain started to dull now that it was gone, other than the tiny jabs of the stitching needle. In a few minutes, I was sitting up with an ice pack over a gauze bandage, the muscle there turning nicely numb.

Piece of cake. Ha ha ha.

Ruse had been examining my loot. "So, our answers are in here?" he asked, nudging the computer.

"I hope so," I said. "They'd better fucking be after all this. The trick is going to be getting them out." I motioned to Snap. "Any chance you can get a sense of a password from that thing?"

Snap considered the metal structure with obvious skepticism. He leaned in, his tongue flitting past its surface here and there. When he straightened up, he shook his head. "It's mostly you, from when you were running with it. The other impressions are much duller. Nothing that tells how to open it."

Of course the owner wouldn't have been petting the computer while logging in or working out nefarious plans. If I'd thought to grab the keyboard too... But then, I'd barely made it out of the store with what I *had* carried.

I rubbed my mouth. "All right. We're going to need a monitor and a keyboard, and I guess I'll have to see if someone from the hacker cabal can talk me through breaking the password encryption... And fast." It was past eleven. At best, we had eight or nine hours before the sword-star bunch realized what we'd taken off with and started cleaning up shop.

Ruse cocked his head. "Wouldn't it be easier to bring the computer to the hackers and let them do the work?"

"I don't know where they are. I guess they probably

know *someone* who could handle it in a city this big." I frowned. "If they'd agree to meet up with us anyway. If that would even be safe."

The incubus's eyes gleamed. "Get them on the phone, and I can handle the rest."

Every minute it took to wait for a response felt like years, but it'd actually only been half an hour before the Fund's contacts had hooked me up with a local associate who reluctantly agreed to a phone conversation. When the call came in, I handed the phone to Ruse.

"Hello there," he said in his smooth voice, and shot me an amused glance as he covered the mic area. "They're using a voice distorter—as if that'll help."

He sauntered around the room, rolling his cajoling words off his tongue, until he'd gotten an address and a promise that our new friend wouldn't mention the visit to anyone. "I'll return with all possible speed," he said, handing me back my phone and hefting the computer.

"Take the devourer with you," Thorn said abruptly.

Ruse looked at Snap, who blinked at the warrior. "What would I do there? I don't know how to get anything out of that box."

Thorn nodded toward Ruse. "He can pick up on whether this 'hacker' has had any contact with our enemies. If they have, we'll want you to test their home and possessions for any useful impressions you can glean that way."

The explanation sounded flimsy, and from the arch of Ruse's eyebrow, he thought so too. He wasn't inclined to fight with the larger shadowkind about it, though. "Come on then. My influence isn't quite as potent without visuals. We want to make sure we get there before it wears off."

Snap cast a concerned look my way, but the need for urgency cut off whatever arguments he might have made. "We'll be back soon," he assured me. "For now, get all the rest you can."

"Believe me, I have zero interest in running any marathons for the next decade or so."

They slipped out, leaving me with just Thorn, looming where he stood beside the bed. I raised my own eyebrows at him. "Couldn't wait to get me alone, huh?"

There was that familiar glower. He appeared to be waiting for something—the rumble of the car engine as the other guys drove away. Then he folded his arms over his expansive chest, but I couldn't feel all that intimidated just from his bulk when I'd seen what he *really* looked like.

"You won't say anything to the others about what I am," he said.

Interesting. "Why not?"

The glower deepened. "It's simply easier not to get caught up in the questions that arise. Even my fellow shadowkind are generally... taken aback."

So I wasn't wrong in being startled that his specific kind existed at all anymore. I scooted away from the pillow to Pickle's snort of dismay, gave the dragon a soothing pat, and gazed up at my avenging warrior. "All right, I'll keep quiet—on one condition. I want you to show yourself again."

Apparently it was Thorn's turn to be startled. "What?"

"You heard me. I'd like to get a look at you when I'm not half out of my mind in pain. Since this seems to be a once-in-a-lifetime-if-that sort of experience and all."

Thorn opened his mouth and shut it, appearing to think better of whatever protest he'd been going to make. He'd correctly labeled me as obstinate just an hour or so ago, after all. "Fine. But only if we're agreed."

"No blabbing your secrets—it's a deal."

I offered my hand to shake on it, and Thorn accepted the gesture with a twitch of his mouth that could have been amusement or irritation or maybe a little of both. His solid fingers engulfed mine in their firm grasp. Then he stepped back from the bed to give himself more room.

Unlike Ruse, he didn't need even the concentration of closing his eyes. The edges of his body flickered, and all at once he loomed half a foot taller, his frame filling out with even more of that sculpted brawn. The smoldering red consumed his eyes. Where his hands had dropped to his sides, his knuckles glinted with their crystalline surface protruding farther and sharper, and the hardened lines of his scarred face caught the light with a diamond-like quality I hadn't seen in the darkness of the parking lot.

And those wings. He kept them partly folded, and still the arc of their dark sweep grazed the ceiling. The feathered tips might have stretched all the way from one end of the room to the other if he'd extended them.

I hadn't seen those wrong. My breath caught. I knew I was staring, but really, if there was ever an excuse to, this was it.

A wave of giddiness propelled my next words. "You're an angel."

Thorn's mouth tensed. "That word belongs to mortals. None of the trappings they add to it have any basis in reality. We prefer 'the wingéd.'"

He placed an archaic emphasis on the end of the word, saying it "wing-*ed*" rather than "wing'd." His voice resonated with the reverb quality I also hadn't imagined. It sent a tingle over my skin.

I hadn't had any reason to believe in a literal heaven even before he'd made his comment about trappings, but if anyone had ever sounded as if they came from on high, it was him.

"I didn't know there were any of you left," I said. "I heard... there was a war?"

The information the shadowkind passed on between each other and to the mortals they interacted with was limited, and where it did exist, the details were sketchy and probably skewed by myth and faulty perception. The little bit I'd gathered was that sometime several centuries ago, there'd been a brief but epic battle of some sort in which angels—okay, the wingéd—had fought in unison with the human factions... on both sides. The clash of uber-powerful beings had left most but clearly not quite all of them dead. No one who'd referenced it had any idea what they'd been fighting about.

If Thorn was a typical representation of his kind, I was going to guess the disagreement had been more serious than which way you hung a toilet paper roll.

He didn't add to my understanding. "Most slaughtered each other. I survived. It's not a time I care to talk about at any length, m'lady."

Fair enough. "And the others really don't know?"

He shook his head. "Not the incubus or the devourer. Omen knows. He was there."

My eyes widened. "Is *he* an ang—er, wingéd—too?"

Thorn chuckled—a sound I'd never heard from him before, thrumming from his throat with heavenly resonance. "No. He's— You'll see, if he wants to show you."

Someone had mentioned the man having claws at one point, hadn't they? I might have prodded the warrior further, but his good humor faded with the last few words. There was more he could have said but didn't need to.

If we ever do find him.

I didn't want Thorn dwelling on that right now. With a twinge from my shoulder, I pushed myself to my feet so I could step closer.

Thorn's stance tensed at my approach, but he didn't disguise his true form. As I reached with my good arm to trace my fingers over the slope of one wing where it left his back, he held himself perfectly still.

The surface of the black feathers was unexpectedly silky, only coarse along the edges, and the ridge of flesh beneath them emanated warmth. I couldn't resist the urge to stroke them more firmly. Was that a slight hitch in his chest, as if that spot might be particularly sensitive to the touch?

When was the last time he'd been close enough to anyone to let them offer this kind of caress, if ever?

"They're magnificent." I glanced up, my pulse stuttering at finding myself so close to that impenetrable face. "*You're* magnificent."

He peered down at me with those smoldering eyes. "Mortals usually flee in terror at this sight."

I grinned. My heart was still thumping double-time, but it definitely wasn't in fear. His musky, smoky smell had coiled around me, and every word that fell from his lips in that tone like low thunder was stirring heat in my core. The jolt of desire that'd rushed through me in the parking lot definitely couldn't be blamed on just adrenaline.

My hand drifted from his wing to rest on his bulging bicep. "Haven't you figured out yet that I'm not your average mortal?"

"It would be exceedingly difficult not to have noticed."

I walked my fingers down to his elbow teasingly. "And you like me, irreverence and obstinance and all, as hard as it might be for you to admit it."

He let out a sound that wasn't much more than a

wordless grumble, and then he proved what I'd just said by clasping the hair at the back of my head and tugging me to him. His mouth collided with mine, hot and steady and unrelenting. I held onto his tunic for dear life and kissed him back, my senses overwhelmed.

Maybe it wasn't the sanest move I'd ever made. I'd already been canoodling with both of his companions, and just one monstrous lover was more than a handful. But—heaven help me even if it didn't exist—I wanted them all, and after tonight, I deserved a little indulgence. It wasn't as if any dalliance between a human and a shadowkind could turn into a real relationship in the long run. Once our battle with the sword-star bunch was over, who knew if I'd even see any of them again?

Thorn kissed me once more, with determined gentleness, before he drew back a few inches. His hand slid from my hair to stroke along my jaw.

"I almost didn't get to you quickly enough tonight," he said, with a rawness I could hear even through the reverb. "We still have farther to go to see this through. I won't insult you by asking you again to back down, but I hate the thought that next time I might fail to protect you."

"You've now saved my life at least a couple times over," I said. "I'm pretty sure any debt you owed me is fully paid."

He made a noise of consternation. "You're worth more than any debt. I didn't kiss you as repayment either."

A flutter passed through my chest with a softer sort of giddiness. "I'm glad we're on the same page, then. Maybe you take the whole protection gig to unnecessary extremes? All Omen could have asked was that you do your best, and I've never asked for anything at all."

I..." His thumb that had been gliding along my chin halted. "I had friends in the war. Brothers and sisters at arms. I would have died for them—I *should* have—but I wasn't there when the need was greatest, and now they are gone and I am still here. I don't wish to repeat that mistake."

He'd spoken in his usual formal diction, but the weight of that loss rang through the words. A lump rose in my throat. How long had he spent roaming the shadow realm alone, tangled up in guilt and mourning? He'd been carrying that wound for centuries, and Omen's mission had brought the pain right back to the surface.

I touched his jaw like he had mine, finding the hardened planes of his face still had the warmth and suppleness of skin against my fingers. "I understand, but I swear to you that if something happens to me, *I* won't blame you for it. All right?"

Maybe it didn't matter what I thought if he'd blame himself anyway, but he inclined his head in acknowledgment. His wings vanished, his body contracting to his normal though still imposing height. The red faded from his dark eyes.

"The others might be back at any moment," he said,

with more his usual brusqueness. "Snap was right—you should be resting while you can."

"Fine," I muttered, but my shoulder was starting to ache more insistently again. I could be satisfied with a couple of kisses for now. Getting more involved with the third member of my monstrous trio—I'd decide later how sane *that* idea was. If we got a later after wherever else our schemes led us tonight.

I sank down on the edge of the bed. As Pickle scrambled up onto my lap to curl up there, my thoughts veered toward my own friends. My best friend, who'd wanted so badly to fight for me too, even if those efforts had ended in disaster.

I grasped my phone. "I should call Vivi. Make sure she found someplace safe to hide out." Get in a few last words with her just in case they turned out to really be my last. It was late, but Vivi tended to be a night owl even when she didn't have a recently-witnessed murder to ruin her sleep.

"I'll give you the room," Thorn said, and wavered away into the shadows to his own room without bothering with the door.

I hesitated over my Frequent Contacts, where Vivi's welcoming face grinned up at me from the top spot. My stomach knotted.

Ten years ago, when I'd been barely more than a kid and she hadn't been much older, we'd been glued at the hip. I wasn't sure how I'd have survived this long without her friendship keeping me sane and human. The thought of someone putting a bullet in *her* still made my innards clench up with an icy panic.

But maybe she'd felt the same way about me potentially walking into danger. She'd screwed up and crossed boundaries, and I was still kind of pissed off about that, but at least she'd done it out of love rather than the intent to do harm.

I tapped the screen and lifted the phone. A few seconds later, my bestie's voice pealed into my ear.

"Sorsha! Are you still okay?"

I ignored the ache in my shoulder. "I've had better days, but yeah. Are *you*? Did you get out of town like I said?"

"Yeah, I grabbed Gran, and we took off for a cottage a couple of hours away that belongs to friends of the family. I—I keep looking out the windows just in case someone's coming." Her voice dipped lower. "I've been worried sick about you. I wanted to call, but I didn't want to interrupt you at a bad time. Obviously I'm not the greatest judge of when or how to interfere."

"You shouldn't have been interfering at all," I couldn't help saying, even though I hadn't meant to restart that argument.

Vivi sighed. "Okay, that might be true. And I'm really sorry I went all stalker on you. But *you* shouldn't have been lying to me. I thought you knew you could count on me... I wish you'd trusted me more."

The dejection in her voice made me wince. I swallowed hard. "It's not that I don't trust or count on you, Vivi. I do, for all kinds of things. But you saw how dangerous the situation is, what kind of people I'm up against... With the things Luna taught me"—and the trio of allies who'd turned up on my doorstep—"I'm better equipped to take them on. I was trying to keep you *safe*."

My best friend was silent for a moment. "I get that. I can even appreciate the thought. But Sorsh, what if I don't *want* to be safe if that means I can't help you when you're in trouble? How do you think I'd feel if you got hurt and I hadn't done anything to stop it? If we're working together, at least we can split the danger two ways instead of it all being on you."

"I don't think it works exactly like that," I said, but her words sent a twinge through me anyway. Had it really been right for me to take away her choice in the matter? I'd told myself she wouldn't fully understand the danger to know what she was getting into—but part of the reason she didn't was because of all the things I'd avoided telling her.

I hadn't liked Thorn trying to send me off to keep me safe, and he'd at least informed me of that decision rather than going behind my back.

"I'm sorry too," I added. "At this point, I think we're both safest if you lay low, but once the immediate crisis is over, we'll talk more. Okay?"

"That sounds like a compromise I can get behind. Are you... Are you looking after yourself?"

"As well as I can. And as you noticed, I've got some friends of another sort who've made that their business too." I smiled wryly. "You don't have to worry about them either. We've reached an understanding."

"If you say so." She gave a short laugh. "Ack, Gran's calling for me. I'd better see what's up. Call me again to touch base tomorrow so I don't go crazy wondering what's happened to you?"

"I'll do that." I'd be worrying about her too.

"Talk soon then. Ditto."

My smile turned painfully bittersweet. "Ditto," I replied.

I lay back against the pillow, Pickle snuggling into the crook of my neck, and closed my eyes. Despite the intermittent twinges of pain, I must have dozed at least a little. One second my mind was drifting through a highlights reel of the past week, and the next all three of my shadowkind companions had burst into my room, talking at the same time.

I sat up, blinking and swiping at my eyes. A glance at the bedside clock told me it was now nearly two in the morning.

We were running out of time.

I held up my hands. "Hold on, hold on. What's going on? What did you find out? Start from the beginning— just one of you."

Ruse came to a stop beside the bed and caught one of my hands in his. His smirk radiated victory.

"The hacker you found cracked all the codes, and we hit pay dirt. We know exactly where Omen is down to the cell number—we've even seen the blueprints to know how to get to it once we're there."

Snap was practically bouncing on his feet with eager energy. "At least, we think it's him. They're all called 'subjects' in the files. But 'Subject 26' was the only one brought in around the time he was captured, and some of the other details sounded like him."

"He's alive," Thorn said with undisguised relief.

"We found the building," Snap went on. "It was one of the other impressions I got from Meriden. Two of them together, actually. There's a big construction site"—he glanced at Ruse as if to confirm he'd gotten the term right —"and in the middle where you can't see unless you go right through, there's the building I saw with the concrete walls and shiny doors."

A secret facility hidden within a construction site? With all the building projects that went up around the city and then took forever to complete, I had to give the conspirators kudos. That was pretty brilliant.

"You *saw* the place?" I said as everything he'd said sunk in. A quiver of nerves raced through me even though the two of them had clearly returned unharmed. "You went in?"

"Not all the way in," Ruse said. "On the way back here, we swung by the address we got to scope things out so we could make more definite plans. We couldn't easily get into the actual building, though. They've got flood lamps all around the place so we can't get close enough to jump to any entry point through the shadows, and obviously we weren't going to stroll over and knock."

"Lots of guards too." Snap made a face. "Some of them standing around, some of them patrolling, with silver and iron protections and those weapons they used before."

"I can smash through their puny equipment," Thorn rumbled.

"Not with this many, even with these guns." Ruse punched him lightly in the arm. "We're going to need a better strategy than 'Charge straight in and hope for the best.'"

I thought of the construction of the toy shop office. "What about the building itself? Is there any silver or iron worked into it?"

Ruse hesitated. "We didn't pick up on anything from outside. The blueprints indicate there were special materials used in the cells, which makes sense. The rest of the building looked clear."

But of course we couldn't know for sure if they'd added more since then.

If the shadowkind couldn't simply slip inside unseen, then getting in would require my expertise. My first impulse was to tell them to lay out the route for me, and I'd get to Omen and release him myself. No need for any of them to risk the same assholes catching and caging *them*, especially when we didn't know how going into the building might affect them.

But as I looked around at the three men—and

perhaps monsters—who'd crashed into my life uninvited days ago, the bizarre fondness that swelled in my chest was tainted with a pinch of shame.

I'd nearly gotten myself killed earlier tonight by insisting I go into the store alone. Shutting Vivi out had made more problems for us than it could solve. The idea of seeing anyone that I, yeah, cared about under threat still made every particle in my body balk. It made me think of my parents' cries and of Luna shattering into mere particles of the woman who'd raised me.

My lungs constricted with the memories. People around me, people who were trying to look after me—they died.

But these three knew the risk they were taking. How could I tell them it wasn't their choice to make—or try to take the choice away from them completely?

If we were going to outmaneuver the sword-star bunch and rescue their boss, it'd take all the wits and skills we had between us. Going in alone could be both a suicide mission and a guarantee of failure.

"We've gotten this far," I said. "No way are they stopping us now. Tell me exactly how the building is laid out and where we need to go, and let's work from there. We need to pull this jailbreak off before the sun comes up."

32

Sorsha

The steel struts of the construction site loomed above the lower rooftops of the neighboring buildings, reflected moonlight making them visible even from two blocks away. They gleamed faintly against the darkness of the night sky like the bones of some massive creature that had settled there to die and had its carcass picked clean. That image fit my mood perfectly as Ruse put the car into park.

"The end is nigh, but I'm holding on," I sang, but not even the inspiration of Blondie could stop my voice from sounding thin in the silence. At this hour, no other vehicles passed us on the road. Not the slightest breeze stirred the warm air. My shoulder still throbbed from the silver bullet Snap had pulled out of me.

The end of our mission was up ahead, sure, but for all we knew it could end *us*.

Out of all of us, I had to admit the one most likely to meet some dire fate was the owner of a mortal body—a.k.a., me. I was prepared for that, but a tightness wound through my ribs as my shadowkind trio moved to get out of the car.

I gave Pickle one last scratch between his wings where he'd perched on my lap and then shifted him to the middle seat so I could get up too, resisting the urge to cuddle him so close he'd squawk. We'd brought him and all my belongings with us because regardless of where this night led, returning to the motel after we faced off against the sword-star bunch directly seemed unwise. Leaving him there in the car, the constricting sensation crept up into my throat.

The three men had gathered around me on the sidewalk. I turned to them when I'd shut the car door.

"If something happens to me tonight," I said, "promise me you'll look after Pickle? He won't get very far on his own."

Snap's expression turned pained. "You don't need to worry about that," he insisted.

Thorn raised his chin, adding to the immense sense of his height. "I don't intend to return without you, but if it eases your mind, you have my word the little creature will be taken care of."

The hairs on the back of my neck rose with the implications of his initial statement. I knew he meant not just that he hoped to make sure I came out alive, but that if I didn't, it'd only be because he fell too.

We had a plan, and I didn't think we could have come up with a better one, at least not without days longer than the hour or so we'd actually had. But so much was still uncertain. Our enemies had caught us off-guard more than once. We intended to turn the tables on them tonight, but we hadn't pulled off anything quite like this before.

An impulse gripped me that I let myself follow, because who knew whether we'd have another moment of relative peace. I grasped Thorn's shirt and bobbed up to give him a light peck on the lips, swiftly enough that he didn't have the chance to return it or pull away, whichever he'd have decided on. I had no idea how he'd feel about the others seeing any softness from him.

The warrior glowered at me after, but the heat in his gaze felt at least as hungry as it did annoyed. Ruse was smirking, wider when I turned to him. He reached for me and tugged me to him by the waist, his eyelids lowering seductively.

"I'll take a little more than that, Miss Blaze," he said in the chocolatey tone that still made my skin tingle. But he let me be the one to lean in the last few inches between us and capture his mouth.

I'd almost forgotten how much skill the incubus could bring to a simple kiss. The press of his lips, languid as if taking his time and yet passionate as if reveling in every second, set a whole lot more tingling than just my skin.

Wouldn't it have been nice to sink into that bittersweet cacao-and-caramel scent of him and leave death-defying capers for another night?

We didn't have any other nights before our enemies discovered how close to them we'd already gotten, though. Reluctantly, I eased back.

Snap's posture had tensed while I'd kissed the other guys. Glimmers of brighter green shimmered through his eyes with the intensity of the reaction he appeared to be reining in. "My peach," he said, shooting a look at the other two that dared them to deny him that claim. The defiance turned his heavenly face even more dazzling.

I touched his soft cheek. I'd saved him for last for exactly this reason. "My devourer?" I said. I wasn't entirely sure what that label meant yet, but the tension in his expression melted at the suggestion.

"Yes," he said with a brilliant smile, and tipped his head to nuzzle my cheek before he brought our mouths together.

I'd expected all sweet tenderness, but Snap was clearly determined to both make a statement and stake a claim. He parted my lips with eager determination, his tongue flicking in to twine around mine as he deepened the kiss. The stroke of the delicately forked tip sent a rush of giddiness through me. As he traced my jaw to tilt it at an even better angle, he all but plundered my mouth.

It was sweet, hell yes, and dizzyingly intense too.

When he released me, every inch of him was lit with satisfaction, deliciously fucking gorgeous. A laugh both delighted and terrified bubbled at the base of my throat until I swallowed it down.

I'd gotten myself an angel, a sort-of sun god, and a guy most mortals would consider a demon. What sort of being was waiting for us inside that prison if we succeeded in freeing him?

It was time to find out. I stepped back and motioned toward the construction site. "Let's do this thing."

As I strode toward the site, my companions wisped away into the shadows to draw less attention if anyone happened to look our way. The site itself was bordered by a solid fence some six feet high, but I made short work of the chain securing one of the entrances with my scorch-knife. Trusting that the trio was following close by, I squeezed inside.

I crept along a meandering path between metal beams and stacks of wood until I skirted a raw cinder-block wall and the glow of the flood lights came into view up ahead. With a few more steps, I made out the concrete walls of the squat two-story building Snap had first seen in the impressions clinging to Meriden's body.

It rose up out of a clear stretch of dirt in the middle of the larger half-finished building. The door on this side was indeed shiny—stainless steel, from the look of it—and the flat gray walls around it held only a couple of small windows, those on the first floor. The holding cells above must have offered no glimpse at all into the outside world.

Figures stalked along the edges of the harsh light that surrounded the place. I counted three patrolling in my view and two others stationed by the door. From what Ruse and Snap had reported, there'd be at least twice that many monitoring the entire area. They all wore helmets and vests that gleamed with plates of silver and iron.

I caught myself just shy of rubbing the bandage on my shoulder. Two guards had been trouble enough. But I wasn't alone here—and if we didn't get going, we'd lose all the advantage of the darkness and surprise.

I lifted my hand with an OK signal. That was Thorn's cue. Tucking myself as close to one of the nearby beams as I could, the metallic odor filling my nose, I braced myself for the chaos.

It started with a thumping like several boards toppling off a pile. All of the guards jerked their heads around to stare in that direction. As one man trotted over to investigate, a sharper clatter split the air. Drawing his gun, he motioned for two of his companions to follow.

They'd just loped out of view when something fell with a clang in the opposite direction. A shout carried from around the side of the building as more guards must have sprung into action. As long as they weren't heading anywhere near me, I was happy.

At an even more distant spot, there came a crash like shattering glass. One of the guards by the door spoke into her radio and then hustled off to help her colleagues. We were down to one between us and the entrance—but just distracting him momentarily wouldn't do the trick. If we wanted enough time to not just get into the building but get Omen and the other shadowkind prisoners out, we needed as many of our foes as possible caught up in a wild goose chase.

Thorn hadn't forgotten that part of the plan. A few seconds later, he charged over to join me, a dazed but thankfully not smashed figure dangling from his hands by the ankles so he didn't need to touch the helmet or vest that would have burned him.

Without a word, he dropped the man on the ground in front of me. Before the guy could regain his equilibrium, I yanked off the tight helmet and jerked at the snaps on his vest, gritting my teeth as the ache in my shoulder grew teeth. The protections hadn't been able to neutralize the warrior's physical strength, but none of my allies' supernatural powers would have any effect until we'd gotten rid of them.

The vest's clasps parted to reveal a faded Guns 'N Roses T-shirt. "Et tu, Brute?" I muttered.

As I tossed the vest aside, Ruse materialized out of the shadows. The guard took a swing at me, shoving himself more upright with a wobble, and Thorn clapped his hand over the guy's mouth the second it opened to yell. Before he needed to intervene any more than that, the incubus started speaking, staring deep into the man's widening eyes.

"Nice to meet you," he said in his cajoling tone. "Tell me, won't you, how many more guards are inside the building?"

The man's pupils had dilated. Thorn loosened his

grip to allow him room to speak. "I— You—" he stammered.

Ruse knelt in front of him. The power rang through his voice so distinctly it tickled my ears even though it wasn't directed at me. "We're going to be very good friends. It couldn't hurt anything for you to tell me."

The guard's posture started to relax. "There are two people monitoring the security cams. Another patrolling the halls. Not that we've ever needed all this manpower on the site... before..."

Ruse made a swift gesture to recapture the man's attention and peered at him even more intently. "Before now. Indeed. Quite the catastrophe that's happening out here. Imagine how upset your employers will be if they find out you all let these intruders get away. They're trying to break down the walls so anyone might wander in and see your secret base."

"No. We can't let that happen."

"Exactly. You know what you need to do? Put in a call on that radio of yours, get everyone you can out here. You can hear the invaders—they're all along the wall—you'll need to keep moving to catch up with them. Don't back down and keep everyone on their trail until you've nabbed them."

The guard nodded with a slow bob of his head. Then his gaze whipped away, his body stiffening all over again. He scrambled to his feet. "You're right—I hear them bashing at the wall right over there. Shit."

He raised his radio as he dashed off toward the

outskirts of the site, hollering for every guard at the facility to join him immediately between pants for breath that only played up the urgency.

Ruse flashed me a grin. "And now..."

The last guard at the door hesitated and then hurried over. One, two, and then a third burst through the doorway to join the defense. Bingo!

Thorn hurtled across the stretch of packed dirt to slam the camera poised over the door into the concrete wall it was mounted on. I sprinted after him. Snap darted from the shadows to meet me by the entrance. With a flick of his tongue through the air over the electronic lock, he smiled and tapped in the code he'd gleaned. The bolt slid over, and I yanked the door open.

As the warrior sprinted back to the shadows to continue diverting the guards outside, Snap, Ruse, and I ducked into the building. We found ourselves in an entry room with lime-green walls and an antiseptic prickle in the air.

Ruse pointed to another doorway at the opposite end. "The stairs are down that hall."

We were hustling along it when a woman in a lab coat emerged, blinking, from one of the workrooms. She didn't have a chance to do more than gasp before I'd spotted the silver and iron badge pinned to her blouse, like a larger version of my own. I snatched at it and wrenched it off her with a rasp of tearing fabric.

"Everything's okay," Ruse said to her in a ridiculously soothing voice. "You have so much work to do. You should get back to it. Nothing's more important than that."

She drew in a shaky voice, her eyes glued to him. "But—"

"Trust me. Nothing going on out here interests you at all. Think of how much you want to accomplish before it's time to leave."

He nudged her toward her office, and she meandered inside looking intent if slightly puzzled. As the three of us jogged the rest of the way down the hall, I tapped Ruse's side with my elbow. "Very impressive. I haven't really seen you in action before."

He chuckled. "I don't normally have to skip so much of the foreplay. Turning the dial up this high is giving me an ulcer. Let's hope I don't have to charm too many more."

We didn't run into anyone else in the hall or the stairwell, but as we reached the second-floor landing, both Ruse and Snap slowed. Ruse's jaw tightened.

Snap gave a little shudder as I pushed open the door to the hall that held the shadowkind prisoners. "A lot of unkind metals in this place."

My gut twisted. "Can you keep going?" We'd known there'd be silver and iron in the cell walls to contain the prisoners, but we'd hoped the effect wouldn't seep into the space outside them. How could we get Omen and the other shadowkind prisoners out of their cells if Snap couldn't reach the locks? Hell, if I got the opportunity, I'd wanted to not just free every being in this place but grab whatever files we could get our hands on quickly to find out what the sword-star bunch had been doing here.

Snap squared his shoulders and marched forward, but I could see the effort it took in the clenching of his hands. Ruse followed, showing similar signs of strain.

The blank walls and solid metal doors offered no glimpse of the creatures inside the cells. I scanned the numbers on the doors as quickly as I could. "Cell 11 was Omen's, right?" He was our first priority. I didn't want to think through the implications of Subject 27 being in only the eleventh cell—or what might have happened to at least sixteen of the subjects before him.

The incubus gave a curt nod. "Let's find it fast. I'm definitely not digging the vibe of this place."

There. I rushed over, Snap close behind me. Fighting a cringe, he bent close to the keypad by the lock. On his first attempt, his tongue flinched back into his mouth before he appeared to catch anything. An even more determined expression came over his face, and he tested the air again.

"4-9-7-2," he spat out, hauling himself back from the noxious surface.

I tapped in the numbers, willing my hand not to shake. How long could Ruse's ploy and Thorn's shenanigans keep all the guards from noticing what we were up to in here?

How were we going to make it *out* of here if they came back too soon?

The lock whirred open. Hallelujah. As soon as we

made sure this was Omen—and that he knew we were his people, coming to rescue him—I'd get Snap to move on to the next cell. If he could even tolerate testing the rest of the locks with all the toxic materials in this place, that was.

I tugged the door wide. The entire ceiling of the cell was one huge panel of light, which glared off the reflective walls and floor and nearly drowned out the twitching form like a streak of shadowy smoke in the middle of it.

"Omen?" I said. "Do you need help getting—"

Before I could finish the question, the blur of darkness flung itself at me with a guttural roar. Yellow-orange eyes blazed at me like twin flames; a clawed hand —or was that a *paw?*—smacked me aside with a scrape of pain through my arm that echoed into my injured shoulder. I stumbled into Snap, who caught me in a tight embrace.

"Omen!" he protested. "She's with—"

The blare of an alarm drowned out anything else he might have said. My stomach flipped over. Sweet stinking cheese. There must have been some other device we'd needed to disable to remove a prisoner safely.

The overhead lights flared twice as bright—and down the hall by the stairwell, a barrier of silver-and-iron-twined bars dropped into place with a clang, cutting off our escape.

"Shit," Ruse muttered. We bolted toward the stairwell anyway. The shadowy figure we'd released was still whipping around us, too swift and hazy to make him out clearly. One moment it looked like a hunched human form, the next some sort of muscular beast, its dark flesh streaked through with a fiery glow. A tail lashed in its wake, taut and sinuous with a triangular protrusion I glimpsed at its tip.

A devil's tail.

I couldn't think about that now. It didn't matter what Omen was if we all ended up dead or jailed tonight.

There was no time to try to free anyone else. Ignoring the guilt that jabbed through my panic, I yanked the scorch-knife from my belt, switched it on, and rammed it into the bars the second I reached them.

The people who'd designed this place had meant the barrier to hold off shadowkind with the power of its metals, not the width of its bars. I cut through one in a matter of seconds, drove the blade against it farther down, and kicked the large chunk out to clatter onto the floor. My heart seemed to be beating right in my throat, my pulse thudding behind my ears almost as loud as the alarm.

As I moved to the next bar, Ruse's voice carried from behind me. "Omen, pull yourself together. We've got you —we're taking you out of this hellhole—but it'll be a lot easier if you get a hold of yourself."

"They did horrible things here," Snap said, with a quiver of anger in his voice. "Horrible things to him. I don't even have to try to taste it."

I'd only cut out three bars when a door banged open

below. Almost biting my tongue at the jolt of panic that hit me, I rammed the knife even harder into the fourth. One more and the space should be just big enough for the shadowkind to follow me through...

A guard barreled into the landing just as I severed the bottom of that bar. I punched it right into her face. As she stumbled backward with a grunt of pain, a form that now looked completely like a man sprang through the opening at her.

The shadowkind man who must have been Omen slammed the guard's head into the ground with a cracking of her skull. He launched his sinewy frame down the stairs, and the three of us bolted after him.

Another guard had just reached the lower landing. With a snarl, Omen crashed into him, slamming him into the door frame and snapping his neck a second later. He flung the body to the side and raced on.

Then, at the far end of the hall where we'd come in, half a dozen guards rushed into the space. Weapons of metals and light flashed in their hands. We all stalled in our tracks.

They stepped forward, wary but ready, a few more of their colleagues coming in behind them to join the blockade. My pulse lurched.

They were prepared for us now, and there were too many of them. I couldn't imagine tearing our way through the whole lot, no matter what Omen was.

My hands shot up instinctively, as if I could ward them off—and one of the guards at the front of the pack flinched as if I'd actually flung something at him. More chickenshit than I'd expected. Omen glanced back at me with eyes now icy blue, as if he'd only just noticed I was still with him and his companions.

But flinging my arms around wasn't going to help us more than that tiny distraction. The guards advanced on us with increasing speed.

"Sorsha!" Thorn's bellow carried through the walls, followed by the crackle of smashed glass. Omen jerked toward the sound. He sprang back to a door between us and him and shoved it open.

We dashed after him to find shards glinting around one of the small windows I'd observed from outside. Thorn stood beyond it, his harsh cheeks splattered with mortal blood.

"Omen," he said hoarsely at the sight of his boss. "Come on, all of you, into the shadows. Sorsha, I've got you."

It wasn't anywhere near the leap it'd been from the apartment building. He swept his arm across the window frame, clearing the splinters of glass. Omen hurled himself through, his form thinning as he soared out into the flood of light. The incubus boosted me after him. As Thorn caught me and swung me onto his back, Ruse and Snap dove after us. Their forms raced through the glow and vanished into the shadows of the construction site.

The alarm was still blaring, frantic shouts breaking through its rhythm. A shot like a sizzling bolt of light smacked the wall less than an inch from us.

Thorn didn't risk tangling with all these attackers. With me clinging to his shoulders for dear life, too grateful to have him to complain about the indignity, he charged off in the same direction our companions had gone. He dodged beams and boards, smashed through one of the gates at the edge of the site, and hurtled on down the street toward the car.

Ruse had already started the engine, the lights flashing on in the darkness. Thorn and I tumbled into the back seat, and he took off with a screech of the tires.

The bleat of the alarm pealed through my ears from deep within that giant steel skeleton. I couldn't catch my breath until the cacophony of our escape finally faded away in the depths of the night.

33

Sorsha

The fire crackled within the ring of stones in the derelict campsite we'd stumbled on, miles outside the city. Its heat, sharper than the warmth that lingered at the tail end of the summer night, grazed my face where I was leaning against the side of the car. Its light washed over all of us arranged around the firepit, including the man we'd risked life and limb to save.

Omen stood poised almost directly across from me, his arms folded over his chest as he watched Snap poke at the fire with a long stick. I couldn't have said he was quite as stunning as the team he'd gathered, though he wasn't exactly hard on the eyes. I suspected if I'd been a regular mortal passing him on the street, I wouldn't have given him a second glance other than maybe to check if his ass looked as fit as the rest of his body. But I wasn't, and something about his presence drew my attention like a moth fluttering to those flames.

Flames that brought to mind the flash of his eyes I'd seen when he first sprang from his cell. He was some kind of shifter, clearly, though not from what I'd glimpsed any standard werewolf or kitsune. And he had more to him than that. I remembered the eyes, yeah, and I also remembered that tail.

Those now icy blue eyes gleamed starkly beneath his sharp brow. His Cupid's bow lips would have looked dainty, his rounded chin soft, if it wasn't for the firm set of his jaw. A sense of power and authority emanated off him so intensely I could almost taste it, like a spike of adrenaline and a tang of blood. He'd been around several centuries ago during the war of the angels, and I'd be willing to bet ages before that as well.

He ran his hand over the short, tawny hair slicked close to his skull and raised his gaze to meet mine. My heart lurched under his penetrating inspection, but I held myself still as if it hadn't affected me. He hadn't bothered to apologize for or even acknowledge the way he'd lashed out at me when I'd first freed him, though at least the scrape of his claws had barely broken my skin through the sleeve of my shirt. Pickle, perched on my shoulder, squirmed closer to my face with a nervous chirping sound.

Omen's mouth curled into a smile as chilly as his eyes. "Would the three of you care to explain the mortal in our midst?" He gave the word "mortal" a disdainful taint.

"They needed a leg up navigating the city and figuring out where you'd ended up in it," I said before the others had to admit to how we'd met. A twinge of protectiveness filled my chest. He didn't need to know they'd gotten themselves captured too—and by ordinary hunters no less. "I was happy to help. I was raised by a shadowkind woman. I pitch in where I can."

I'm not afraid of you. Well, maybe a teensy weensy bit, but he didn't need to know that either.

"She's part of that group of humans that advocate for mortal-side shadowkind," Ruse put in with a wave of his hand. "The something-or-other Fund."

Omen grimaced. "The do-gooders who haven't the guts to do half enough good to make a real difference. I know of them."

I bristled at his bland dismissal, but Snap leapt to my defense before I had to. "I don't know anything about the people Sorsha works with, but *she* doesn't have any shortage of courage. Or any other useful quality. We wouldn't have managed to find you, let alone break you out, if it wasn't for her."

Thorn, looming by the hood of the car, inclined his head. "She's lost a great deal serving our cause and yet refused to back down. I wouldn't hesitate to fight at her side again."

Omen considered his three compatriots with the same piercing focus he'd aimed at me. I wasn't sure what they might have given away about the other directions our relationships had veered in. Maybe the fact that they respected me on any level irked him.

"I thank you, then," he said finally, turning his attention back to me for a brief moment—and not sounding particularly grateful. "Forgive me my skepticism. I've just spent the last innumerable weeks being tortured by your kind; I'm not feeling the friendliest toward anyone mortal at the moment."

His gaze lingered on me a little longer, as if searching for some reaction to that statement beyond my tight smile of acceptance. A creeping sensation ran over my skin.

"Is that all they wanted?" Ruse said. "To torture higher shadowkind? It seems like an awful lot of trouble just for that."

"Oh, no, I'm sure they had a much more complex agenda." Omen rubbed his jaw. "They were attempting to accomplish something with their torment, to *discover* something, but they were careful not to say very much about it in my presence, so I can't say what. I do know, given their techniques, it can't bode well for us. As I suspected, there are humans making some sort of bid to sway the balance of power between mortal and shadowkind."

My stomach knotted. And we'd left that place standing and full of other captive beings who'd be subjected to even more of that torment. The words tumbled out. "We have to stop them."

Omen raised his eyebrows at me. "You sound as though you're including yourself in that 'we.'"

I lifted my chin. "Of course I am. The same bastards *killed* the woman who raised me. Even if it wasn't for that, they deserve to go down. I'm already all in. The rest of the Shadowkind Defense Fund will help as much as they can too, whatever you think of them."

"So you plan to go running back to them. Or did you think you'd join our little company? Keep in mind that the way we're going won't be easy even for us."

The truth was, I hadn't had much of a chance to think my options over. I hesitated for a second, but the answer came with a swell of certainty.

Maybe it was the connection I'd started to feel with all three of my trio. Maybe it was the fact that I suspected sticking around would *really* piss off the man who'd asked the question, and the more he talked, the more the idea of annoying him appealed to me.

Or maybe it was simply because I had to believe that if I was dealing with a devil, I'd be better off having him at my side than anywhere else in this battle.

The other three shadowkind were watching me too: Thorn in solemn silence, Ruse with a slyly crooked grin, and Snap braced, his face aglow with an indomitable hope that suggested he'd tackle me if I made any move to go.

Not that he'd need to. I shrugged as if I wasn't concerned about how much danger I'd face and said, "I'm here now. We ended up making a pretty good team."

When Omen smiled, his teeth glinted, even and white. I hadn't yet located the shadowkind part of him that lingered even in this guise. "Welcome on board," he said, in a tone that seemed to say, *We'll see about that.*

In that moment, I wasn't sure whether I faced more peril from the jailors we'd just fought off or the shadowkind man we'd rescued from them.

*　*　*

Oh, you were here for the end of the world, scores of death and destruction—what about that, you ask? I never promised it would be a *short* story. Stick with me. We're getting there.

Want to find out how Sorsha and her monstrous lovers will tackle the rest of the sword-star group—and what complications Omen's arrival will bring? Grab *Twilight Crook*, the second book in the Flirting with Monsters series, by going to this URL or using the QR code below: https://smarturl.it/FlirtingMonsters2

Eva offers a free fantasy novella to those who sign up for her author newsletter! Get it here: https://BookHip.com/ZCQRBM

ABOUT THE AUTHOR

Eva Chase lives in Canada with her family. She loves stories both swoony and supernatural, and strong women and the men who appreciate them. Along with the Flirting with Monsters series, she is the author of the Cursed Studies trilogy, the Royals of Villain Academy series, the Moriarty's Men series, the Looking Glass Curse trilogy, the Their Dark Valkyrie series, the Witch's Consorts series, the Dragon Shifter's Mates series, the Demons of Fame Romance series, the Legends Reborn trilogy, and the Alpha Project Psychic Romance series.

Connect with Eva online:
www.evachase.com
eva@evachase.com

Made in the USA
Middletown, DE
13 October 2021

50233061R00213